TOWER OF TERROR

At the back of the tower was a door with a window about twenty feet above it. Just once, Sally thought she saw a flicker of movement at the window, but it may have been imagination bred by fear.

She crouched and ran the remaining distance, until she stood with her back pressed against the wall of the tower. The stone felt hot. She found herself panting to get her breath back.

The next step was obvious. It was to turn the iron handle and see if the door would open. And yet, she didn't want to try that handle.

Why not? You must.

I can't.

You can! You will!

She reached out and turned the handle. It was open. Inside the tower was dark and musty. A narrow circular wooden stairway led to an upper room.

She moved toward the stairs, and as she did, caught a glimpse of movement out of the corner of her eye.

Too late.

There was a tremendous boom, and the boom hurled her backwards against the wall.

MICHAEL ALLEN

NO HOLDS BARRED

BART

NEW YORK

ISBN: 1-55785-096-8

First Bart Books edition: April 1989

Bart Books
155 E. 34th Street
New York, New York 10016

Manufactured in the United States of America

From *The Spectator*, 19 March 1881:

A great and successful crime has startled Europe. The Nihilists, after four known and several unknown attempts, have succeeded in killing the Emperor of Russia. Though warned from abroad, and by his Minister of the Interior, Count Melikoff, the Emperor persisted on Sunday in attending a review. He had nearly returned to the Winter Palace when a bomb exploded beneath his carriage, wounding some Cossacks in attendance behind. The Emperor alighted, and, in spite of a remonstrance from his coachman, insisted on seeing to the wounded, when a second bomb thrown by a man standing near, fell between his legs, and exploding, broke both legs, laid open the bowels till they protruded, and tore the left eye from its socket. From eighteen to twenty other persons were also seriously wounded. He was rapidly borne to the Palace, but according to the best accounts he never recovered perfect consciousness, though he whispered, "I am cold," and at four o'clock he died.

Please to remember the Fifth of November,
Gunpowder Treason and Plot.
We know no reason why gunpowder treason
Should ever be forgot.

Traditional English rhyme

1

On the Monday, when it didn't matter one way or the other, Sally felt fine.

On the Tuesday, when it mattered more than anything had ever mattered before, she felt terrible.

Tuesday was the day she had to fight the Russian.

It was Tuesday, July 29, 1980. The place, Moscow. It was the day the Olympic judo finals for women were to be held.

Sally Denning woke up and looked at the quartz alarm clock which she had brought with her from home.

Two A.M. She had been woken by a clattering of dustbins in the small courtyard outside the window of her room. But now that she was awake she realized that she didn't feel at all well. And she knew immediately that the Russians had given her something. Some kind of drug.

Nonsense. Ignore. Turn Over. Go back to sleep.

3

That was what she usually did when she felt nervous before a major competition.

Except this time Sally wasn't able to sleep. The symptoms were definitely there: a restless churning of the gut; the headache; the aches and pains in the muscles. It was an unnerving feeling, like fingers on your leg in the dark of a cinema.

At 4 A.M. the same thing happened. There was another disturbance, in the corridor this time. Lights came on and shone through the pane of glass above the door to Sally's room. Then the door opened and a voice apologized in slurred Russian. The door closed again. Loudly.

Natalie Zasulich was not disturbed, of course. Natalie Zasulich slept in a soundproofed room.

I will eat breakfast. I feel perfectly O.K. There is nothing whatever the matter with me. It's all an illusion. I will eat this Russian porridge and I will enjoy it and it will do me good. It will make me strong and I will beat that Russian bitch Zasulich again. I've beaten her before and I'll beat her again today. I will beat her and beat her and beat her. Always provided, that is, I can eat this porridge first.

Sally realized that the drug was a clever cocktail, with the dosage carefully judged. It contained some kind of hallucinogen which made the world seem unreal. It crippled but it did not paralyze. It sneaked up on you, hit you hard and went away. And then just when you thought you had managed to eat the porridge, it came back and slugged you again. And after that you were sick.

Ben Meadows, the team's coach and manager, came and stood by Sally as she wiped her mouth with a towel. She saw his face turn pale with anger, and although she didn't really hear what he said to the other girls, she understood his reaction perfectly.

And she smiled.

He is furious, she thought happily. *Ben feels for me! He cares for me. Hold my hand, Ben, I love you.*

Why do I always want the things I can't have? Like Olympic gold medals, for instance. And Ben.

You're crazy, Sal. You're a fruit-case. How could you possibly be stupid enough to imagine that the Russians would let you win? Didn't you know how important it was to them, here in Moscow of all places? They have Zasulich's name engraved on that gold medal already.

And how could you possibly have imagined that Ben would care for you? He's married, don't you know that? He's married, do you hear?

Yes, yes, I hear you.

Sally knew that the women's judo finals were to be held in the huge Central Stadium, a vast oval complex of buildings named after Lenin. Altogether the complex contained twenty-six swimming pools, three hundred soccer fields, and twelve hundred gymnasiums. The corridors stretched for miles.

"Here, come with me." Ben took her arm and

made her walk beside him. They were inside the hall now, but she didn't remember how they had gotten there. He took her arm. Made her walk. Corridors.

The hall was high and airy, with the seats in steep tiers. The mountainous seats were ahead of her. Blurred. They seemed to climb right into the sky.

"There," said Ben. "Do you see?"

She tried hard to see what he was pointing at. But there were tears in her eyes. Blurred again.

"No. I can't see."

Ben turned her shoulders so that she was looking in the right direction.

"There," he said after a moment. "Can you see him now?"

And at last she *could* see. Her father was there, just beyond the barrier, perhaps five yards away. He was a spectator and she was a competitor and never the twain shall meet. *Security, you understand*.

Sally looked at him across the no-man's land between the barriers, her eyes focussing as if down a funnel. A small man. Surprisingly small. He seemed old and vulnerable. And he had a pipe in his mouth, as always.

Don't frown, Daddy! Don't look so worried. I'm all right, really! Look at me, I wave and I smile reassuringly. I'm all right, really I am.

There were two tables in the under-61-kilos competition, Sally remembered that, and she reminded herself of it over and over again. Table A and table B. Sally herself was in table A, Natalie Zasulich in B. They were seeded one and two, and the system was designed to keep them apart until the final. If Sally should get that far.

Sally's first fight was against a Rumanian. The judges stopped it after a few seconds because someone complained that the contests were being held in the wrong order. But it didn't make any difference. Eleven seconds after the restart, Sally won. She was strong and fast. No stamina, of course, but she was strong and fast to begin with.

Afterwards her stomach churned again. She was sweating one minute and shivering with cold the next. The other girls in the team did what they could to look after her.

In the second fight Sally beat a Swiss girl by *ippon*. No problem.

I am fast, I am strong, I am winning.

Yes, but you're sick, you fool, don't kid yourself, these are the flotsam, the makeweights, the girls who can't even convince themselves that they might win. They aren't even surprised when they lose. When you throw them they shake their heads and almost smile, because they always knew you were a winner.

There was a break then. Lunch, was it? Sally tried hard to eat something but couldn't. She was O.K. though. She said so frequently, whether asked or not. But no one in the team seemed to believe her.

The semifinals were held in the afternoon. Sally's opponent was from the People's Republic of

Korea: a tough and vigorous little girl. Just before the contest began, the Nigerian judge objected to Sally's jacket. There was nothing unusual about it. She had worn it in dozens of contests, including today's, but apparently it wouldn't do: the sleeves were too short.

Sally shrugged, went off and changed it, and then came back.

The judge objected again. The jacket still wasn't right. Sally went off for a second time, and came back in the jacket she had worn the first time. Ah, that was much better! Of course. *And how much did you earn for that, little man?*

All this hassle had been arranged deliberately; Sally knew that perfectly well. It was standard procedure for the Russians. But it bothered her not at all, because she was high, floating, quite above small matters of this kind.

She won in twenty-eight seconds with *Uchimata* for *ippon*. Hard. Fast. Unbeatable, for the moment at any rate.

Ben pounded her on the back with praise. "Fantastic!" he shouted. "Fantastic! You've made the Olympic final! Fantastic! You'll be our first-ever gold medallist! I know you will, I can feel it in my bones!"

Sally beamed. *If I win today he will hug me. I'm sure of it. Dear God, Ben, how I love you! But it's not fair. You have no right to be married. It's not fair. . . .*

*   *   *

Sally and her teammates watched Natalie Zasulich as she made swift and dramatic progress through table B. They watched her closely, noticing how she looked, how she moved, whether she was quick, slow, nervous, tense, confident, or angry. The one thing they could be quite sure of was that Natalie Zasulich did not feel sick. Not cripplingly, achingly sick.

In the semifinal for table B, Zasulich left a Czechoslovakian girl flat on the mat with a leg twitching uncontrollably. The injury looked ugly and the doctors rushed the Czech competitor away. Sally smiled. Judo means "the gentle way" in Japanese, but there was nothing gentle about the Russian. Not today.

Eventually the time came for the final to begin.

Sally ignored the clock and stayed where she was. She felt totally unconcerned.

Everyone else was very concerned. A large, bosomy Russian official began screaming at Sally, her face contorted by rage. But Sally herself remained calm; and she also remained seated in the changing-room, until at last Ben was sent in to talk some sense into her. He came and stood in front of her and put his hand on her shoulder.

"They're waiting," he said quietly. He looked worried.

"Let them wait."

Ben paused. "They may disqualify you."

Sally laughed out loud. "No, they won't!" she said. "Don't be so stupid, Ben! They want to win out there, on the mat. Not here, by default. If I stay here and complain that I've been poisoned, it's an international incident. If I go out there and get beaten, it's sour grapes. So they *won't* disqualify me and I am *not* going out. Not yet, anyway. Let them wait. Let them sweat a bit. God knows, I need an edge of some kind."

Ben stared at her for a moment and then broke into a grin. "O.K.," he said. "When you're ready."

Sally closed her eyes.

Her mind was clear now, clear and rested. So she thought about her family: about her father, who was here; and about her mother and her brother, who were both dead. And then, when she was ready, she went out into the hall.

"Hajime!" Begin.

The foul-smelling, vile corruption of the Russian's breath hit Sally like a brick wall. It was deliberate, of course, like everything else that had happened that day, but it was a shock all the same.

"Whore!" snarled the Russian in English. "Dirty, filthy, shit-eating whore! I am going to crush you! Kill you! Destroy you!" And then, as if to prove the point, Zasulich began to fight with a ferocity which Sally had never experienced before.

Show no weakness, thought Sally. *Attack.*

She went for *Tsuri Goshi,* a lifting hip throw. She pulled with her left hand to break the Russian's balance, stepped in with her right foot, turned on it. Her right hand let go of the lapel, reached over the left arm and grabbed Zasulich's belt.

Straighten the knees, give a strong pull, turn and throw her over your hip.

But it didn't work, of course. Zasulich countered by jumping to her left, causing Sally to lose her balance. She stumbled and fell.

On the mat the groundwork was hard. Hard, grinding, and exhausting. There was the stink of the Russian's breath, the occasional gasped insult, the strength, the power, the grip. It was all so very hard.

Attack.

Sally went for *Kesa Gatame*, but the Russian freed her upper arm. The hold was broken and the count stopped.

Now it was the Russian's turn: *Mune Gatame,* a very strong hold. Zasulich put her weight on Sally and relaxed fully. Sally's only hope was to turn over. She had to catch the Russian's left foot in her right hand and lift, combining it with a turn.

I'm not going to be able to do it. I have no strength. I can't do it.

Yes you can! You can!

She made it and broke free.

A shoulder throw, *Seionage,* but it has to be done with speed, and Sally had no speed. Not now. Her time perception had slowed and her muscular response was flagging. She stumbled and fell, expecting an attack.

But Zasulich did not attack.

Why not?

Zasulich went on the defensive, seeking only to

survive, and Sally couldn't understand why. It was not until five years later that she understood.

And the rest became a blur. Sally attacked and failed, attacked and failed, over and over again.

It seemed to go on, and on, and on, but eventually the contest ended. They stopped struggling and bowed to each other instead.

The exhaustion was so complete, the aches and pains so numerous, that she couldn't even begin to count them. But they didn't matter any more. It was over, that was the main thing.

The judges indicated the result. The hall whirled around her.

"What happened?" asked Sally.

"It was two to one," said Ben.

"For me?"

"No . . . against you."

There was a tremendous roaring in her ears. It was the roar of the Moscow crowd, of course: they were acclaiming Natalie Zasulich.

Sally couldn't believe it. "But . . . I won, didn't I? Surely everyone could see that? I attacked more— and that means I was the winner."

"The judges define attacks," said Ben. "Not you, Sally, and not me." He said it gently, to comfort her, but she could not absorb his meaning.

Hug me, Ben. Hug me, please. Pull me in close and tell me it doesn't matter. Tell me you don't care that I lost. Tell me you love me, because I love you!

Ben turned his face away from her, and she didn't understand why: she confused his distress and anger with rejection, for her brain was even more fatigued than her body.

She sat down heavily, collapsed almost, her head slumped over her knees. In her ears there was a continuous roar of applause and she wanted to weep with rage and pain. She felt robbed—robbed of the title, robbed of the gold medal, but most of all, robbed of Ben.

If I had won, she thought despairingly, *Ben would have loved me. If I had won he would have held me tight. . . .*

2

Monday, March 25, 1985.

The car was at least ten years old, and as soon as Jane saw it she made up her mind to tell Flettner exactly what she thought of his arrangements. The back seat was filthy, but there appeared to be no alternative means of transport, so she got in.

Jane was not looking forward to the journey. The camp lay two hundred miles into Libya, across an endless expanse of dunes.

It was hot, even early in the morning, and they had to stop several times when the radiator boiled over. The driver, Mahmud, was a Berber; he was about thirty, but his teeth were already deformed and black. He had strapped four goatskins full of water to the outside of the car to keep them cool, but even so the water was lukewarm when they drank it.

For the first hour, Mahmud glanced in the mirror every few seconds. Jane realized that he was looking at her, rather than checking for a tail, and she had made a point of wearing slacks to avoid getting him worked up. Unfortunately, Mahmud could not take a hint, and the first time they stopped he leered at her as she got out. But when he put out his hand to touch her bare arm she was ready.

"Aieee!" Mahmud sucked the base of his thumb where Jane's knife had drawn blood.

Jane smiled at him. "Do that again, Mahmud, and the next time it'll be your cock that's bleeding." She smiled again, more genuinely this time.

Mahmud said nothing and looked hurt, as if he had been treated unjustly. But he gave no more trouble after that.

Only twice in two hundred miles was there any relief from the monotonous sand: once they came to an expanse of black rock which gave way almost immediately to amazingly green fields, and after that it was sand again. Shortly afterwards Jane suddenly saw hundreds of palm trees on the horizon, waving gently amidst a deep blue sea.

"Look!" she said. "Over there!"

Mahmud looked, and then shrugged to show his indifference. "Aywa, sarab," he said. *Yes, a mirage*. Big deal.

It was noon when the camp came into view: a few huts, a bare flagpole, and some tents. It was not an exciting prospect, but it would be home for the next four weeks.

When the car stopped, Jane took a quick look around and decided that the scene didn't seem to have changed much from last year. She got out, picked up her bag and walked towards the largest hut, which was the commandant's office. Through the open window of one of the other buildings she could see several heads staring at her, but she ignored them.

Jane went in through the open door and dropped her bag with a thud.

Klaus Flettner looked up; he had a pipe in his mouth.

"For Christ's sake give me a drink," said Jane with a croak.

Flettner indicated a pitcher on a table beside his desk. Jane picked it up, drank deeply, and then tipped the rest of the water over her uplifted face. She rubbed some round the back of her neck. Now she felt a great deal better.

Flettner was not pleased. He took the pipe out of his mouth. "Water is very scarce around here."

"Then you should get yourself better organized, shouldn't you?" said Jane.

She quite liked Flettner and she knew from experience that he was a very capable camp commandant. But she was determined to remind him that she was not just a meek little *hausfrau*.

"I thought you Germans were supposed to be good at administration," she went on. "Precious little sign of it around here. I suppose it's another of those myths, like Latin lovers."

Flettner grunted. "Huh. Still the same Jane as ever, I see. Good-humored, tolerant, easygoing. What a pleasure to have you with us." He puffed away, blowing out clouds of blue smoke. "And how are you, my dear? Are you well?"

"That's a stupid, bourgeois question." Jane came and sat down in a canvas chair in front of the desk. "If I wasn't well I wouldn't be here."

Flettner shrugged. "As you wish. I was only trying to be polite."

"Don't bother."

Jane wasn't sure why she felt so angry. It was a combination of factors, perhaps: the weather, the journey, and most of all the risk. That bugged her, she decided. The risk: in this situation other people's mistakes could so easily put your life on the line.

From where she was sitting Jane could see into the adjoining hut. The heads that had turned to look at her when she first arrived were now staring straight ahead, listening to a lecturer.

"What's the subject?" she asked.

Flettner followed her glance and then consulted the timetable on his desk. "Codes."

Jane sighed. "Fascinating. And who are your instructors this year?"

"Palestinian Rejection Front, most of them. Plus a few guest speakers, such as yourself."

Jane leaned forward. She was beginning to recover from her exhaustion. "And tell me, Klaus, have you got anyone for me?"

Flettner paused before answering. "We have with us twenty fine young men and women." His manner could be very germanic at times. "Well-educated, intelligent, fit . . ."

"Yes, yes, I know all that, Klaus. But have you got anyone for *me?* Specifically for me."

"Well, take your pick," said Flettner with an expansive gesture. "They are all absolutely first-class material."

"No doubt. But how many are English?"

"One."

"One!" Jane was horrified. "Only one?" She stood up. "Now listen, you bastard, I told you I wanted a choice!"

"Yes, indeed you did, Jane. But I'm afraid it could not be arranged."

Jane's mouth narrowed. "Get him in here."

"Who?"

"The Englishman."

Flettner puffed a little smoke. "My dear Jane, let me remind you that *I* am the camp commandant here, not you. I give the orders."

"Yes, dear, I know you do," said Jane, as if to a retarded child. "But get him in here anyway. I want to see what he's like."

Flettner smiled, revealing a gold tooth which had not been there the previous year. Then he returned to his paperwork. He plainly had no intention of being dictated to or provoked, and after a moment Jane admitted defeat. She went out into the sunshine to look around the camp.

After the evening meal break Jane was finally granted her request. The delay did not surprise her; the camp was run on military lines, and she knew that although she could be rude to Flettner in private and get away with it, she could not give him orders.

At seven o'clock Jane and Klaus Flettner sat behind a trestle table in one of the lecture rooms, with an empty chair in front of them.

The interviewee was called in.

Neither Jane nor Flettner said anything to him, but after hesitating for a moment he sat down in the obvious place.

Flettner puffed smoke.

Jane read the papers in the folder in front of her.

Eventually she looked up. "So you are Gordon Tate?"

"Yes."

Jane examined a photograph of Gordon which had been taken on his arrival two days earlier. It was full-length, and he had been required to strip naked for it.

Jane was rarely stirred by pictures, but she had to admit that this one was interesting. She glanced up at the subject, comparing the bulge in his jeans with the photograph.

"You're a big boy, Gordon, aren't you? A very big boy."

Gordon stirred in his chair.

"A pity you can't use it, though." She looked up at him and smiled thinly. "It says here that you're impotent."

"That's not true."

"Isn't it?"

"No . . . I just had a bad dose of the clap, that's all. It sort of . . . put me off."

Jane laughed. "Well, we'll see. We'll soon see."

Gordon actually wriggled, and Jane was delighted. It was clear that he hated this whole business, and that was fine as far as she was concerned. *Let's pile it on some more*.

"How old are you?"

"Twenty-three."

"Did you fill in this form?" Jane waved one of the documents.

"Yes."

"Well, you said how old you are on the form. So why answer the question when you know I have the information in front of me?"

No response.

"You say here that you've never been in any trouble with the police. Are you sure about that?"

"Quite sure, yes."

"You've never been arrested, never been charged with any sort of crime?"

"No, never."

"You could get into a great deal of trouble if you're lying, you know." A strong touch of the schoolmarm entered Jane's voice.

"I am not lying!" said Gordon. Sweat was running down his cheeks.

"Are you straight?"

"How do you mean, straight?"

"Sexually straight, that's how I mean."

"Yes, of course I am."

"There's no *of course* about it, sunshine. With that moustache of yours you look like a 1970s Village faggot. In fact I think that's what you are.

A fag. All this crap about catching a dose is just a lie. I'm going to have to keep a careful eye on you, Gordon, I can see that. What's your earliest memory?''

"My . . . earliest memory?'' The sudden change of tack had thrown him, just as she had hoped it would.

"Yes, that's what I said.''

"Well—of my mother, walking away from me. Leaving me crying.''

"Tell me how you got here. In your own words.''

"How I got here? Well, by plane and lorry.''

Jane rolled her eyes skywards. "Jesus H. Christ, Klaus, do you seriously expect me to take this idiot? The man's a fucking moron.''

Flettner took the pipe out of his mouth. "What Dr. Challoner means, Gordon, is that she would like you to tell us something about your political background. How you came to hold your present views, how you came to be recruited, that sort of thing.''

"Oh. Yes. I see.'' Gordon began to look more at ease. "Well, I suppose I first got actively involved when I was at the polytechnic.''

"Where you took an extra year to get a very poor degree,'' Jane commented.

"Well, yes . . .''

"Go on, Gordon,'' said Flettner; his tone was encouraging.

"Well, I got interested in politics then, as I say. I met a lot of people who felt very strongly about various issues. And I did, too. So we went to a lot of demos, some of them pretty violent. And it . . . sort of went on from there. Wherever there was trouble we would go along and sort of . . . give it a helping hand.''

"In what way?" asked Flettner.

"Well, just throwing stones, writing slogans, that sort of thing at first. But then we got a bit more professional. We made firebombs, roadblocks, dropped bricks off the roofs, that sort of thing.''

"And where did you do these daring deeds?" asked Jane.

"Well, Liverpool, Manchester, Brixton. Wherever . . .''

"You got paid, of course?"

"Well, sometimes, yes.''

"Who by?"

Gordon looked sly. "Ask no questions, tell no lies.''

"And how did you get invited to come here?"

"Um, it was last February, in Liverpool. There was some trouble up there—''

"At the by-election?"

"Yes. And a guy who knew me, knew my record, asked me if I wanted to train as an urban guerilla.''

"What sort of man was this?"

"Well, I don't know, really. I think he's a Maoist.''

"I see. Why did you accept?"

"Well, because I hadn't got anything else to do, so I thought I might as well.''

"And you were afraid to refuse.''

"Well, yes. He did suggest it might not be a good idea to say no." Gordon grinned sheepishly.

"I see . . . State your political position. Succinctly, please, we haven't got all day." Jane used a handkerchief to wipe the back of her neck; it was dripping.

"Well, I'm a socialist," said Gordon. "I believe in the abolition of private property." He paused.

"Is that it?"

"Well, yes."

"Which political thinkers have influenced you most?"

"Umm, Marx, I suppose."

"Have you read any Marx?"

A hesitation. "No."

"Who have you read?"

More hesitation. "Well . . ."

"Have you read Frantz Fanon?"

"No."

"Carlos Marighella?"

"No."

"Regis Debray?"

"No."

"Agatha Christie?"

No response.

Jane laughed. She hadn't enjoyed herself so much for a long time. "You haven't read much, have you, Gordon? And when you go back from here, after you've been trained as an urban guerilla, as you put it, what are you going to do then?"

"Well, it depends, I suppose."

"What do you hope to achieve, exactly? What revolutionary change do you hope to bring about? What is your objective?"

Gordon leaned forward, twisting his hands together. "Well, I'd like to help to destroy the class structure—put an end to bourgeois capitalist society."

"Bourgeois . . . capitalist . . . society." Jane repeated each word, as if savoring the taste of them. "I see. And if you succeed in that, we shall all live happily ever after, shall we?"

"Well, we'll be better off than before, yes."

"Like the Russians, you mean? Or the Chinese? As well off as they are?"

No answer.

"Have you ever killed anyone?"

"No, not that I know of."

"Could you?"

"Well . . . yes. Sure."

"You are quite certain?"

"Yes."

"What are you specializing in while you're here?"

"It's on the form," said Gordon, pointing towards the folder. "I'm not supposed to answer if it's on the form. Isn't that right?"

Jane's expression scarcely flickered but her euphoria received a nasty jolt. *Oh-ho, so we're going to have to watch you, aren't we, Gordon? A clever little dick, it seems*.

"On your form," she said thoughtfully. "Well

now, let's see. Oh yes, here it is: explosives.'' She looked up again. ''Tell me, Gordon, do you think one man can ever alter the course of history?''

Gordon thought about it for a moment. ''Yes, I think so.''

''Give me an example.''

Gordon shrugged. ''Well—Adolf Hitler.''

''Not a very good example,'' said Jane briskly. ''I'm talking about people who change the balance of power by a single act of violence. Name me one of those.''

Gordon's face was blank. His hands worked in his lap.

''Very well,'' said Jane. ''I'll give *you* one—Lee Harvey Oswald.''

After the interview, Jane was restless and dissatisfied. She walked around the room to dissipate some of her nervous energy. Flettner remained seated, puffing his pipe.

''He won't do,'' she said eventually. ''He's absolutely useless.''

Flettner paused before speaking. ''He is not useless. He is intelligent, willing, and strong.''

''Intelligent? Him?''

''He is not a Doctor of Philosophy, I admit. He cannot debate on quite such a high plane as yourself. But, I repeat, he is good material. He has a degree in electronics, and physically he is exceptionally fit. He is very well trained in judo and karate. And we will do much with him here.''

Jane frowned. ''Yes, but he's so . . . I don't

know. He's such a *moron*. Look at his psychologi-
cal profile. Afraid of posh hotels and restaurants.
A health-food freak. Worries about being consti-
pated. One job since he graduated, as a TV technician. And he was sacked from that because he was
suspected of petty theft. It's a *pathetic* record.''

"I think," said Flettner patiently, "that what
you are trying to say is that Gordon is one of the
led, rather than a leader. But that, my dear Jane, is
precisely what you need."

"Oh, he's a sheep all right, I can see that."

"And since you are so worried about his psy-
chological background, you will have noticed, I'm
sure, that he is motivated by a perfectly genuine
grievance?"

"No," said Jane sharply. "I didn't see that. Tell
me about it."

"Oh, it's in the papers somewhere. There was a
car crash which killed his father and mother, and
left his younger brother with serious brain damage.
He's in a home for the handicapped. Gordon himself grew up in an orphanage."

"And that's a genuine grievance?"

"No, not that in itself. But the family should
have gotten some sort of compensation, and didn't.
The case got lost in the courts. Later on, when he
was eighteen, Gordon tried to pursue the matter.
But he was too late. Even the negligent solicitor
was dead. So he and his brother got nothing. Your
wonderful British justice had failed. And, naturally, Gordon has a grudge against the system."

"Hmm, well, maybe. But what I need is someone with teeth. Do you think this man can kill?"

"In due course we shall find out—just as we did
with you. Remember?"

Jane turned and looked at Flettner in surprise.
Then she smiled. Yes. She did remember. She
remembered very well.

After four weeks, Gordon Tate believed that he
was the fittest man in the camp.

He thought he was fitter than Klaus Flettner
because when all was said and done, the German
was forty years old. Gordon was also fitter than
the Palestinian instructors, because in their view, a
spartan life was sufficient to strengthen a man in
itself, without the need for further effort. And
Gordon was sure that he was fitter than any of the
other trainees, because unlike them he had not
smoked marijuana, had not indulged himself sexually, and had not been involved in drunken fights.
He had eaten regularly, slept long, and trained
hard.

Gordon had now come to know his fellow trainees quite well. There were seventeen men and
three women. They were all Europeans, all in their
twenties and all with several years of higher edu-
cation: one or two held doctorates. Most came
from comfortable backgrounds: their fathers were
doctors, lawyers, and civil servants. And yet somehow or other, these totally respectable parents had
produced highly rebellious children. For among
the other attributes which Gordon had noticed in

all the trainees was a determination to destroy the society in which they lived. That was why they were here: to learn the techniques of violent revolution.

Much to his surprise, Gordon had enjoyed most of the training. He was surprised by that, because he had never enjoyed any previous educational process: learning had always been a problem for him. But this time he had found it all quite easy. He was better at some things than others, of course: good at guns, codes, radios, and explosives. Not very good at disguises, leadership, or problem-solving.

Now, after four weeks, it was over. Today was a Friday, and tomorrow they would all return to Tunisia and fly home. Gordon was looking forward to that. He wasn't sure what he would do next: get a job, perhaps. Nor was he sure that he would use his new skills. Maybe he would, but maybe not. Poisoning water supplies was a bit different from painting slogans on walls. It was a different league altogether, and Gordon wasn't sure that he wanted to get involved in it. In fact he wasn't at all sure how he had come to be involved in it in the first place.

In the middle of this reverie, one of the Palestinians tapped him on the shoulder and told him that he was wanted in Flettner's office. Good. Gordon found Flettner easy to talk to: he was firm and stood no nonsense, but he was friendly and jolly, a bit like a bachelor uncle.

Gordon entered the now-familiar wooden hut

and found Flettner standing up, obviously waiting for him.

"Ah, come in, Gordon, come in." He indicated a chair.

"Thanks." Gordon sat.

Flettner puffed on his pipe for a moment, and then resumed his seat behind the desk.

"Well now, Gordon, you've come to the end of the course."

Gordon nodded happily. This reminded him of the end of term at school. No problems so far. "Yes," he said. He nearly added "sir" but bit it off at the last moment.

"Yes, come to the end of the course," said Flettner again, flicking through the papers in front of him. Gordon recognized his file: it seemed to have gotten a good deal thicker since the interview with Jane Challoner.

"Well, Gordon," Flettner continued, "before you graduate, so to speak, I want to show you something. Something which I think you will find very interesting."

He turned in his swivel chair and closed a venetian blind so that the light level was reduced. Then he pressed a button on a video recorder beside his desk, and a television set behind it flickered into life.

"This is a recording of what happened at this time last year," said Flettner. "Same camp, but different people."

The camera picked up a group of about twenty-five young Europeans, sitting on the ground in front of a blackboard, listening to yet another lecturer. Mercifully there was no sound.

"Now," said Flettner. "Watch the door of the hut."

The camera zoomed in on the door of the hut—*this* hut, Gordon realized. His heart began to beat faster. He wasn't sure why, but his instincts told him that something bad was about to happen.

Nothing did happen for about a minute, but then the door opened and Jane Challoner appeared. The camera pulled back to a wide-angle shot.

The trainees took no notice of Jane and went on listening. Gordon watched her closely.

She went round to the rear of the group and brought her hand out from behind her back. She was holding a pistol.

She cocked it, and in his mind Gordon could hear the click. He stopped breathing.

The trainees looked round now. The lecture had suddenly ceased to be interesting and the instructor moved to one side. He was smiling, Gordon noticed.

Jane spoke. She said a name perhaps, and the girl she had addressed stood up; she was open-mouthed, incredulous.

Jane shot her once, and then again; she hit the girl both times. The force of the bullets knocked the girl a long way; they sent her sprawling into two or three of the other trainees, who pushed her away from them, on to the ground. The trainees who had touched the dying girl leapt to their feet in revulsion, wiping their hands on their clothes.

Everyone else stood up too, edging well away

from Jane. She went over and looked at the girl on the ground. Then she fired down at her once more. Gordon could almost feel the concussive effect as the bullet went in.

Flettner switched off the machine.

Gordon wanted to moan. *Oh no no no no no*. It was horrible, dreadful. He didn't want to have *anything* to do with that. Not to watch it or think about it or know about it. But deeply engraved on his brain was a truth he had learned the hard way: you must never, never show weakness. So he said nothing. He tried hard not to flicker an eyelid, but his pulse was pounding and his palms had gone cold.

"Well now," said Flettner calmly. "Wasn't that interesting?"

Gordon said nothing.

"What do you think of our Dr. Challoner now?"

Gordon knew that he had to say something. "She's all right," he said, as neutrally as he could.

"All right," repeated the East German. "What a useful phrase that is. It can mean so many different things in English, according to the inflection. All right . . . Hmm. Let us be more specific. What do you think of Dr. Challoner as a lecturer, for example?"

"She's very good."

"Yes, well, so she should be. It's her profession. It's fascinating, you know, that she should have chosen locks and security systems as her specialty. Locks are terribly Freudian, don't you think?"

Gordon raised an eyebrow and listened carefully: the danger was not yet past.

"I seem to remember that locks and keys come into *Faust*, don't they?" said Flettner. "Have you ever read *Faust*?"

Gordon shook his head. Not only had he never read *Faust*, he had never even heard of it.

"Yes, I think they do," Flettner mused on. "And the key, of course, represents the penis. Yes, I think that's the way it works. How interesting it would be to think it through, Gordon, if only one had the time. Anyway, the fact is, I showed you that videotape in order to demonstrate to you what happens to some of our students. In the case of those we value highly, like Jane, they are given a chance to prove themselves, and then they go out into the world and make their mark on history. Jane has spent the last year helping the IRA. In her spare time, of course, I must emphasize that. Officially she has remained a university lecturer. And now, tell me: what do you think of her as a woman?"

"As a woman?"

"Yes."

"How do you mean?"

"Well, do you find her attractive, for instance?"

"Yes, I suppose so." *More caution. Be careful, Gordon. Mind what you say.*

"Everybody else certainly thinks she is attractive," Flettner assured him. "She is young, and she takes great trouble over her appearance, even here. Everything color-coordinated. And you may have noticed, Gordon, that in the past four weeks Jane has slept with many of the men in this camp, with two notable exceptions: you, and me. She has avoided sleeping with me in order to make it clear that I do not own her. Last year, you see, we were lovers for the whole time she was here. And in your case, of course, she has avoided sleeping with you because you are impotent.''

"No I'm not." The denial came out fast, but after a moment Gordon thought he had better add to it. "Look, I'm a bit fed up with people being rude about my sex life. I don't know where you get your information from, but I can screw just as well as the next man. But I told you—I had a very bad infection. It was bloody painful. And if you'd suffered the way I've suffered you'd think twice before shoving it into someone new."

Flettner shrugged. "As you wish. But do you think you could work with Jane?"

Careful, Gordon. Watch what you say. "Yes, I suppose so."

"You suppose so." Flettner rose, relit his pipe and began to pace about. "Tell me, Gordon, why do you think you were invited here?"

It was Gordon's turn to shrug. "I don't know."

"Why do you think you, of all people, had all your expenses paid, while some of the others paid as much as five thousand U.S. dollars to come here?"

Gordon's eyes widened.

"Oh yes, indeed they did. Believe me, Gordon, I would not lie to you. The Scandinavians and the

Italians particularly, they will *pay* to be taught how to destroy things. So, why do you think you were invited to come here free?''

''I don't know,'' Gordon repeated. It was true, and it also seemed the safest answer.

''Well, I will tell you. You were chosen because Jane needs someone. She has an ambitious plan—a plan which Moscow approves and wishes to build on. Because Moscow, of course, pays for all this, as I'm sure you realize.''

Gordon hadn't realized, but he decided not to admit it.

''So that is why,'' Flettner continued, ''that is why you were selected and brought here and trained. To create a small cell of two people to carry out a very important mission.''

He paused. And waited. And then: ''Don't you want to know what that mission is?''

Gordon's mind could work fast at times, especially under pressure. His brain ran through the alternative answers, considering the implications. Whichever answer he gave would involve danger, but a positive answer seemed the least dangerous.

''Yes,'' he said. ''Yes, of course I want to know.''

Flettner nodded. ''Good. The plan,'' he said carefully, ''is to kill the British prime minister. Very simple.'' He spread his hands. ''Quite straightforward. And what I must ask you is this. Why do you think Moscow would want to do that?''

Gordon groped for a moment, and then came up with the stock answer which appeared perhaps half a dozen times in his lecture notes. "Well, because every time a public figure in the West is assassinated, it creates panic, uncertainty, and confusion. The stock market suffers, the economy dips, and . . . well, all that sort of thing."

"Good," said Flettner with a nod. "Good. I see you have studied well. To be more precise, Gordon, there are two motives behind this plan of Jane's. One personal, and one political. The political motive is that the present British prime minister is a very right-wing gentleman. He is strongly pro-American, and is cooperating with the U.S. in strengthening the American nuclear presence in Great Britain. However, a great deal of his authority is based on his dominant personality—and if he himself is disposed of, then the balance of power will shift sharply to the left. We have very good reasons for supposing that if the prime minister dies, then the plan to accept more American missiles on British soil will be quietly shelved. That is the political motive behind this operation, and I'm sure you can follow its logic."

There were voices and sounds of movement outside the hut, and Gordon shifted nervously. Flettner appeared not to notice.

"But you know, Gordon, whenever someone approaches us with a plan, we usually find that there are personal motives, too. And that is so in this case. When Jane was a child, the man who is now prime minister was then an unknown politician. But he was a friend of her father's, and round about the time when Jane was fourteen, he became her lover. You can imagine what she was like in those days, Gordon. A temptation to any man. And although she was by no means naive and foolish, Jane fell in love with this man. As is the way with young girls, even intelligent ones, she had dreams that he would divorce his wife and marry her. All of which, of course, came to nothing.

"So now Jane feels that the prime minister used her, lied to her, and rejected her. In her eyes he also ruined her father financially. Anyway, Gordon, the fact of the matter is, Jane now wants her revenge. And since what Jane wants is what Moscow wants, too, you and I are going to help her."

Gordon twisted his hands together as he fought to gain control of himself. He didn't want to have anything to *do* with all this. It was lunacy, and bloody dangerous with it. And yet what else could he do? Where else could he go? Answers: nothing, and nowhere.

"There will be no direct involvement, of course," Flettner emphasized. "Moscow much prefers not to be directly involved in matters of this kind. You yourself are not even supposed to know what Jane is planning. Not yet. And certainly not supposed to know that Moscow is behind it. But I thought it best that you should."

Thanks very much, thought Gordon. *With friends like you . . .*

"I thought it best that you should know," said Flettner steadily, "because I thought it would make it easier for you to do what you have to do next."

Gordon suddenly became still. He wanted to

moan in protest all over again. *Oh no no no no no no no.*

"You have done very well here," Flettner continued. "Very well indeed." His voice was calm and soothing. "But the question is, can you now put what you have learned into practice? Do you graduate with honors, Gordon, or do we have to judge you a failure? Do we use you for our mission, with great fame and great rewards to follow—or do we cast you aside and start our search again? Do you go on from here—or do we discard you?"

Oh please stop. Please please stop, I can't stand it. I can't stand all this horrible killing.

"What do you want me to do?" Gordon asked. He hoped that his voice did not sound as desperate as he felt.

Flettner adjusted the angle of the venetian blind so that the two of them could see through the window. Outside, the trainees were seated on the ground, just as they had been on the videotape.

"It's very simple, Gordon. I know you can do it. I'm sure you can. You see the Dutchman, over there, Hendrik Vreede?"

Twenty-six, six feet tall, light brown hair, glasses. Jeans and a T-shirt. "Yes, I see him."

"I want you to go out there and shoot him."

Gordon swallowed. "Why?"

"Why? Good question, Gordon. Why . . . Well, partly because he is useless. A rich, spoiled brat, too idle to do anything except screw and talk big. But mostly because he has been turned by Dutch intelligence."

"Turned? You mean he's a spy?"

"Yes. When he gets back to Holland—*if* he gets back—he will report on all of us. And then we shall all be on everyone's computer. Do you understand?"

Gordon nodded.

"Here." Flettner handed him a Russian pistol.

Gordon checked the magazine: eight shots.

Oh God I don't want to kill anyone.

But if you don't they'll kill you. You've been told too much. Too many secrets.

Yes, I know.

Well get on with it then. It won't be as bad as all that.

Oh, won't it?

No. It won't.

Gordon cocked the Tokarev pistol. Cocked it indoors, not outdoors, as Jane had on the video-tape. His body felt light and his hands tingled.

He opened the door and went out into the sunshine, keeping his eyes almost shut to guard against the dazzling light.

Hendrik Vreede was sitting at one side of the group. That was fortunate, because there was no one else to stop the bullet if it passed through Vreede; no one to be spattered with his brains.

Gordon walked up to Vreede without hesitating, put the gun on the back of his neck, right on the base of the skull, and pulled the trigger instantaneously.

Vreede hadn't even looked around.

The body jerked forward in a violent spasm, the

arms waving like those of a giant doll. Then: no further movement.

Gordon walked back and replaced the gun on Flettner's desk. As he let go of it, his hands started to shake uncontrollably and he stuffed them into his pockets. Even then the shaking traveled up his arms, and he was sure that Flettner could see it.

Outside there was pandemonium. One of the girls was screaming hysterically and some of the male trainees were shouting at each other.

Flettner closed the venetian blind again. "Not bad, Gordon," he said with a smile. "Not bad at all."

"Have another drink," said Flettner.

"Thanks," said Jane, "I will."

Flettner poured her another gin, and Jane watched it come out of the bottle with an almost tactile pleasure. She had already drunk one large glass, and it was improving her mood no end. That plus the knowledge that tomorrow morning she would be leaving this god-awful place and would soon wash the sand out of her hair for good.

Jane was already slightly high and she looked forward to getting completely piggly wiggly. If Flettner played his cards right she might even let him fuck her—he *was* pretty good, after all. A little heavy, but big and never in a hurry. Yes, if Flettner played his cards right . . .

"I want to have a little talk with you, Jane," said the East German.

"Oh?"

"Yes . . . I thought Gordon stood up pretty well this afternoon, didn't you?"

Jane became wary. "He passed the test, I suppose."

"Oh yes, he passed it very well. It is never easy to kill in cold blood."

Jane thought about it. "No, but that's the trouble with Gordon, you see. Cold blood. He's too cold a fish altogether. No life in him."

Flettner poured himself another whiskey. "There's not much life in his cock, that's true. But then, that's not everything. And he has many, many virtues. He's anonymous. Forgettable. He has no job, no girlfriend, and no police record. He takes orders. And he's strong."

"I don't like him," said Jane. Flettner was taking altogether too much for granted. "He's second-rate. Third-rate. And I wanted a choice— three or four people to pick from. Why didn't you give me a choice?"

"That's not as easy as you might think, Jane. English recruits of any quality are few and far between. I don't know why."

"I do. It's because of the detection rate. Most of those who volunteer find themselves doing thirty years in high-security prisons. So only the very brave and the very thick come forward. Gordon's one of the thick."

"I think you underestimate him."

"No, I don't." The gin had loosened Jane's tongue and she was talking fast now. "Anyway, I won't use him. I could find someone better in my own university. I could find some green young kid, seduce him, make him my slave. Do it that way.''

"Yes," said Flettner slowly. "You could try. The trouble is, you see, Moscow wouldn't let you.''

Jane almost choked as she tried to laugh with a mouthful of gin. "Wouldn't let me? They couldn't stop me! Not if I wanted to do it that way.''

Flettner's manner became quiet and serious. "Oh, yes they could, Jane. There's no doubt whatever that they could. And they *will* stop you, believe me, unless you do it *their way*.''

Jane paused. She suddenly didn't feel piggly wiggly any longer. "How would they stop me?''

"How do you think?''

Jane shivered, despite the heat. "They wouldn't.''

It was Flettner's turn to laugh, and she realized that her expression must be comical.

"Oh, yes they would," he said. "It's hard to believe, isn't it? Amazingly hard. But take my word for it, Jane, they would kill you without even thinking about it. . . . A year ago you put up your scheme. It was slightly wild, but then a lot of these things are. However, I passed it up the line as usual. Mine not to reason why, as you English say. And Moscow checked it out. They checked you out, too, as they always do. And the fact is, they *want* it done. But they want it done *right*. They need a good, disciplined team. And you and Gordon are a matched pair.''

"Matched by whom?''

"The computer."

Jane sneered. "The computer . . ."

"And I mean by that," said Flettner, "that you have both been measured, judged, and found suitable."

Jane turned away but Flettner followed her.

"See how much he has improved already. You saw how the others reacted to him tonight. He was a hero—a professional among amateurs. He has killed, and they haven't. And you saw how he responded to them—he *loved* it. For the first time in his life Gordon has found something he can succeed in, something which will earn him respect."

"Well, maybe. But I'm still not going to use him."

Flettner raised his voice. "You take him, or the deal is off."

He's recording this! Jane suddenly understood. *He's actually recording this whole bloody conversation. And if I don't say the right thing, it'll go all the way back to Moscow and some stupid little prick in the KGB will— Hellfire and shit!*

She put down her glass in a hurry. "Klaus," she said with a grin, "you Germans have absolutely no sense of humor, have you? You never understand when I'm joking."

"I hope you understand that I am not joking at all," said Flettner.

"Of course! Of course!" Jane went across the room and placed her hands on Flettner's shoulders. "The fact is, Klaus, Gordon is perfectly O.K. I certainly had reservations about him at the start, but not now. Now I agree with you. He's proved himself to my complete satisfaction.''

Why do my face muscles not work properly? I want to look amused and confident, but I must surely look drawn and frightened. Why why why?

Because I am frightened, that's why. Was the change of heart too sudden? Is it too obvious that I changed my mind under pressure? And does it matter, either way?

Yes, it does matter. It matters to me, if not to them. It's a matter of pride.

''What I want to say, Klaus, is that I really am very grateful. I'm grateful to you and to everyone else who had a hand in selecting Gordon. It's not easy to find promising material, I realize that, and I appreciate the time and trouble you've put in, I really do.''

How's that then? Are you listening up there in the Kremlin? Is that smarmy enough for you? Does it sound loyal and safe enough to let me go on and do what I want to do?

''Good,'' said Flettner. He was obviously very pleased. ''And now that you have accepted Gordon as your partner, I am authorized to give you a letter. Read it, and then we will burn it.''

Jane felt a sudden urge to burst into hysterical laughter. *Don't you think we ought to eat it?* she felt like saying. *Chew it slowly, thirty-two times to the mouthful, just like Nanny used to tell us?*

But she restrained herself and solemnly took the sealed envelope from the East German's hand.

She read the letter several times. And when she

had read it she could see why Flettner was treating the matter so seriously. It was signed by the head of the KGB himself.

The letter ordered her to extend the scope of her plan. Jane's first proposal had been to assassinate the British prime minister. Now the letter instructed her to do more than that. She was to wait until the president of the United States was also in England, on one of his occasional trips to Europe, and then—she was to kill them both. Together.

Jane stood there and thought about the implications. The ripples would spread and spread, she thought. Spread out through the world of today and through time. She genuinely wanted to change the world, to make it a better place for ordinary people to live in, and she could see how this plan would achieve that end. True, a lot of innocent people would be hurt in the process, but that was inevitable in any process of change.

Eventually she looked up.

"And now we must burn the letter," Flettner reminded her.

"Yes, I think we'd better."

Flettner lit a match and Jane watched as the paper was consumed. Then Flettner ground it into smaller specks, and finally he went outside and mixed the fragments of ash into the desert sand. When he came back, he took a large drink before speaking.

"I am to be your linkman, Jane. Very remote, of course. I shall be seconded to London and you will communicate with me only through a dead-letter box. But you must keep me in touch with progress.''

Jane stared at him hard. ''Are *you* happy with the plan?''

Flettner nodded. ''Yes. And I must say I was very impressed. Your original proposal was bold enough. But this—this is far more ambitious. It will change the course of history.''

''Yes,'' said Jane. She was almost whispering. ''Yes, I think you're right.''

3

Monday, April 22, 1985.

Sally Denning closed the lift door on the fourteenth floor of New Scotland Yard and pressed the button for the computer section in the basement.

As the lift went down she took another look at the photograph which her boss had just given her. It was a fuzzy full-length shot of an Italian terrorist named Antonio Volinia: he was a short man, already stout despite the fact that he was only twenty-eight years old. He had black hair, dark eyes, and wore an open-necked shirt and slacks.

After she had found the right door in the computer section, Sally knocked and then almost collided with a man coming out.

For a moment she didn't recognize him. Then, when she did, her mouth fell open in shock. It was Ben Meadows.

Sally was so surprised that at first she couldn't say anything except: ''Oh!''

''Oh indeed!'' said Ben with a wide grin. He

had obviously recognized her immediately. "What are you doing here?"

"Well, I work here," said Sally. She cursed herself as soon as the words were out; they sounded so defensive and stupid.

"Yes, I can see that," said Ben, indicating the identification card on her lapel. "But what I really meant was, whom did you want to see?"

Sally recovered her wits. "Oh, well, I've just started work in Tracing and Vetting, and Superintendent Fitch sent me down to follow up this." She waved the photograph of Volinia.

"Ah, that," said Ben cheerfully. "Yes, I know all about that. Follow me and all will be revealed."

With a smile he set off down the corridor, and after a slight hesitation Sally followed.

She felt distinctly taken aback, but also delighted. She had not so much as set eyes on Ben Meadows for five years, and now here he was in Computing. It was all very unexpected, and she was surprised to find how excited she was, but she forced herself to act normally.

Calm down, you stupid cow, she told herself. *He'll think you're a complete idiot, gasping and spluttering like some tongue-tied schoolgirl.*

Ben opened a door numbered 01.14 and ushered Sally in, switching on the light.

"Here we are. Come in and make yourself comfortable. Then we'll show you our box of tricks."

Sally smiled at him and sat down in the obvious chair.

Ben sat in front of a large television screen with

a complicated control board below it and banks of other electronic equipment on either side. He began pressing buttons and the screen flickered into life.

Sally tried not to look as flustered as she felt.

"I saw you the other day," Ben told her. "In the distance. But you didn't take any notice of me, of course. You were with a man." He smiled at her mischievously to check her reaction.

Sally almost blushed, and she felt annoyed with herself. She had forgotten how Ben used to tease, and he hadn't changed a bit. He probably hadn't really seen her at all.

"Oh yes?" she said, obviously doubting his word.

"Yes." Ben peered intently at the TV screen. "Before that I hadn't seen you for . . . oh, ages. Not since Moscow."

"No," said Sally. "No, I don't suppose you had."

The memory of Moscow hit her with an almost physical pain. She took a deep breath. She had tried so hard to forget Moscow, but now she could feel the agony of it all over again: the vomiting, the headache, and the flashing in front of her eyes. But most of all, the pain of that medal ceremony, when she could hardly stand up long enough to receive the silver, and Natalie Zasulich had waved her arms with joy as the crowd shrieked its approval.

Moscow. It spoiled the joy of seeing Ben again.

"That was a very long time ago," she said quietly. "It's all past history now."

"Yes," said Ben, "I suppose it is."

If I had won he would have loved me. Sally had never succeeded in eradicating that idea. And yet it didn't make any sense.

She glanced at Ben out of the corner of her eye. He still looked the same: tall, wide-shouldered, muscular. Not handsome exactly—he wasn't a male model—but he *was* very attractive. Thirty-five, perhaps—ten years older than herself, but still young. And still able to make her feel as if she wanted to throw herself at him. She sighed.

It's not fair.

Life never is.

"How's your father?" asked Ben as he continued to twiddle the dials.

Sally hesitated. "Well, he's not too bad for his age. He married again, you know."

"No, I didn't know."

"Yes, four years ago."

Ben looked at her for a second. "You don't sound very enthusiastic."

Sally laughed shortly. "No, I'm not, really. I don't get on with her, to be honest. But she's a pleasant enough person and Dad's very happy so it's not a problem. But he's not been too well recently—he had a heart attack."

"Oh dear, I'm sorry to hear that." Ben sounded concerned. "Give him my best regards when you see him."

"Thanks, I will."

Ben selected a cassette of videotape from a rack and clicked it into place.

"I don't manage the women's judo team any longer, you know. It all got a bit too much to handle. But I keep in touch, and they miss you."

"No, they don't," said Sally placidly. "There are lots of talented young girls these days. Better than I was. And they get younger every year."

"Yes, well, there are some very good girls about," Ben admitted. "But I'm sorry you dropped out."

"I'm not. It was absolutely the right decision. I never had time to breathe in those days. No time to read, or go to the theatre or art galleries—nothing but training, training, training. But in the last few months I've started teaching the kids at a club near my flat for a couple of evenings a week."

"Ah well, that's better," said Ben. "I wouldn't like to think you'd given up judo completely." He pressed more buttons, and the reels of tape began to revolve. "How long have you been in the Metropolitan Police?"

"Oh, five years."

"Ever since university?"

"Yes."

Ben grunted. "You're an old hand compared with me then. I've only done six months."

"How do you come to be working here at all?"

Ben chuckled. "Well, I've always worked with computers, as you know. The last job I had was in a company which made sausages—and then one day I saw a woman being mugged in the street. I was on a bus, so I couldn't do anything at the time. But that same evening I saw a job advertised at Scotland Yard—and it suddenly dawned on me that there are more important things in life than sausages.''

He said it with such a droll inflection that Sally laughed out loud. ''And what are you actually called?''

''Here? Well, I'm simply manager of the computer unit. You name it, I'm responsible for it. Data processing, programming, security and so on. I don't usually deal with anything so minor as this type of inquiry, but in your case I'll make an exception.''

More teasing. Sally smiled and took it in good part.

''And you're in Tracing and Vetting now, are you?'' Ben asked.

Sally looked away from him. Somehow she couldn't bear to meet his eyes: his gaze was so open that he seemed to be absorbing part of her being.

''Yes. I just started today. But I've been in Special Branch about a year.''

''Oh. And what have you been asked to do, precisely?''

Sally looked down at the photograph. ''Well, apparently this man Volinia was spotted in an airport in Tunisia last Saturday afternoon. And as I understand it, the idea is to look at the videotape of the airport and to track down anyone he spoke to, to see if they're involved in anything illegal.''

''O.K.,'' said Ben. ''Let's play the tape and see what we can find.''

He pressed a button and a picture appeared: it was just a standard airport lounge.

"This is Monastir," said Ben. "Now, the modern terrorist is a mobile animal, so in the past few years strenuous efforts have been made to keep track of any known villains. The CIA were the first; they could match faces seen on a TV screen against their computerized files in Langley as long ago as 1973. Since then all the other good guys have followed suit, and we all cooperate pretty closely. Which is how people like Volinia get noticed."

"But how did he come to be noticed in an out-of-the-way place like Monastir?"

"Well, that's because Tunisia has a very long border with Libya, and a number of so-called holiday-makers are in fact sneaking across the desert to the terrorist camps there. Last Saturday Volinia came into the airport lounge, and the surveillance man on duty thought he was worth running a check on. It turns out that Volinia is a member of a very dangerous group called the Milan column. Part of the Red Brigade. So, from then on the duty man kept track of him. What you're watching now is a recording of Volinia killing time as he waited for his flight."

"Killing time is right," said Sally. "He doesn't seem to be doing anything—just mooching about."

"Ah yes, but just see what we can do with a simple tape like this."

For the next hour Ben demonstrated the full potential of the computerized system. Volinia's prowlings lasted just over twenty minutes, but from time to time Ben stopped the tape and enlarged that section of the picture which included the head of another passenger in the lounge. Then he checked the image of that person against the files of passport photographs in other British computers linked to the one in New Scotland Yard. At the end of an hour he had identified for Sally no less than sixteen British subjects, and the printer had clattered out their names and addresses, together with any other known information. One passenger had a blue file, which indicated active political involvement. Two other travelers had criminal records.

"There you are," said Ben, as he handed over the printout. "All you have to do now is trot round and see if they're guilty of treason."

"Thanks very much. That's really very impressive," said Sally. And she meant it.

"Oh, we can do a lot more tricks than that," Ben assured her. "And don't be too impressed. You may find that some of those identifications are wrong. The failure rate is about four percent."

Sally folded up the list of names and addresses and stood up to go.

Ben glanced at her. "So—er—you're still not married, then?"

"No. No, I'm not."

"Are you spoken for?"

"No." She smiled. "I can't say I've ever been short of boyfriends, Ben, but they never seem to stay for very long. They don't like police work, you see. The uncertainty of never knowing whether you can go out on Friday night or not."

"Ah yes, I know what you mean. But I was wondering whether you'd like to have dinner with me tonight, for instance."

Sally felt shocked. "But I—I—aren't you still married, Ben?"

"No. No, my wife died, about three years ago."

"Oh, Ben!" Sally was genuinely upset; she sat down again. She had never been a very close friend of Ben's wife, but she had met her many times at judo competitions and she was distressed by the news. "Oh Ben, I'm so sorry. I had no idea."

Ben shrugged. "Well, that's the way things go. It took me a long time to get over it, I must say. But I'm back to normal now." His face brightened. "So, what about dinner tonight then?"

"Well—yes, Ben, I'd love to. Thank you very much indeed."

Sally could hardly get home fast enough. She had a bath, changed, rejected the first dress she put on, changed again, fretted about the time, worried about her hair, laddered her tights putting them on, and arrived at the restaurant far too early.

She took refuge in the ladies' loo.

There is no need to worry. Will you stop? You're acting like a sixteen-year-old. He has not stood you up. He's just late, that's all. People do get delayed—it happens all the time. So just stop repainting your face and go out and see if he's there.

He won't be.

He will! Go out and see.

"Oh—hello, Ben."

"Oh! Hello, Sally. Look, I'm sorry I'm late, but my taxi got stuck in a traffic jam. I do apologize."

Smile. "Oh, that's all right, I only just got here myself." *Liar. You've been here for bloody hours.*

"I hate it when other people are late, it's such bad manners, so I feel very annoyed with myself. I should have known, I suppose. The traffic doesn't get any easier, does it?"

"No, not a bit."

"I hope you'll like this place. It's sort of old-fashioned. Candlelight, and music you can actually dance to—like they did in the thirties. Do you think it'll be O.K.?"

"Oh Ben, it looks lovely, it really does. Thank you so much for asking me out."

Smile.

There, that's better. Now he's smiling, too.

Finding and interviewing sixteen recent visitors to Tunisia proved to be more time-consuming than Sally had expected. The task took nearly a week, as opposed to the two days which she had originally estimated.

After interviewing fifteen of those on her list, Sally sat down and reviewed her notes.

She was well aware that not everyone felt comfortable about giving information to the police, so she had told the interviewees that one of the passengers on the plane from Tunisia, a mythical

Mrs. Robinson, had fallen ill with Legionnaires' disease after arriving home. Sally had said simply that Mrs. Robinson was known to have spent a lot of time in the company of a young couple (or an elderly lady, or a middle-aged man, depending on whom she was talking to), and that "the authorities" were anxious to trace these contacts. So far, everyone had been willing to answer questions on this basis, and it had not been necessary for Sally to state openly that she was a police officer.

None of the first fifteen interviewees seemed remotely likely to have been in Tunisia, or Libya, in order to train as a terrorist; they could scarcely produce a parking ticket among them. The sixteenth subject was, however, a different matter.

After five years in the Metropolitan Police, Sally had developed a nose for trouble, and there was something about Dr. Jane Challoner which made her cautious. For one thing, the name was vaguely familiar. And for another, Special Branch had a blue file on Dr. Challoner.

The blue file simply indicated active political involvement. It was certainly no indication of a criminal background, and there were times when Sally was uneasy about the Big Brother aspect of the Special Branch's records. Nevertheless, there were times when the existence of a blue file was invaluable in tracking down extremists, and Sally began to read this one with interest.

The records showed that Dr. Challoner had considerable spirit and initiative. While at Oxford she had joined a number of moderately left-wing societies and had been present at a number of peaceful demonstrations—mostly Ban the Bomb. But she had also been involved in ferreting out some semisecret information for a series of articles in the *New Statesman*. Her photograph had been taken standing in one of the communications tunnels lying deep under Whitehall. And she had played a part in preparing an article on the transportation of nuclear missiles by train.

Nothing very sinister in any of that, Sally decided. All good, clean, undergraduate fun, you might say. And Sally knew that similar files existed on literally thousands of other students.

And yet. And yet . . .

There was definitely something which made Sally pause. And when she came across Dr. Challoner's photograph, she realized at last what it was. She and Jane Challoner had crossed swords once before.

Sally could remember the previous incident all too painfully now. During her first year at university, there had been a debate in the students' union about Northern Ireland. Still bitter about the fact that her own brother had been killed while serving with the army in Belfast, Sally had attended the debate. In retrospect, that had been a mistake. It had also been a mistake to intervene in the discussion, and to try to outargue one of the invited speakers, a representative from the University of Oxford Troops-out Movement, if Sally remembered correctly. What she could remember, without any difficulty, was that her own speech had been torn into tiny shreds and she had been made to look ridiculous by a confident and ruthless opponent: Jane Challoner, no less.

Sally sighed. Dr. Challoner was clearly going to be no sort of pushover to interview, so she decided to give herself a slight advantage by not arranging the meeting in advance.

The next morning she took a car from the Special Branch pool and drove down to Winchester unannounced.

The University of Hampshire was located five miles from the center of Winchester.

When she arrived Sally found that physically the university consisted of perhaps fifteen major buildings set in a valley and surrounded by woodland. Spring had come early in Hampshire, and the branches of the trees were already tinged with green.

The security guard at the main gate directed her to the history department, and a map in the entrance hall of the building gave her the location of Dr. Challoner's office.

Dr. Challoner, however, wasn't in. "Gone to coffee," said a note on her desk.

Sally went back to the entrance hall and had a cup of coffee herself, out of a machine. Then she tried again.

"Come in."

Sally entered. "Dr. Challoner?"

"That's me."

Sally was already alert, but she realized at once that she was going to have to be at her best to deal with the woman now facing her. The eyes that met hers were brown and very intense. The face and figure were feminine enough, but the eyes remained wide open even as Dr. Challoner sucked on a cigarette, and they were very, very hard.

One glance was enough. Sally decided to be absolutely frank: her subject was too smart for anything else.

"My name is Sally Denning," she began. "I'm a police officer. I'd like to ask you a few questions if I may."

Dr. Challoner smiled politely. But it wasn't a genuine smile. It said: *I don't really want to talk to you at all. I don't like you, and I don't want to have anything to do with you; but I am prepared, just, to give you this tight little smile so that you will take the hint without my having to be rude.*

"If you're quick," Dr. Challoner said aloud. "I really am very busy."

"May I sit down?"

Dr. Challoner said nothing, so Sally seated herself in the only vacant chair.

With a trained eye Sally recorded Dr. Challoner's description on her memory. She took in the fashionable jeans, expensive blouse, and the light but expert use of makeup. Dr. Challoner's hair was dark brown, carefully cut and recently washed; she wore a gold bracelet and a gold necklace. All in all she was a woman who took great care over her appearance but tried hard to look casual.

"Could I just check first that you are Dr. Jane Challoner, living at Number 16 Springwood Drive, Winchester?"

Dr. Challoner inhaled cigarette smoke. "Yes, that's right. But before we go any further, perhaps I could see your warrant card?"

"Yes, of course." Sally extracted it from her handbag and held it at arm's length to be read.

"Yes. I see. Detective Sergeant Denning of the Metropolitan Police . . . Rather a long way from home, aren't you?"

"This is a matter which originated in London," said Sally calmly. Inwardly, however, she didn't feel calm: she felt under attack. Everything about the lecturer's manner demonstrated that she considered herself to be far superior to any mere policewoman.

"I see," said Dr. Challoner again. "O.K., so what is it you want to know?"

"I believe you flew back from Tunisia last Saturday afternoon."

"Yes . . ." The admission was guarded.

"One of the passengers on your flight, a Mrs. Robinson, has become seriously ill, and we're anxious to trace anyone who had close contact with her."

Dr. Challoner said nothing, so there was no alternative but to plough on.

"Which hotel did you stay at?"

"The El Djem, in Hammamet."

"I see. Well, that was Mrs. Robinson's hotel, too. I wonder if you came across her while you were there?"

"I don't remember being introduced to her, but if you tell me what she looks like, I might be able to remember talking to her."

Very clever, thought Sally. *If you really were at the hotel, then obviously you can't remember Mrs. Robinson because she doesn't exist. And if you were actually in Libya, and not at the El Djem at all, then you're too bright to say, no, you don't remember her.*

"Mrs. Robinson?" said Sally. "Well, I haven't met her myself, but I understand she's a short, stout lady. About fifty. From Lancashire."

Dr. Challoner shook her head. "No, I don't remember anyone like that. What's the matter with her, anyway?"

"She's got Legionnaires' disease."

"Oh. Really." Dr. Challoner was clearly skeptical, and Sally began to wish she had read up on Legionnaires' disease. But then she realized that it didn't matter. If pressed, she could pretend that she was just a dumb policewoman, sent out without proper briefing.

"Well, that's it then," said Dr. Challoner briskly. "Can't help you, I'm afraid. Sorry." And she made as if to stand up.

"Er, if I could ask you just one or two more things," said Sally hastily.

Dr. Challoner sighed. "Oh, if you must."

"How long did you spend in Tunisia?"

Dr. Challoner looked peeved. "Well, not that I consider it remotely relevant, but four weeks, if you must know. The whole of the Easter vacation."

"And what did you think of your hotel?"

"What the hell has that got to do with anything?"

"What I mean is," said Sally patiently, "did

the drains smell, or was there any problem with the drinking water?''

''No, everything was fine, thank you, just fine.''

Keep at her. She's openly annoyed now. If she has anything to hide, this is when it might slip out.

''Did you travel around much?''

''Not a lot, no.'' Another weary sigh.

''Where did you go?''

''Oh, Sousse, Skanes, Monastir. But why are you asking me all this?''

''Well, we're trying to get an idea of what Mrs. Robinson might have been doing. She's too ill to tell us herself.''

''Oh. I see.''

''And what sort of things did you do in Sousse and Skanes?''

''Oh, all the usual things. What every tourist does. Look in the travel books—it's all there.''

''Yes,'' said Sally sweetly, ''it is, isn't it?''

And then she regretted her remark. She had allowed her pride to get the better of her. By demonstrating that she was brighter than she appeared, she had given Dr. Challoner—if she needed it—a warning. *Shit.*

''I'm afraid I've never been to any of the places you mention,'' Sally continued. ''Are they very dirty? The sort of place where you could easily pick up an infection?''

''I should imagine it's more than likely,'' said Dr. Challoner dryly. ''I much preferred the hotel myself. And again, not that it's relevant, but I should point out that mine was very much a working holiday. I took a lot of books with me, and I spent most of my time reading.''

''I see. But the weather must have been good—you've got a lovely tan.''

The thin, pitying smile appeared on Dr. Challoner's face once again. ''Yes. I tan very easily.''

Sally decided not to push her luck. She stood up to go. ''Well, that's all, thank you.'' She looked around at the piles of books and papers. ''I'm sorry to have kept you from your work.''

''Er—just a minute,'' said Dr. Challoner, holding up her hand.

''Yes?''

''This Mrs. Robinson—how long has she been ill?''

''Since Sunday. So I understand.''

''I haven't seen anything about it in the papers.'' The statement was almost a question.

''No.'' *Don't say anything more.*

''And what about the rest of us—are we supposed to get injections or something?''

''No. If you weren't in close contact with Mrs. Robinson there's no need. Just go and see your doctor if you feel ill.''

''You bet your sweet life I will.''

Dr. Challoner gave Sally a black look, making it clear that she didn't believe a word of what she'd been told. But of course that was no proof of anything, except that the lecturer was nobody's fool.

While Sally had been interviewing her sixteen subjects, Ben Meadows had been carrying out his usual duties in the computer unit at New Scotland Yard. But he had not found it easy to carry on as usual: ever since taking Sally out to dinner he had found himself constantly thinking of her—and of the other woman in his life. Between them they were causing him a few problems.

Almost as soon as he had begun work at the Yard, Ben had been introduced to the woman who worked as secretary to Sally's boss, Detective Superintendent Walter Fitch. Her name was Denise.

Denise was married, with two children aged twelve and fourteen. Her marriage was not a happy one, and she had been only too willing to snatch what pleasure she could from a liaison with Ben.

Ben's relationship with Denise was based on mutual interests such as sport, the cinema, and sex—chiefly the latter—and nothing had ever been said about divorce. Denise had always maintained that she had no great wish to break up her marriage, at any rate while the children were still at school, and Ben had never felt the urge to change her mind. But there were two serious snags to the relationship: one was the degree of guilt which he felt about making frequent love to another man's wife; and the other was the sneaking suspicion that if and when he did break off their affair, Denise was going to be seriously hurt and upset.

That was the Denise problem. The Sally problem was different.

Ben had to admit that he had enjoyed his dinner date with Sally enormously, and ever since that evening he had been almost obsessed by her. He had tried to shut her out of his mind, and had failed.

But why, asked another part of him, why on earth *should* he try to forget Sally? Why shouldn't he admit, quite openly, that he found her devastatingly attractive, and always had? He was single, she was single, they were both young, healthy, and active—it was natural that he should find himself drawn to her, and there was nothing whatever to feel guilty about.

Or was there?

Yes, there was.

Ben realized now that he had failed Sally in Moscow. And that was what prevented him from ringing her up and asking her to go out again on Tuesday evening, and on Wednesday—because he had failed her. And even if Sally didn't hold it against him consciously, she almost certainly had the knowledge of his failure engraved on her subconscious mind.

And what was the precise nature of his failure? Ben sat at his desk and thought about it.

In the months before the Moscow Olympics, Sally Denning had been one of Britain's hottest prospects for a gold medal. She should have won. But she didn't.

In retrospect, Ben realized, the whole British team, and he himself in particular, had been desperately naive.

To the Russians, sport was politics and politics meant war. Survival and victory were everything, and the methods used in winning counted for nothing. And they had acted accordingly.

That was where Ben had failed. As manager and coach of the women's team he should have anticipated the danger. He should have set up defenses against it. But he had not done so. He had allowed the Russians to give Sally some kind of drug, and in a sense that drug had destroyed her.

Sally had never competed in judo again after that day in Moscow. She had never wanted to, never been capable of it psychologically—perhaps even physically—and Ben realized now that he should have encouraged her and helped her to recover from that traumatic experience. But he hadn't. He had allowed her to drop out of sight, to cease competing, and to lose contact with anyone and everyone who had been involved in the Moscow fiasco.

Ben sighed deeply.

He looked at the photograph of Sally which he had cut out of an old judo magazine. She really was very beautiful.

It was six o'clock on Thursday evening, and Ben was just about to leave his office, when there was a knock on the door and Sally came in.

It gave Ben a shock to see her in the flesh once again. He was struck by the difference between the image in his mind and the reality which now faced him.

The reality was so much more rounded, more vibrant, more *alive*. Sally radiated energy and confidence. She was happy, energetic, concentrated. He wanted to reach out and grab her, to kiss her full on the lips and to squeeze her body close to him. And as a result he wasn't listening to a word she was saying.

"I'm sorry, just run that past me again," he had to say.

Sally laughed and pushed her fair hair out of her eyes. "What I was saying, Ben, is that I would like to have another look at the Monastir airport tape. If you've still got it, that is."

"Oh yes, we've still got it all right. Come with me."

Select, lock in, switch on. Ben performed these functions on the machine automatically, which was just as well because his whole being was focussed on Sally's physical presence, on her perfume and warmth. Her eyes were deep blue, her complexion creamy and clear. He could not remember when he had last experienced such an intense longing for physical contact; he was not even sure that he had ever felt it so intensely. And yet this was not the time and place to show how he felt.

Ben ran the tape. Sally watched the television screen carefully. Ben tried to watch it, too, but who the hell cared about passengers in an airport lounge? The girl beside him was much more fascinating.

After a few minutes Sally clutched his arm. "There. You see that?"

"No. What?"

"Wind it back and run it again."

Ben did so.

"There. Hold it there."

Ben froze the frame.

"You see that woman there, on the left?" Sally pointed.

"Yes."

"That's Dr. Jane Challoner. I interviewed her this morning. Now, just run the tape on a bit, normal speed."

Ben pressed the appropriate button.

"You see what she does there? She walks past that man with the moustache sitting on his own, doesn't look at him, but says something out of the corner of her mouth. Can you identify him for me?"

"I think so."

Ben operated the computer controls. He zoomed in on the man with a moustache, ran a check on his profile, and grunted with quiet satisfaction as the printer began to chatter out the required information.

"Good, this is an easy one," said Ben. "His name is Gordon Tate. Passport issued for the first time in March this year. You were lucky—if he'd grown that moustache after his passport photograph was taken we probably wouldn't have been able to trace him."

"Anything else on him? Any blue file, for instance?"

"No, not a thing." Ben tore off the printout sheet and handed it to Sally, who immediately made for the door. "Hey, what's the rush?"

Sally flashed him a stunning smile. "I have to interview Gordon Tate."

"What, tonight?"

"Yes, why not?"

And with another smile and a hasty wave, she was out of the door and gone.

According to the computer, Gordon Tate lived in Room 203 at Number 9 Talbot Terrace, Bayswater. Sally used the underground to take her as far as Queensway and then walked the rest of the way.

Number 9 proved to be a warren of bed-sitting rooms; the front door was wide open.

Sally made her way to the second floor. The green paint was peeling off the walls, there was a smell of cabbage, and the stair carpet was so threadbare that in another month or two it would be dangerous. It was not a house she would have cared to live in herself.

She found Room 203 at the end of a dark passage.

"Come in," called a muffled voice in response to her knock, and she opened the door.

The occupant of the room was busy eating cold baked beans, straight out of the tin. He looked up in surprise, the spoon frozen halfway to his mouth. "Oh!" he said.

"Mr. Gordon Tate?"

"Yes." Tate put down the baked beans and looked for something to wipe his fingers on; he settled for using his jeans. He did not stand up.

"I'm here on behalf of the local health authority," said Sally. "I need to ask you a few questions."

"Oh. Yes? I see."

"May I sit down?"

"Oh, yes, of course." Tate cleared a pile of jazz magazines off a wooden chair. Sally sat down and took out her notebook.

"I believe you travelled on Flight BA 212 from Tunisia last Saturday afternoon."

"Er, yes, that's right, I did."

Tate seemed nervous, Sally thought. He couldn't keep his hands still and his eyes glanced around the room.

"One of the passengers on that flight has since been taken ill with Legionnaires' disease."

"Oh, really?"

"Yes, I'm afraid one lady has been very poorly indeed. So naturally we're interviewing everyone who came in on that flight to see if they had any close contact with her."

"Oh. Yes. I see." Relief showed on Tate's face.

Now what have you got to be relieved about?

"The lady in question is a Mrs. Robinson. She'd been on holiday in Tunisia for about two weeks. I wonder if you had any contact with her?"

"No, no, I didn't."

Very quick, thought Sally. "But how do you know whether you met her or not? I haven't described her yet."

Tate was embarrassed. "Oh, well, what I meant was, I don't remember meeting anyone of that name. I wasn't introduced to her, that's what I mean."

"Oh, I see." Sally pretended to accept this

explanation. "And how long were you in Tunisia, Mr. Tate?"

"Er, four weeks."

Slight hesitation. "Four weeks?" Sally raised the pitch of her voice to express surprise.

"Yes . . ." said Tate defensively.

"That *is* a long holiday."

Sally looked around. The walls were bare, the floorboards were exposed, the furniture was third-hand, and the gas fire was badly cracked. The only item in the room which had any value was a music center.

"Four weeks in Tunisia must have cost an awful lot of money," Sally continued.

"Yes, well, as a matter of fact, my uncle paid for me."

"Ah, I see. He must be a very generous man."

"Yes, he is. He, er—I've been unemployed, you see. For quite a long time. And you get a bit low when you're unemployed, so he thought it might buck me up a bit."

"And did it?"

"Oh, yes, yes, it did, thanks."

You could have fooled me, thought Sally. "And where did you stay in Tunisia, Mr. Tate?"

"Oh, at the El Djem Hotel, in Hammamet."

"Oh really? That was where Mrs. Robinson stayed, too. Which floor was your room on?"

"The, er, the second. Overlooking the swimming pool."

"Oh, very nice. And I see you're very brown. You must have done a *lot* of sunbathing." Sally made the remark sound lewd, but there was no response. "Did you get about very much?"

"Oh, quite a bit. We did all the usual touristy things, you know."

"We?"

Tate almost flushed. "I—er—well, I mean, wherever you went there was a crowd of people. I didn't mean I was with anyone particular."

"I see. You didn't take a girlfriend then?"

"No." Tate looked down at the floor between his feet.

"And what did you see while you were there?" *Let's see if you answer that one, Mr. Tate. It's got absolutely nothing to do with Legionnaires' disease or Mrs. Robinson. Let's see if you have any objections.*

Tate apparently didn't mind answering at all. "Well, I went to Sousse and looked at the old city. And there are some catacombs nearby, I looked at those, too. And on another day I went to Skanes, to see the president's palace. And I went to the ruins of Carthage, of course. They're very famous. . . . I think those were the main things I saw."

"Gosh," said Sally, "you sound just like one of those travel brochures!"

Tate said nothing, but his eyes seemed to narrow in anger.

Move on. "Well, as a matter of fact I've interviewed someone else who stayed at the El Djem Hotel," Sally told him.

"Oh, who?"

"A Dr. Challoner. Dr. Jane Challoner."

The eyes skidded away again.

"Did you meet her, by any chance?"

"Yes, yes. As a matter of fact I did."

Pause. Wait. Let the silence stretch. Make him need to fill it. And after a moment Tate spoke.

"I, er—well, Dr. Challoner and I spent some time together."

"Really?"

"Yes."

"Did you meet her out there, or had you known her before?"

"No, we met out there."

"And you went around together quite a bit?"

"Yes."

"Funny," said Sally ruthlessly. "She didn't mention you at all."

It was past eight o'clock now, but Sally didn't feel at all tired, so after stopping for a hamburger and a glass of milk she made her way back to New Scotland Yard.

Ben Meadows had long since gone home, but there was a night officer on duty in the computer unit, and he willingly helped her to play the Monastir airport tape yet again. Sally was beginning to know it well by now.

According to Gordon Tate, he and Jane Challoner had spent a lot of time together, and they had been on holiday in the same hotel for no less than four weeks. If Tate was telling the truth it was hard to believe that they had not gone to bed together during that time, what with all that warm sun, and soft hotel beds at their disposal. And yet in the airport lounge they ignored each other. Apart from what looked like a few words spoken out of the side of Dr. Challoner's mouth, there was no contact between them at all.

Why?

Before she went home Sally made one further check. She phoned the manager of the El Djem Hotel in Hammamet, and eventually discovered how to communicate with him in fractured French.

Did Monsieur Fourati by any chance recall two English visitors, Dr. Jane Challoner and Monsieur Gordon Tate, who were believed to have stayed at the hotel for the four weeks ending last Saturday?

Why yes, as it happened Monsieur Fourati remembered them very well indeed. Monsieur Tate had a grand moustache, no?

Yes.

And Dr. Challoner, a most beautiful brunette, no?

Well, yes, if you like that sort of thing. But could Monsieur Fourati confirm that these two young people had been resident in the hotel throughout the entire four weeks?

Yes, indeed he could, Mademoiselle, he could confirm it from personal knowledge.

Oh. Pity. Merci, Monsieur Fourati, et bonsoir.

So, that was the end of that idea.

Or was it? Sally recalled what her boss, Superintendent Fitch, had said to her: "Remember that if any of these people actually did cross into Libya, they're bound to have a pretty good cover story."

It was ten o'clock by now, but Sally made one last telephone call, to a fat, cheerful little lady called Maisie Williams, whom she had interviewed earlier in the week.

Maisie Williams had also stayed at the El Djem Hotel, and had thought it only fractionally less satisfactory than paradise.

After a certain amount of introductory chat, Sally described Gordon Tate and Jane Challoner in great detail and asked Mrs. Williams if she could remember meeting either of them.

"No, dear," said Maisie apologetically, "they don't ring any bells at all." Which was strange. Because Maisie Williams had bad feet, and had stayed in the hotel almost all the time. And she loved to talk. She had talked to anyone and everyone—except, it appeared, Challoner and Tate.

Curiouser and curiouser, thought Sally.

But it was, after all, a very big hotel. There was probably nothing to it.

She gave up worrying about it, went home and went to bed.

4

Jane Challoner rolled over in bed and looked at the alarm clock: it was half past seven.

For a second she thought she would have to get up, but then she realized that today was Saturday, so she could stay where she was.

Towards nine o'clock Jane was woken again by her two cats, Vinca and Claude. Vinca was a Russian blue, sleek and beautiful; Claude was just an ordinary alley cat. Between them they had decided that it was high time they were fed.

Jane went downstairs and tended to the cats, chatting to them as she spread out their food. Then she had some breakfast herself. A little later she went to the telephone in her living room and dialed the number which Gordon Tate had given her.

Gordon had no phone of his own, and the number was that of a pay phone situated in the hall of Number 9 Talbot Terrace. According to Gordon, it was a matter of luck as to who, if anyone, answered it.

Jane let the phone ring for a full two minutes. Eventually it was picked up by a sleepy-sounding young woman, who reluctantly agreed to see whether Gordon was in. There was another long pause, and then a deep male voice said tentatively: "Hello?"

"Is that Gordon Tate?"

"Yes."

"Good. This is Jane." She was reluctant to identify herself fully just in *case* anyone else was listening.

"Oh. Hello," said Gordon. His voice sounded dull and flat.

"How are you, Gordon?"

"Oh, all right, thanks."

Jane paused, but nothing happened. *Well, don't ask me how I am, will you?* she thought. *Self-centered sexist pig.* "You don't *sound* too good," she told him. "You sound a bit down."

"Well, things could be better."

"Hmm, well, listen, Gordon, I've been thinking. I'd like you to come and see me. We could have some lunch together. I've had the photographs of our holiday developed, and I'd like to show them to you."

"Photographs?"

"Yes."

"Oh . . . When do you want me to come?"

"Today, of course!" *Numbskull.*

"Oh. Sorry, I can't do that."

"Why not?"

"Well, I—er—I'm having lunch with a friend, that's why not."

Liar, you haven't got any friends. "Tell him to get lost."

"I can't."

Jane bit back the violent language which she was strongly tempted to use. She had the feeling that it would be in her interests to handle Gordon carefully. "Why *not*, Gordon?" she asked, in a dangerously polite tone of voice. "What's to stop you coming to see me?"

"Well, because I haven't got any money, for a start."

Oh, so you were lying about the friend. "I see. Well, I suggest you pawn something."

"I already have, and I'm still broke."

Jane sighed. Her patience was wearing thin. "Well then, *steal* something, Gordon. For Christ's sake, haven't you got any initiative at all?"

"I don't know," said Gordon doubtfully. If his general attitude was any guide, it was going to be Christmas before he went anywhere.

By now Jane had had more than enough. "Listen, Gordon," she said peremptorily, "and listen good. I want you here, today, for lunch. If you're completely broke then borrow the train fare for God's sake, and I'll give you a loan when you get here. But get here, and get here fast. Do you understand me?"

Gordon paused, and Jane could hear the background hum which her father had once told her was the wind blowing across the telephone wires. And then it was Gordon's turn to sigh.

"Yes," he said. "I understand you." And he put the receiver down.

Four hours later Gordon phoned her from Winchester railway station.

"What took you so long?" Jane asked with undisguised contempt. "Did you get lost on the underground?"

For the first time Gordon showed some spirit. "You should be bloody glad I'm here at all!" he shouted back down the phone. "I had to pawn my stereo gear to get the train fare, and so far I don't think this place is bloody well worth it!"

Jane laughed. "All right, Gordon. You just stay where you are, and I'll come and find you."

Jane drove into Winchester to collect her visitor, and after parking her car she took him to a Berni inn.

After they had been sitting at the table for a couple of minutes, Jane suddenly noticed that Gordon was eyeing the menu with some concern.

"And just what," she asked crisply, "is the matter now?"

Gordon pointed to the list of prices. "Who's supposed to be paying for all this?"

"I am."

"Oh, well, that's all right then. Do you mind what I have?"

"No."

"Oh. Good," said Gordon. He seemed genuinely relieved, and proceeded to order the most expensive steak available. He didn't seem at all inclined to talk until it arrived, and when it was served he attacked it with such ravenous zeal that Jane was taken aback.

"How long is it since you last had a good meal, Gordon?"

He didn't even look up. "Two days. Thursday night was the last time. Baked beans."

Oh. Jane picked at her own plate ruminatively. "And how do you come to be so completely and utterly flat broke? You really seem to have worked at it."

Gordon shrugged. "Well, I'm unemployed, aren't I? I thought you knew that."

"I do. But aren't you on the dole or whatever it's called these days?"

"Yes, of course I am, but . . ."

"But what?"

Gordon shrugged again. "Well, my holiday seems to have upset them."

Jane put down her knife and fork. "You surely weren't dumb enough to tell them you'd been on holiday, were you?"

"No. I told them I'd been up north, doing some painting for an old auntie. But I don't think they believed me." His eyes were full of resentment. "They seem to think I'm a bloody crook," he complained.

"No!" said Jane, but her sarcasm passed clean over his head.

"Yes. They don't believe a word I say. Any-

way, they're refusing to give me any money. . . .
It's not bloody fair, you know.''

Jane almost laughed but a glance at Gordon's
face restrained her: she could detect no hint that he
was joking. ''You're not Irish, by any chance, are
you?''

''Me? Irish? No. Why do you ask?''

''Well, because your logic has an Irish lilt to it.
You sound just like the boys in the IRA. They
have just the same clarity of mind as you have.''

''Are you still working for them?'' Gordon asked
between mouthfuls.

*Who told you that? Who told you I had anything
to do with the IRA?* ''I never worked *for* them,''
she said carefully. ''I worked *with* them.''

''Well, whatever. Are you?''

Jane paused before answering. ''No, I'm not.''

''Why not?''

She thought about it. ''You'll find when you're
a little older, Gordon, that all revolutionary movements claim to represent the working class. But
the Provisional IRA is the only such movement in
the world which is actually recruited from the
working class. Which means that they are thick.
Which in turn means that they're bloody dangerous to work with. And that's why I've given it
up.''

''Oh.''

''Yes.'' Jane decided to get down to business.
''But anyway, Gordon, I didn't get you out here to
talk about that. What I really want to know is

whether you've had a visit from anyone asking about Legionnaires' disease.''

Gordon had now finished his steak and chips; he wiped his mouth on a napkin. "Oh," he said, "yes, as a matter of fact I have."

"When?"

Gordon squinted. "Well, Thursday evening, I suppose it was."

"Tell Jane all about it, Gordon, there's a good boy." She smiled her most encouraging smile.

"Well, there's not much to tell. This girl from the council came to see me. She said that some woman on the flight we came back from Tunisia on had gone down with this Legionnaires' disease, and she wanted to know if I'd met her. That's all."

"I see. What did you tell her?"

"Nothing."

"Didn't she ask any questions?"

"Oh yes, a few. But I just used our cover story, as agreed."

"Good."

The waitress brought their desserts at that point.

"Did you—er—did this girl visit you as well, then?" Gordon asked when they were alone again.

"Yes, she did, as a matter of fact. But she wasn't from the council—she was from the police." Jane took a spoonful of ice cream and allowed it to melt in her mouth.

"Oh!" said Gordon in surprise. "But—er—even so, I don't think there's anything to worry about, is there?" He looked across the table anxiously.

"I mean, people who travel on the same plane as anyone who gets a nasty disease, they often do get followed up, don't they?"

"Yes. So I believe, Gordon. So I believe."

"So—well—it was just an ordinary inquiry. There's no need to worry, then, is there?"

Jane smiled at him. "No, Gordon, no need at all."

He seemed to accept her assurance and relaxed.

"Well now, it's time to move on a bit," Jane told him. "Time we got organized. I've been doing some planning, and I think I've got a pretty good cover story for you. Something for you to pretend to be doing while you're actually working for me."

"Oh? What is it?" He sounded cautious rather than curious.

"Well, you're unemployed, you've got nothing particular to do, so you're going to take a post-graduate degree. Become a student at the University of Hampshire."

Gordon shook his head. "I couldn't do that," he said firmly.

"Why not?" Jane felt an immediate flush of anger, deep in her throat. Every time she made a suggestion to this bastard he thought of forty-three different reasons for not accepting it.

"Well, because I couldn't get a grant."

Jane sighed. "You don't have to get a grant, Gordon. I will support you. You can register as a self-supporting student and I will find the money."

Gordon was unconvinced. "I couldn't do it anyway. I haven't got a good enough first degree."

It was all Jane could do to stop herself giving a great scream of frustration. "Gordon—for Christ's sake—we can forge your references. We can make it *look* as though you've got a good degree. Didn't you learn anything during your month in Libya?"

He might just as well not have heard her. "I couldn't do it anyway," he said flatly. "I'm not brainy enough to do a research degree."

"No, you are absolutely correct there," Jane admitted. "I congratulate you on your perspicacity. But *I* will do all that for you. *I* will write your research outline, *I* will get it approved, and *I* will act as your supervisor."

Gordon chewed meditatively. "Won't I have to be interviewed?"

"As your prospective supervisor, I will interview you."

"But—wouldn't I have to appear at the university?"

Jane nodded. "Research students occasionally do, yes."

"Well then, I don't think that would work out, would it? I mean, I live too far away."

Jane did just wonder if her guest was teasing her, but she could see from the worried frown on his face that he was not. No one could possibly be that good an actor. She felt almost sorry for him.

"But what I'm suggesting, Gordon, is that you should give up your bed-sitter in London and come down here and live with me."

Gordon was clearly astonished. "Come and live with you?"

"Yes. What's so terrible about that?"

"Well. Nothing. Not if I was a lodger. But, I mean, wouldn't people talk?"

"Of course they would talk. That's the whole point. Not only would they talk, but they would accept the arrangement as perfectly normal. In practice, as you say, you would be a lodger. But as far as the rest of the world was concerned, you would be my live-in lover. A handsome young man whom I met on holiday, and who I am now leading by the hand as he embarks on a distinguished academic career. Nothing unusual about that, Gordon. It happens all the time."

The troubled frown had not left Gordon's face. He shook his head. "Oh, I don't think I could do that."

"For Christ's sake stop saying that!" shouted Jane.

Heads turned on the far side of the restaurant, and she hid her face in her hands until she was back in control of her emotions. Her temper had a short fuse at the best of times, but Gordon was taxing her patience beyond endurance.

I ought to be used to this, she thought. *But the Irish weren't as bad as this, were they? Or were they? God, I don't know. . . .*

She looked up again. "Why not, Gordon? Why can't you do what I suggest?"

"Well . . ." said Gordon, in a tone which implied that there were innumerable reasons.

"Well what?"

"I just can't, that's all."

Something inside Jane seemed to snap. She leaned across the table and hissed at him, her eyes staring. "Now listen, Gordon, just listen to me, you stupid little shit, and listen very carefully. There is absolutely no reason at all why you shouldn't do what I suggest, no reason at all, do you hear? How many employers are queueing up for your services? None. Are there books you want to write, concerts you have to give, girls you need to screw—have you talents I know nothing about? No. You're just an idle, useless, impotent bloody layabout, but you're all I've got and by God I'm going to knock you into shape if it kills me. When you flew to Tunisia you accepted military discipline—and that means you have to obey orders. You were taken to Tunisia for one reason and one reason only, and that was to assist me. And you'll do as you're bloody well told, Gordon Tate, or you'll pay the penalty. And the penalty in this case is death!"

Gordon sat very still throughout this tirade. But as he listened, the blood gradually drained from his face, and when Jane had finished he put down his spoon and fork, wiped his mouth on his napkin and walked quickly out of the restaurant.

Gordon was very upset. It always made him upset when people shouted at him. One of his most vivid childhood memories was of being shouted at in the orphanage by one of the women who worked there. She had shouted at him every time he wet his bed, and eventually she had threatened to rub his nose in it if he ever did it again. And inevitably he had done it again, the very next night. She had shouted at him once more, and had rubbed his nose in it, just as she had promised. And ever since then he hadn't liked being shouted at, hadn't liked it one bit.

Fortunately, he didn't have to put up with that sort of thing any longer, and he wasn't going to put up with it now, so when Jane started bellyaching he'd just got up and walked out on her. And serve the silly bitch right.

Gordon went home, back to his bed-sitting room in Talbot Terrace, Bayswater.

After his latest visit to the pawnshop he still had some money in his pocket, so he bought some groceries and cooked himself a meal on his small gas ring. After that he went out again, to see a Clint Eastwood movie. Finally he retired to a dimly lit pub where a rock band was appearing, and did his best to get drunk.

The next morning Gordon woke up slowly. He had a headache and felt very depressed.

Eventually, after several cups of coffee, he began to feel more human, and he realized that he had to make some sort of decision about what to do.

He groped in all his pockets and counted the money he had left. There wasn't much: fifteen pounds and fifty-three pence. That wouldn't take him very far, particularly as he was behind with the rent.

He looked around the room at his few possessions. His collection of jazz and blues records
represented his total worldly wealth. He owned
none of the furniture, and his beloved stereo set
was gone, for the time being at least. There were
two pairs of jeans hanging in the wardrobe, three
shirts in a drawer, plus what he had on. Apart
from those items, and a suitcase, all he had to
show for twenty-three years of life was some dirty
underwear and a few pairs of socks.

"Shit!" said Gordon aloud. He got up and walked
around the small room, eventually ending up at the
window.

So, he told himself, *here I am, twenty-three
years old, living in a dingy bed-sitter. No friends,
no future, no hope. A failure: on the scrap-heap.*

But do I have to go on the same way?

He made himself another cup of coffee and
thought about it some more. And in the end he
was forced to acknowledge that although he enjoyed feeling sorry for himself as much as anyone,
there was one arena of life in which he *had* achieved
some success.

That arena had been in Libya.

When he thought about it, Gordon had to admit
that his fellow trainees, and the instructors, had
considered him quite outstanding, in some respects
at any rate. And that had been only a week ago.

Yes, the more he thought about it the more he
came to realize that in Libya he had really done
rather well. Klaus Flettner, the East German camp
commandant, had been pleased with him. He had

said so. And all the other people in the camp, well, they had sort of looked up to him at the end. Even the Palestinian instructors, surly bastards for the most part, even they had grinned and slapped him on the back when he shot the Dutchman.

Yes, he hadn't done too badly there at all. So, Gordon asked himself, why not go with Jane, as she suggested? She was a bossy little bitch, of course. Arrogant, snobbish, and rude, but not so very different from anyone else. The whole world seemed to treat him pretty much the same, so he was, in a sense, quite used to it.

The more Gordon thought about it, the more reasonable the idea seemed, so eventually he began to pack his few possessions into his battered old suitcase. It was the only item he possessed which had once belonged to his mother, but he made up his mind that as soon as he could afford something better, he would throw it away.

Jane Challoner was still in her dressing gown when she opened the front door. She looked astonished when she saw who was there. Gordon noticed that two cats had followed her to the front door, and they looked equally wide-eyed.

"Oh!" said Jane. "It's you."

"Of course it's me, you stupid tit," he said. "Who the hell did you think it would be?" He began to lift his various belongings over the threshold.

"Well, I'm just a bit surprised, that's all," said

Jane. She ran her hands through her dark brown hair. "This is a bit unexpected, isn't it?"

"Not to me it isn't. I thought you wanted me to come. In fact, I thought you ordered me to." He lifted the last of his record cases into the hall and closed the front door. "Which is my room?"

Jane stood with her hands on her hips, her head on one side, looking at him curiously. "Are you sober?" she asked.

"I am now, yes. I had a few drinks last night, but so did you by the looks of it. . . . Well? Have you decided which is my room or not?"

"Yes," said Jane. She seemed to recover some of her normal self-assurance. "You can have the guest room. Turn left on the landing."

Gordon put one foot on the stairs and then paused. "No," he said slowly. "No, I don't think that will do. I'm supposed to be your boyfriend, aren't I? I mean, that's the cover story."

"Yes, I suppose so."

"Well, in that case I'd better sleep with you. After all, that was what they taught us in Libya, wasn't it? Always make sure your cover story is watertight—remember?"

Jane shrugged, and Gordon was amused to see how discomfited she was. "Please yourself," she said. "It's all the same to me." And she began to examine her nails.

They went out to lunch that day, and after lunch they went for a walk along the banks of the river Itchen.

Eventually they found a quiet spot where they could talk unobserved, so they sat down in a patch of shade.

"Well now, Jane," said Gordon, "isn't it about time you told me what I'm going to be doing?"

She looked sideways at him. "You mean for your research?"

"No. I mean for you."

Jane paused for a moment and then nodded. "O.K. Well, whether you realize it or not, Gordon, you and I are both revolutionaries. You by instinct, and me by conviction. You like breaking things, you're surly, resentful, and destructive. The only times when you feel good are when you've done something violent. When you've hit somebody and hurt them."

Gordon smiled ruefully. She had him there.

"We both feel that society is rotten and corrupt. It has to be broken down and replaced with something else. So we're both agreed on the need for change. And I mean sudden, radical, violent change. Are you with me so far?"

"Yes."

"Right. Well now, about a year ago, when I went to the Libyan training camp for the first time, I put forward a plan which would produce some quite dramatic changes quite quickly. And because of the kind of plan it was, it was submitted upwards for approval, right to the very top. Do you know where the top is, Gordon?"

"Yes. It's Moscow."

Jane looked at him with a degree of grudging

respect. "Yes, as a matter of fact it is. Anyway, the plan was approved. And not only did Moscow say yes, but they also added to the plan considerably."

"And what is this plan now?"

"I'm not going to tell you that," said Jane. "Not yet, anyway. But you know more or less what's involved. And before we go any further, I want to make it quite clear to you that this is the point of no return."

"Here and now?"

"Yes. Here and now." Jane gazed at him. He could see that she was trying to impress him with the seriousness of what she was saying. "I want an answer from you, Gordon. I want to know whether you are with me to the very end, or whether you're going to go home now and forget you ever knew me." She paused and stared at him frankly.

Gordon glanced once at the river, and then looked Jane straight in the eyes.

"I'm with you," he said firmly.

5

Nearly three weeks went by.

They were busy weeks for Sally. At work she was involved in further interviewing of the same kind as she had undertaken during her first week in Tracing and Vetting, and the hours were long.

In the evenings, she was equally busy. Three girls in her local judo club had won through to the regional finals, and she kept her promise to give them individual coaching. And finally, in what little time was left, she continued to see Ben Meadows.

By now Sally was happily in love. In a way, she always *had* been in love with Ben, but five or six years earlier, when he had been manager of the British women's judo team, she had loved him almost unconsciously. In those days Ben had been married, but in the past month she had been able to face her own feelings squarely, and she was simply delighted that he had come back into her life after such a long absence.

One reason for feeling particularly happy was that Ben clearly felt the same way about her. Not that he had actually said anything, of course—he *was* English, when all was said and done—but when he kissed her she could feel how relaxed he was, and how completely the tension went out of his body. He had even bought her flowers on one occasion, and if that wasn't a sign of deep commitment in a man, she didn't know what was.

She and Ben had not yet become lovers in a physical sense, and perhaps, she thought, that was being old-fashioned. But there was no need to rush. She was quite certain that it would happen before long, and that when they did make love the experience would be all the more intense and satisfying.

The phone rang in Sally's flat and her heart began to pound. She laughed at her own reaction: how silly it was that a bell should cause such alarm. But of course it wasn't the bell which had raised her pulse rate—it was the thought of who might be on the other end of the line.

"Hello?"

"Hello, Sal, it's me."

"Hello, Ben." She smiled.

"Are you free tonight by any chance?"

"Free for what?"

"Well, dinner initially."

Sally laughed. "Yes, I dare say I am. You're not giving me much notice, but I am free, as it happens. Where and when are you suggesting?"

"Well, there's a little Japanese restaurant in Victoria Street. Do you know it?"

"Yes, I do. How about seven-thirty?"

"O.K. See you then."

"Fine. Byeeee!"

Frantic showering.

What about my hair? Will it do?

Yes.

No! Quick shampoo. Where the hell is the hair dryer? Oh my God I'm going to be late.

But in the event Sally was not late: she arrived first.

It was a warm evening, the fifteenth of May, and she was wearing a new cotton dress in yellow and gold which turned heads as she came into the restaurant.

She sat down at a table for two and ordered a drink. She wasn't sure whether it was correct to drink saki as an aperitif, but she had some anyway and let it relax her until Ben arrived some ten minutes later. He kissed her cheek as he sat down and smiled at her across the table. He was wearing the dark blue suit which she liked so much: it made him look so handsome and successful.

"Sorry I'm late."

"You're forgiven. But I've ordered for you in your absence. I was hungry."

"Good."

"And it's my treat tonight," Sally told him. "I'm paying. Women's Lib and all that."

Ben grinned. "Well, we'll see about that when we get the bill."

Their first course arrived; it was an hors d'oeuvre of small pieces of chicken, and they ate in silence for a while. The starter was followed by soup, and when the main course arrived Sally acted as cook; she transferred the pieces of meat and vegetable from the bowl in which they had been delivered to the electric hotplate which had been placed on their table. An appetizing sizzle soon quickened their appetite.

"Well," said Ben, when the cooking was well under way, "while you're doing that I think I'd better pass on a message I've been given for you."

Sally looked up at him.

"I don't think you'll like it very much, but I've been asked to pass it on, so I will. . . . You remember Natalie Zasulich?"

Sally gave him a very old-fashioned look. "My dear Ben, how could I possibly forget?"

Ben nodded. "Well, the fact is, she wants to meet you again."

Sally was astonished. "Wants to meet me?"

"Yes."

"Whatever for? And how do you know she does, anyway?"

"Well, first things first. Just after lunch I had a phone call from George Payne. I don't know if you remember him but he was quite a good competitor in his day, back in the fifties. Anyway, George is with the Foreign Office, and last week he was in Prague. While he was there he met a girl who's secretary to their minister of sport. She's also very keen on judo, and mixes a lot with the girls on the international circuit. What this girl told George was that Natalie Zasulich had asked her personally to get a message to you to say that she would like to see you again.''

Sally's mind was buzzing and she could no longer be bothered with the cooking: she passed the spatula to Ben and let him fiddle with it.

"But—if she wants to meet me, why didn't she contact me direct?''

"Well, because this is all highly confidential. The Russians don't know about it, and apparently they mustn't find out, or Zasulich will be in very big trouble. This meeting between the two of you is to be secret, and it's to be arranged as soon as possible.''

Sally snorted. Her pulse was racing again, this time with anger, and her cheeks were flushed. "This is ridiculous," she said. "How can I possibly meet Zasulich? I can't ring her up and arrange a lunch date, now can I?''

"No," said Ben, "but with a bit of luck you *could* arrange to meet her quite soon.''

"Oh? And just supposing I should want to, how would I do it?''

"At the European championships, in East Berlin. Ten days' time.''

Sally thought about it. "Hmm, well, I *could* I suppose. But why on earth should I bother?''

"Ah, well, that's the crux of the matter. Normally there would be no reason at all. It's just a third-hand message of a very vague kind. But according to George Payne, this request deserves to be taken very seriously.''

''Why?''

''Because there are rumors that Zasulich wants to defect.''

Sally continued to bristle. ''I expect she does. But so what? What's that got to do with me?''

Ben pressed his case. She could see that he was doing his utmost to be tactful, and she knew that it was unreasonable to feel so angry with him. But she did feel angry—bitterly, hurtfully angry. Moscow was the place where she had been poisoned and cheated and abused, and now here was the girl who was responsible for all that, calmly asking for a meeting as if they would be delighted to see each other again!

''What you've got to remember,'' said Ben, ''is how things look from Moscow. You're in Special Branch now, and it's my guess that Natalie knows that. And in her eyes, it means you have political influence. I think Natalie wants you to put in a good word for her, to ensure that if she does leave Russia she'll be granted political asylum.''

That was too much. ''What, me use my influence to get her in here? In the first place, no one who matters would listen to my opinion, and in the second place, why on earth should I?''

It's not fair. It's not fair. I won!

Ben reached out and took her hand in his. ''I think you should help her, Sally, because whether you like it or not, you know how she thinks and feels. You shared a unique experience with her—an

Olympic final. That's why Natalie is asking for you, and that's why I think you should help.''

He squeezed her hand, obviously trying to reassure her. But Sally didn't feel reassured; she felt angry and confused.

Ben continued: "It wasn't Natalie herself who cheated you, all those years ago—it was those who controlled her. In fact, the people who did it are the ones she's now trying to escape from. You know the kind of pressure they put on athletes over there—you understand it better than anyone."

Sally gave a deep sigh. For some extraordinary reason she wanted to sob her heart out, and she covered her eyes with her hands. Her shoulders shook violently, and tears fell onto her plate.

It was a minute or two before she began to recover.

Well, that's your makeup shot to pieces, she thought, *not to mention your relationship with poor Ben. God, what a disaster. What must the other diners think? Better pull yourself together, girl, you're making a complete fool of yourself.*

Eventually Sally wiped her eyes with a tissue from her handbag. "I'm sorry, Ben," she said chokingly. Then she looked up at him and smiled through her tears.

"Are you all right?" he asked anxiously.

"I am now, yes." She smiled again and paused. "Do you really think I ought to help Zasulich?"

"Well, I think you ought to bear in mind that if she really does want to defect, that could have very big political repercussions. And I got the strong feeling from George Payne that unofficially the Foreign Office would like you to follow this up.''

Sally nodded. ''Yes,'' she said. ''I see. Well, I can't say I'm convinced by any of what you've told me. But, on the other hand, I don't mind going to see the European championships. I wonder if we can get any tickets?''

Ben smiled. ''To quote what you said earlier this evening, it's a little short notice, but just you leave that to me.''

6

For three weeks Jane waited. She wasn't quite sure why she waited, but she knew that she *was* waiting—deliberately doing nothing.

Doing nothing, that is, about The Project.

On reflection Jane had decided that Gordon should not attempt to register for a research degree. It was much simpler if he stuck to what was essentially the truth: he was unemployed, he was looking for work, and if he couldn't find a job he might think about taking a higher degree in the autumn. In the meantime he made use of the university library and the other campus facilities just as if he *were* a student; nobody bothered him. He also filled Jane's house with health foods, and played his dreadful jazz records at every possible opportunity. But she managed to put up with that—most of the time, anyway.

True to her promise, Jane financed Gordon's new life entirely. She paid him a weekly allowance, and to his amazement she even bought him a

car. Not a new car, it was true, but a good one
nonetheless. It was a four-year-old Talbot Alpine
with automatic drive, which made it easier for him
to control. He had a driving license but he had
never been able to afford a car of his own and was
short of practice.

Not surprisingly, Gordon asked where the money
for all this was coming from, and again she stuck
to the truth: she told him that it was a legacy from
her grandmother, and that it amused her to spend it
in this way.

"How much did your grandmother leave?" was
the next question.

"Sufficient," said Jane. "That's what they say
when you ask the horsepower of a Rolls-Royce,
Gordon. Sufficient. And that's all you need to
know."

One Sunday lunchtime they got drunk. Both of
them. Getting piggly wiggly, Jane called it. They
went out for a meal, had sherries before and wine
with it, and then came home and drank brandy.
Jane's cats, Vinca and Claude, jumped anxiously
on and off her knee: they could tell that she was
not her usual self.

After a while Jane got so drunk that she was
sick, but the act of vomiting made her feel better,
so she drank some more brandy.

She got drunker and drunker and drunker. *Yo-oh
heave ho.* The world went round and round and
round.

Eventually, Gordon tried to take her glass away

and she stopped him at first but then he succeeded. He put his arms around her.

Oh hold me, hold me, hold me!

He carried her upstairs, and she trailed her hands against the wall as she went, her head hanging back and looking at the ceiling. *Take me to bed, Daddy. Cuddle me. I want to be cuddled.*

At five o'clock, at perhaps the fourth or fifth attempt, Jane woke up. Gordon was asleep on the bed beside her; he was fully clothed.

She sat up and considered how she felt.

Not too bad, she decided after a moment. A damn sight better than she deserved to feel. Thirsty, though.

She went downstairs and drank a whole pint of orange juice, which was supposed to be good for hangovers. The cats watched her approvingly. Then she went back upstairs and had a hot shower.

The shower revived her still further, and she felt fully relaxed as she wrapped a towel around herself and went back into the bedroom. Gordon was also awake now, and she gave him a rare smile. A genuine one. "How are you feeling?" she asked.

"O.K.," he said guardedly. "How about you?"

"Oh, I'm fine. Just fine." She sat down on a stool in front of her dressing table.

"I was a bit worried about you earlier on."

"Oh?"

"Yes. When I put you to bed you were crying and moaning and sobbing. In a hell of a state."

Jane shrugged it off. "Oh, I was just drunk,

that's all. But I'm O.K. now. Feel terrific, in fact.''

She loosened the towel which was covering her and let it fall around the stool, leaving her naked. She lifted up her left arm to apply a deodorant. As she did so she noticed that Gordon was sitting up on the bed, looking at her.

A moment later she used the deodorant roller on the other side of her body. Gordon continued to stare.

''What are you looking at?''

He smiled shyly. ''You.''

''Why?''

''Well, why not?''

''I've seen you looking at me before,'' she said teasingly. ''You look at me whenever I sit down here, don't you?''

''Well, you've got a very good figure.''

''Yes, I have, haven't I? I've got fantastic tits, even if I do say so myself.'' She cupped her hands underneath her breasts, lifting and rolling them as she and Gordon both looked in the mirror. ''It's a shame you can't fuck, Gordon, it really is.''

Gordon said nothing but glanced down briefly. Then he looked up again and gazed at her frankly. Jane continued to fondle herself. She pressed her breasts hard against her rib cage, shuddering as the sensation in her nipples shot down her spine.

I'll get this bastard stiff, she thought, *if it's the last thing I do*.

She turned round on the stool to face him. ''Take your clothes off, Gordon. That's an order.''

Gordon looked at her for a moment, as if deciding what to do.

Go on! Do it!

His expression did not change. Then he swung his legs off the bed and slipped out of his clothes.

When he was standing naked she went over and pressed herself against him. He was about eight inches taller than she was, and she had to reach up to stroke his shoulders. She ran her hands all over his powerful, muscular frame, all the way down to his groin.

"All these weeks you've been sleeping beside me, Gordon, but you've never once reached out and fondled me. Why not?"

He gave a tiny shrug. "Never felt like it," he said simply.

"But you're not queer, are you?"

"No."

"And you're so big. You've got a cock like a horse. It ought to be in the Guinness Book of Records."

Gordon grinned.

"God only knows what it would be like if it was ever raised in anger." She stopped playing with him and reached up to pull his head down towards her. "Kiss me, Gordon. Kiss me."

He did so, kissing her with surprising skill and passion. He put his arms around her and lifted her up on to the bed. Then he began to kiss her in earnest, kneading her breasts with his hands.

After a while he moved his mouth down and

sucked both her nipples in turn. The blood began to pound in Jane's head.

Later he moved his mouth lower still on her body, using his tongue and his lips until she screamed with pleasure.

Eventually Jane turned away from him and rested. When she had recovered she turned back again. He opened one lazy eye to see what she wanted. She laughed.

"You enjoyed that, didn't you?" she said.

"Yes."

"But it still didn't turn you on?"

"No."

Jane sighed heavily. "Ah well. Never mind, Gordon. Perhaps it will one day."

7

Ben Meadows was standing on the westbound
platform of the Knightsbridge underground station.
It was Friday morning, and he was waiting for
Sally. She was fifteen minutes late.

Through a friend in the travel business Ben had
been able to reserve two seats on a weekend pack-
age trip to the European judo championships in
East Berlin. The tickets had become available
through a cancellation, but fortunately they were
exactly what he wanted. He would be sharing a
room with one of the British men's team officials
whom he knew quite well, and Sally would be
sharing with one of the girls who had originally
competed at the same time as herself, but who was
also now retired. All of which solved the problem
of whether to book separate rooms at the hotel or a
double one, if they had been making their own
arrangements.

So now here was Ben, standing on the underground platform, waiting for Sally, with the tickets

for the flight to Berlin tucked in his wallet. They were cheap tickets, they were convenient tickets, and Ben considered himself damn lucky to have got them. But unless Sally got a move on they were going to be wasted.

Ben was restless, and not just because Sally was late. Ever since being appointed to his post at New Scotland Yard, he had been involved in a long series of discussions about replacing the Yard's computers, most of which were nearing the end of their life. It was hard to get away from the office, even for one day, and in order to be free to go to Berlin he had been forced to rearrange an important meeting.

But the pressure of work wasn't what was *really* bugging him. The real problem was woman trouble. Two-woman trouble, to be precise.

Yesterday evening Ben had finally made it clear to Denise, the married woman with whom he had been having an affair for the previous six months, that he couldn't continue their relationship. It had not been an easy thing to say, and he had tried to be as tactful and kind as possible.

He had explained to Denise that however unhappy her marriage might be, he had always felt bad about making love to another man's wife. He had also explained that he thought it was unfair to go on seeing her unless he was prepared to ask her to divorce her husband and to marry him—which he wasn't. So he thought it best that their affair should come to an end.

Just as he had feared, Denise had wept bitterly—

which, when all was said and done, was understandable. So now Ben felt guilty about having slept with her, and guilty about telling her he was not going to sleep with her.

He groaned aloud, causing some of the other passengers to look at him curiously.

As if that was not enough to cope with, Ben had also come to the conclusion, during a largely sleepless night, that he also felt apprehensive about taking Sally to Berlin.

He wasn't sure how Sally would react, that was the crux of the matter. The forthcoming European championships would be the first major judo event which she had attended since Moscow, five years earlier. And who could tell how it would affect her? Perhaps she would realize at last how badly she had been let down in 1980. And if that happened, how would she feel about the man who was supposed to have been protecting her? It wasn't a happy thought.

Ben looked at his watch again, for the nineteenth time that day. As he did so, he saw Sally coming down the steps towards him.

She looked so beautiful, so radiant and stunning, that she took his breath away. He forgot his fears and his guilt, and his frown dissolved into a smile.

Sally was wearing a smart blue mackintosh which matched the color of her eyes. She had a black overnight bag swinging from one shoulder, and she clip-clopped along the platform towards him in high-heeled shoes. She pecked him on the cheek and apologized.

"Sorry I'm late, Ben, have I messed everything up?" She gave him a dazzling smile.

"No, no, not at all," he assured her. "We'll make the plane all right. And I've only been here five minutes myself."

The European championships were being held in the Karl-Marx-Halle on Karl-Marx-Allee. To reach this venue they had to pass into East Berlin through the international transit point at the corner of Friedrichstrasse and Zimmerstrasse: the famous Checkpoint Charlie. Sally was fascinated by it, though it wasn't the most beautiful place in the world.

As soon as she entered the Karl-Marx-Halle Sally felt lightheaded with anticipation. It was so long since she had last attended a big event like this that she had forgotten how much of the competitors' tension communicated itself to the crowd. And she could see immediately that the competitors' nerves were stretched taut: their faces were drawn and haggard, their cheeks were pale, and their eyes burned with frightening concentration.

Sally was shocked. She had never seen such rampant fear of failure. It made her thank God that she was no longer a competitor herself: if she had ever had any doubts, she was convinced now that she had been right to quit when she did.

Not one of the competitors seemed to enjoy the event: there was no vestige of the Olympic ideal of taking part simply for the joy of participating. Sally sensed that in this arena winning was everything; to lose was to forfeit your soul. The championship seemed more like a convention of robots than a sporting occasion, and each and every robot was programmed to test the others to destruction.

Natalia Zasulich fought at about 9 P.M. From her seat high up in the gallery Sally had an excellent view. She saw Natalie glance up at the crowds and wave to all quarters of the hall in response to the applause which greeted her appearance. But although Natalie's eyes seemed to scan each row of seats, Sally doubted whether the Russian girl could pick out the face of her former opponent among so many.

Sally noticed that there were now even more people in Natalie's entourage than there had been in 1980. She counted no less than nine individuals with some apparent connection to the Russian champion. There were two obvious coaches, a masseuse, two bodyguards, and a number of others who might be anything from bag carriers to psychologists. Whoever and whatever they were, the team of nine clearly had one function only, and that was to ensure that their protegée won yet another gold medal.

And tonight Natalie made a dramatic start: she won her first contest in short order, by *Uchi-mata* for *ippon*, one of her favorite moves. She was still fast and still ruthless, and Sally could only shake her head in wonder at the vast amount of time and effort which must have gone into maintaining this judo machine at peak efficiency.

Afterwards, the crowd of Russian officials gath-

ered together in a hollow square and marched their
star performer away. The autograph hunters were
ignored.

Sally sighed. At first she had not been keen to
come to Berlin, but now that she was here she was
determined to talk to the Russian girl. And as she
had expected, getting close to Natalie was not
going to be easy.

The next morning Sally arrived at the hall as
early as possible, thinking that with a bit of luck
she might be able to talk her way into the competitors' dressing room. But before long she realized
that it was a hopeless task: security men were
everywhere, and not even a British team official
could have gotten near a Russian competitor.

Sally abandoned all hope of talking to Natalie
inside the competition hall and resigned herself to
watching the morning's contests.

She had been looking forward to seeing some
high-level competition again, but now that it was
taking place she found that she was not enjoying it
at all. The contestants were all so dour and humor-
less, they met defeat with such a poor grace, and
they contrived to win by such blatantly unsports-
manlike maneuvers that Sally found the whole
thing depressing.

Ben seemed to enjoy the event, but he was also
conscious of Sally's reaction and did his best to
cheer her up. So much so that Sally felt she ought
to apologize over lunch for not being more responsive.

"I'm sorry I'm not being better company, Ben,"

she told him. "But I'm beginning to think that this might be a wasted journey."

Ben nodded. "Well, I must say I don't think you stand much chance of having a quiet chat with Miss Zasulich. At least, not on the basis of what we've seen so far. On the other hand, what you ought to remember is that if Natalie is as keen to see you as you think she is, she may possibly find a way to contact you."

Sally's mood brightened. "Do you think so?"

"Well, it's a possibility. Being a double Olympic gold medallist ought to provide her with a certain amount of clout, even in East Berlin. And if she really wants to contact you, surely she can bribe or blackmail someone to help her?"

"Yes," said Sally. "Yes, I think there's something in that."

In the afternoon and evening the championship continued, with Natalie Zasulich carving her inexorable way through the opposition. In the final of her weight, she scored a stunning victory by *Yoko-shiho-gatame*. Many of the spectators were saying that this would be Zasulich's last competition, and certainly she fought with a ferocity which indicated that she intended to go out on a high note.

But what, Sally asked herself, *what is she going to do about meeting me?*

It was only when the medals were being presented that Sally saw a glimmer of hope.

The victory rostrum was directly in front of the balcony in which Sally was sitting, and as Natalie climbed on to the winners' stand, she raised her head and looked up into the crowd.

She seemed to gaze straight into Sally's eyes. She looked up, right through the lights, all the way through the sweat and the tears, through the flashes of the photographers' cameras, and through the almost tangible roar of the crowd. And she looked directly towards where Sally was sitting.

She smiled triumphantly and lowered her head as the gold medal was placed around her neck. Then she looked up again. And *Yes* her expression seemed to say: *Yes! Yes! Yes!*

Something important was going to happen. Sally could feel it.

And something important did happen. But not straight away.

On Sunday a number of other finals and repêchages were being held, and Ben was anxious to watch them. For her part, Sally could think of nothing else to do which would be likely to improve her chances of meeting Natalie, so she accompanied him to the Karl-Marx-Halle as usual.

Sally's ticket was for the same seat she had sat in on the previous two days, and as she reached it she found a printed programme lying on it. She picked it up and sat down. Ben was still talking to a friend at the end of the row, so Sally opened the programme and began to glance through it.

Pinned to the inside cover was a note. It said: *Konditorei Grüner Baum, Alexanderstrasse, 1100.*

Sally closed the programme at once, grateful that Ben was not sitting beside her. She unpinned the note and slipped it into her handbag.

She did her best to hide her mounting excitement, but some of it apparently showed, because when Ben finally sat down he looked at her and smiled.

"O.K.?" he asked. He was obviously pleased that she was looking less gloomy.

"Yes, fine, thank you," said Sally, and tried hard to look less keyed up than she felt. She had no idea where Alexanderstrasse was, or who would be there to meet her, but at least *something* was happening.

While they were waiting for the morning's contests to begin, Sally glanced through the Berlin guidebook which she had bought in Tegel Airport. Fortunately Alexanderstrasse was easy to find—it was close to the hall. And Sally knew enough German to be sure that a Konditorei was a café or restaurant, but whether it was big or small she had no idea. The guidebook was silent on the matter.

At five to eleven Sally excused herself and pushed past Ben. "Shan't be a minute," she said.

During the long wait, she had several times been on the point of showing the note to Ben and asking his advice, but eventually she had decided to leave him in blissful ignorance. If Natalie Zasulich really was going to meet her, she would expect her to come alone.

Leaving the hall was easy: the security staff were only concerned with people going in. Outside, the streets were almost deserted; it was a Sunday morning.

Sally checked the map in her guidebook. She

needed to go out of the hall, turn left, and then go down the Karl-Marx-Allee.

She set off at a brisk pace.

Two East German policemen were standing on one of the corners of her route. They were laughing over some private joke. Sally pretended to ignore them, and although they gave her an appreciative whistle they made no attempt to stop her.

When she reached Alexanderstrasse she turned left. It was one minute past eleven. And suddenly, there on the opposite side of the road, was the Konditorei Grüner Baum.

It was a small and discreet café, up-market by the standards of East Berlin. It was also open.

Sally stepped inside. A bell rang in the rear but stopped when she closed the door.

The café was larger than the exterior had suggested. Several groups of East Berliners were sitting at the tables; some of them seemed surprisingly well dressed. But no Natalie.

Sally moved to the far end of the room and picked herself a chair with its back to a pillar, facing the door. She sat down.

A waitress approached her. "Ein Kaffee bitte," said Sally with a smile, and the waitress disappeared.

The coffee arrived. Sally drank it slowly.

Time passed. She tried to read the guidebook, but found that her mind refused to take in the words.

Half past eleven.

Sally sighed. Should she order another coffee and stay? Or should she go?

She thought about it. Perhaps she was in the wrong place, at the wrong time. Misunderstanding. Delay. Abort.

She tried not to feel disappointed. But she couldn't stay here forever: Ben would begin to worry.

Sally sighed again. She stood up and began to leave. But as she did so the door of the café opened, the bell rang once more, and Natalie Zasulich walked in.

Natalie was alone, and she came and sat down at Sally's table as if they met here at the same time every week.

The waitress noticed Natalie's arrival and approached her. In fluent German, the Russian girl ordered black coffee for two. Then, when the waitress had gone, she put her left hand on top of Sally's and smiled at her. "You are well?" she asked.

"Yes, I am well," said Sally, and smiled back. It was easy. There was no logical reason for it, but she felt delighted to see the Russian again, and for a moment her eyes filled with tears.

"Good. That is good," said Natalie, and patted her hand. She took a packet of Gauloises out of her handbag and lit one with a Zippo lighter.

Sally smiled again.

"Why do you laugh?"

"Oh, because you have French cigarettes and an American lighter."

Natalie chuckled. "Ah yes. Of course. We are

such snobs, we Russians. Anything foreign must be better than our own. Or so we think, anyway.''

Sally said nothing for a while. She felt too overcome by Natalie's presence to say anything. At home, the Russian girl was a star: and here, in East Berlin, she walked like a star, she was dressed and groomed like a star, and she gave off all the vibrations of a star.

All of which left Sally temporarily speechless. But when she looked closer, she was shocked by what she saw. Natalie was thirty years old now, which was positively antique in the world of judo. And what a price she had paid for her long list of achievements. Her face was lined, and under the immaculate makeup her complexion seemed gray. The eyes, in contrast, were black, and they gazed at Sally with disturbing intensity. The strain of all those years and all those contests had left its scars on her features; and Sally sensed that below the surface there were wounds on the soul.

Sally shuddered.

"You are cold?" asked Natalie, suddenly concerned.

"No. No, I'm all right." Sally smiled reassuringly.

The Russian girl leaned forward. "I have not long, Sally. It is difficult for me to get away. So I will talk, and you listen. *Da?*"

"*Da.*"

"Good." Natalie nodded and then sighed. "First I must make a confession. . . . It is not nice, but I have practiced hard, so I will say it quick. . . .

Five years ago, in Moscow, you were drugged for me to beat you. You know that, I suppose?''

''Yes.''

''But you did not complain?''

''No. There was no point.''

Natalie lifted a hand in understanding. ''Well, it is all old history now. But you should know for your own peace of mind that there was more than drugs. Other things were done, too. A judge was fixed—if he had not voted for me he would have been disgraced in his own country. Some unclean photographs, you know what I mean?''

''Yes.''

''So there was no way you could win, Sally. But you deserved to win. In my heart I know that, and I tell it to you now. Anyway, I do not ask you to forgive me. But I ask you to understand.''

Natalie looked up, and Sally shivered again. ''Yes, I understand.''

''Thank you. . . .'' The Russian inhaled deeply on her cigarette and then continued. ''Winning made many good things for me, Sally. Many good things for me and for my family. We have a better flat, a television, a car, good jobs. My father and mother are dead now, but my sister and I, for five years we have the good life.''

The door of the café opened and Natalie turned to look. At the door was one of the two East German policemen who had whistled at Sally. He glanced in, said something to his colleague outside, and then closed the door again. Through the window of the café Sally could see them as they continued along the pavement.

Natalie glanced at her watch and then resumed her conversation.

"I say a good life, Sally, but it is not a truly good life. We are afraid all the time. Sometimes we are right to be afraid, sometimes not. But the fear never goes away. And when I stop winning, all that we have will gradually fade away. I have no talents other than my ability to throw people onto the floor!" She laughed sadly.

"So, Sally, I will stop beating the bush and I will tell you the truth."

"You want to come to the West," said Sally. "Your sister and yourself."

Natalie smiled and nodded. "Yes. That is right."

"And you want me to arrange it for you?"

"No. No, I cannot ask that. I ask only that you pass the message."

"But why me?" Sally was genuinely puzzled. "Why do you ask me to do this?"

The Russian hesitated, and Sally could see that this was the moment when Natalie had to decide whether to trust her or not; the moment when she had to commit her life to a stranger, or draw back.

Without hesitation Sally reached out and grasped Natalie's left hand between both of her own. The hand was cold and it shook. Sally pressed it firmly, willing warmth and trust into it.

"You must tell me, Natalie. What do you want me to do?"

The Russian's lips trembled. "You are with Special Branch. Political police, no?"

Sally hesitated. "Near enough."

"But you can pass an important message? You know who to tell?"

"Yes, I know who to tell." It wasn't true, but she could try.

"Very well. Of course I understand that my sister and I, we are nothing. The West will not want us. And so, like brides, we bring a dowry with us."

In the back of Sally's head the warning bells began to ring. Natalie was confirming what she had suspected all along: that there was more to this incident than mere defection.

"And what is your dowry, Natalie?"

The Russian lowered her voice. "My sister, as I told you, has a very good job. She is a typist in the Kremlin. Sometimes she types very important documents. Sometimes papers for the Politburo itself. You understand Politburo?"

"Yes."

"Good. Three weeks ago my sister read about a plan. A plan to kill two people."

"In England?"

"Yes."

"Who are these people?"

"I cannot say."

Sally's mind was an uproar of possible questions. "When is this to happen?"

"Soon."

"And who's going to carry out these killings?"

"A young man, and a woman."

"Are they English?"

"Yes."

"You have their names?"

"Yes."

"Can you give them to me?"

Natalie shook her head. "Sally, please. You must understand. It is my *dowry*. Mine and my sister's. I can say only that two men are to be killed, and that they are two of the most important men in the world. If they are killed, the West will be greatly weakened. I know who they are, and I know who is to kill them. And if you arrange for me and my sister to come over, we will bring the papers with us."

Sally rubbed a hand over her eyes. There was so much to think about, but so little time. "Natalie, if you want this story to be believed, you must give me some sort of proof. Can you give me one page of the document, something which will prove that you're telling the truth?"

Natalie shook her head. "No. It is too dangerous."

"But who are these two men who are to be killed?" Sally waited, saying nothing more, because this was the key to the whole matter. If Natalie would not tell her, the story was worthless. No one would be interested in helping her to defect, gold medallist or not.

Natalie leaned forward again. "Very well. I will tell you. But whether it will help or not I do not know. The plan is to kill both the British prime minister and the president of the United States."

Sally said nothing but her reaction must have been visible in her eyes.

"Yes," smiled Natalie with a nod. "Now you

understand why I can tell you only so much, and no more. But I have *seen the papers*. I know it is true. The man and the woman who are to do this thing have been trained in Libya. They have been trained in the use of explosives.''

"They are going to use a bomb?''

"Yes, so I believe. The next time the American president is in England, he will be killed, together with the British prime minister. It is a plan approved at the very top level in the Kremlin. And if your people will arrange for my sister and me to live in the West, we will bring proof of all this with us. There is nothing more I can say.''

The café was filling up, this time with an extrovert group of about a dozen Germans. Natalie gathered together her coat and handbag. She seemed quite composed now, like a smart housewife who was off to do a little more shopping. She stood up, and Sally made a move to go with her.

"No, no, you stay here, Sally. I will go first. It is best if we are not seen together.''

"But . . . how will we contact you?''

"Your people will find a way. They always do.'' She bent to kiss Sally's cheek and then turned to go.

"Natalie!''

"Yes?''

Sally stood up and embraced the Russian girl, hugging her close. She smelt of expensive perfume and fur. Sally was crying and she could not for the life of her understand why.

Natalie cupped Sally's face in her hands and

beamed at her. "Ah, my little English champion, how kind and generous you are. I knew I was right about you! I knew that in spite of everything I had done to you, you would help me."

"Of course!" said Sally. "Of course."

Natalie kissed her on the forehead for the last time and then walked away. The bell rang as she went out through the café door.

Sally sat down again. She felt paralyzed in both body and mind.

She rewound the tape in her memory and played the conversation back: and it all remained convincing. Natalie Zasulich was sincere. She believed what she had been saying. She really had a sister, and the sister really had seen the papers.

Sally walked to the counter at the front of the café to pay her bill, and just as she was putting the change into her handbag she heard a scream of brakes outside.

In a moment Sally was out of the door and sprinting down the road. And as she ran she saw a black Mercedes, fifty yards ahead. The car reversed, the tires smoking, and it bounced as the wheels mounted the body lying in the road. Then it came forward again, crushing the broken creature beneath it with both sets of wheels.

Sally ran out into the road, and as the Mercedes hurtled towards her she saw the driver's face.

He smiled.

And at the last moment he flicked the steering wheel to the left so that the vehicle missed her by a foot.

Sally ran forward. Her breath choked in her throat, sobs and words jumbling incoherently. "Natalie! Natalie!"

She reached the Russian girl's side and turned her over. The head was crushed, almost unrecognizable. "No! No! No!" she screamed. She felt the Russian girl's chest: no heartbeat.

A crowd gathered about her, chattering with horror.

"Natalie! Natalie!" She wept.

A hand seized her by the shoulder, pulled her back, spun her around and dragged her away through the crowd.

"They killed her!" Sally cried in anguish. "They killed her, Ben, they killed her!"

"I know," said Ben. His face was white with shock. "I saw it. But we can't stay here! We must go. Quickly. Come. . . ."

He took her by the hand and forced her to run along the pavement, her blonde hair flying in the air behind her.

8

Gordon was doing it again. Jane made him do it every day now, ever since she had discovered how good he was at it.

And oh my *God* he was good.

"Lower. Just a little bit lower, Gordon. Slowly. Slowly! Oh. Oh my God, that's so good."

Oh Gordon you're fantastic your tongue sets me on fire oh my God please don't stop. Please don't stop. Please. Please don't. Stop. Stop. Please.

"Please stop, Gordon. Please."

Jane separated herself from his mouth with a conscious effort of will.

She had never been worked on like that before. Never. His mouth was like a drug: unbelievable.

Oh my God.

With a groan Jane sat up on the side of the bed. She was running with sweat, and she wiped her face with a towel.

"I don't know who taught you how to do that, Gordon, but she deserves a medal, whoever she was. All I have to do now is get that prick of yours operational, and then I shall put you to work as a male prostitute and make a fortune.''

Gordon grinned sheepishly, but he was pleased, she could see that. He was always pleased when she praised him. *And God knows*, she thought, *that's pretty seldom.*

Jane began to rub herself down with the towel. She needed a shower really, but there wasn't time. A few quick dabs of perfume would have to do instead. She began to get dressed.

While she was dressing she dictated a list of shopping which she wanted Gordon to do during the day. Then she flipped open her briefcase and rapidly checked the contents. Her first lecture was at 10:15; she might just about make it.

''Now, I'll be back about five,'' she told him. ''And I want a meal ready so that we can leave here not later than six. On the dot.''

''Yes, ma'am,'' said Gordon. He gave her a mock salute, which was made all the more ridiculous by the fact that he was naked.

''I mean it, Gordon,'' she told him with a warning look. ''Don't you bloody forget.''

''Where are we going to?'' Gordon asked as they drove through the night.

''Kilburn.''

He laughed. ''So, it's an expedition to County Kerry then, is it?''

Jane was surprised by his astuteness. ''It is so,'' she agreed.

"Perhaps we ought to be tooled up."

"We are 'tooled up,' as you put it."

"You've got a gun?" asked Gordon.

"Yes."

That really intrigued him. "Where'd you get it?"

"I stole it."

"When?"

"Oh, years ago, when I was twelve."

"How'd you come to steal it?"

"Well, when I was a little girl, I had a boy-friend called Nigel. And Nigel's father had a revolver which he kept in a locked drawer in his desk. And one day, just to impress me, Nigel took the revolver out and fired a shot from it."

Gordon chuckled. "What did he shoot at?"

"Oh, nothing much. He just lay down on the ground, with his arm outstretched, and fired into a compost heap at the bottom of the garden. I suppose we were lucky—he could easily have killed me, or himself, because he didn't really know what he was doing. As I say, he was just trying to look big."

"Oh. And did he succeed?"

"Oh yes," said Jane. "I found it very exciting. I let him put his hand right down my knickers after that. Anyway, I never forgot that gun. And when the opportunity arose, four years later, I simply stole it. And some bullets, too."

Gordon was impressed: she could tell by his manner. "And no one ever found out?"

"No, of course not. Who would suspect a demure little schoolgirl of stealing a revolver? Nigel's father probably never even reported it. I don't suppose he had a license."

After that they didn't talk much until they arrived at their destination, which was a pub in Kilburn where Jane was to meet her contact. She made Gordon wait in the car while she went inside.

She returned half an hour later. Then she drove another two miles, following her contact's van, until he turned into a dark side street. There Jane handed over the agreed sum of money, and her contact loaded fifty pounds of gelignite, in six-ounce sticks, into the boot of her car; as part of the deal he also included some Number 6 detonators.

On the way home Jane stopped at another pub, and in the floodlit car-park she opened the boot and let Gordon look at what she had bought.

"Irish Independent Explosives," said Gordon thoughtfully, as he read the name of the manufacturer. "Ever-Soft Gelamex."

Jane laughed. "The IRA's favorite brand."

Gordon looked up at her. "Will he talk, the man you bought this from?"

"No," said Jane firmly.

"Are you sure?"

"Certain. If he talked, his friends would kill him for making a profit on the side."

"Oh," said Gordon. "Well, that seems a pretty

convincing reason. But isn't it about time you told me what this stuff is going to be used for?''

Jane closed the boot of the car with a solid thump. ''It's going to be used for killing people,'' she told him. ''What else could we do with it?''

9

Monday proved to be a busy day for Ben Meadows and he had no chance to speak to Sally during working hours. Back at his flat in the evening, he decided to ring her up to see how she had fared when reporting the events in Berlin to her boss, Superintendent Fitch.

The answer, apparently, was not very well. Ben had never heard Sally sound so depressed. She had gone back to work determined to get the British authorities to take Natalie Zasulich's story seriously, but the only outcome of her meeting with Fitch seemed to have been a reprimand for going to East Berlin without permission. One of the rules of her department was that visits to communist countries required clearance in advance; Sally had known about the rule, but had chosen to ignore it.

Well, too bad. Ben made a number of sympathetic noises, but his private view was that if you break the rules you must expect to pay the penalty.

It was soon obvious that he wasn't going to

produce a change in Sally's mood, so before long he rang off, promising to talk again the next day.

On Tuesday Ben tried to ring Sally twice, but she was out of the office both times. As a last resort he left a message telling her the name of a restaurant where he would be having dinner, and suggesting that she might like to join him.

Unfortunately, Sally didn't appear at the restaurant at the appointed time. Ben waited in the bar for half an hour and then abandoned hope. He ordered a meal and buried his head in the evening paper.

Halfway through the soup there was a tap on his shoulder.

"Started without me, I see," said Sally cheerfully.

Ben began to apologize, but Sally's laugh put him at ease. She sat down and raised one beautiful eyebrow at the waiter, who came galloping across the room to see what he could do for her.

While Sally was ordering, Ben wondered whether to broach the subject of her painful interview with her boss or talk about something else. Sally resolved this dilemma by plunging straight into conversation, while he still had his mouth full of soup.

"Well," she said, her eyes shining with enthusiasm, "I've decided what to do."

"Oh? What about?"

"About the Russians, of course!"

"Oh . . ." Ben's heart sank.

"Yes. If Fitch won't do what's necessary, I'll bloody well do it myself!"

"Oh," said Ben again. "Don't you think you'd better start at the beginning, so that I understand what you're talking about?"

"Yes, all right. Well, early yesterday morning I sat down and typed out a full report on what happened in Berlin. I even added an appendix, saying what I thought should be done to identify the people Natalie told me about."

"I see," said Ben. He could imagine how well that would have gone down. Senior members of the police force do not take kindly to being told how to do their job. "And what was the response?"

"Pathetic. After a long wait I was told that my report had been considered at a very high level, but nothing whatever would be done about it. And I've been forbidden to take any further action."

"Oh—who told you that?"

"Fitch. But he was just passing on the word from higher up. Apparently the official story in East Berlin is that Natalie was killed by a drunken driver."

"What, at half past eleven on a Sunday morning?"

"Yes, exactly. Ben, I *saw* that driver. I looked him in the eye. And believe me, he was *not* drunk. I think she was killed because she wanted to defect. And that's why the East Germans let us get away, of course. They didn't want any witnesses who could say what actually happened."

"Yes, I agree. And what about the warning Natalie gave you about a possible assassination? What was Fitch's reaction to that?"

Sally sniffed. "Huh. Well, first of all he said

that whatever Natalie's sister may or may not have seen, it certainly wasn't the details of a genuine plot. Either it was some sort of war game, or else it was a deliberate KGB forgery, designed to give us something to worry about. And even if the warning was genuine, they wouldn't worry about it too much. The American Secret Service has a list of four hundred high-risk assassins in the U.S. alone. The average number of threats against the president is about twenty-five thousand a year.''

"Oh," said Ben. "Well, at least you tried."

"I'm not finished yet, Ben. Not by a long chalk. There's quite a lot I can do on my own, without any assistance from anybody."

Ben began to feel irritated. Sally seemed to be forever running headfirst into things. But he tried not to sound as impatient as he felt. "What have you got in mind now?" he asked.

"Well, a computer search, for a start."

"What for?"

"For the suspects, Ben! Wake up."

At that point Sally's soup and his own steak arrived, so Ben kept his head down for a while and said as little as possible.

"Let me remind you what Natalie told me," Sally continued. "First, that there is a plot to kill the British prime minister, together with the American president. Second, the crime is to be committed by two young people, a man and a woman. And third, they've been trained in Libya. So, you feed all that information through your computer, and you'll come up with a list of suspects."

"Well, yes, you will. The trouble is, Sally, you'll come up with several hundred names, so you won't be much farther forward."

"We'll narrow it down."

"How?"

"I don't know, but I'll think of a way." Sally pulled a bread roll to pieces as if it had offended her. "There's the explosives angle, for a start. Natalie said that these people had been particularly well trained in the use of explosives. We could try that."

"Yes, we could. But you're still going to be left with a long list of suspects, and the only way to narrow it down further is by legwork. Which involves a great deal of time and effort. And if I understood you correctly, Walter Fitch has ordered you not to spend any more time on this business."

Sally looked up with an expression which told him that she was not pleased. "Whose side are you on, Ben?"

"I am on the side of truth, justice, and freedom," he told her. "As always. But I think you've got to be careful to see what Natalie Zasulich told you in some sort of perspective."

"Well then, put it in perspective for me," said Sally with a note of steel in her voice. "Show me how it shapes up."

Ben decided to plough on. "I think that what Natalie wanted, above all, was to defect to the West. But ask yourself: who needs a Russian athlete? From the government's point of view, defectors like Zasulich are just a damn nuisance. They upset the Russians and they're quickly forgotten by the media. And I think Natalie knew that, too.''

"So you're saying she made this story up?"

"No. But what I do say is that she had an obvious *motive* for making it up."

"She didn't make it up. Natalie wasn't like that."

"Wasn't she? She cheated her way to an Olympic gold medal. And just think for a minute. A double assassination of the kind you're talking about could start a third world war. What possible motive would the Russians have for taking a risk like that?"

"Oh, Ben," groaned Sally. "That's the stupidest thing I've ever heard you say. Do you really want me to answer that question?"

"Yes, please," said Ben coldly. He did not appreciate being called stupid.

"Very well. In the first place, the U.S. has just elected a new president. He's idealistic and vigorously opposed to communism. Agreed?"

"Agreed."

"Secondly, our own prime minister is a man with very similar convictions. And not only does he think like the president, but their wives are actually sisters."

"I am *aware* of that," said Ben.

"Well, in that case you'll know that this particular president and this particular prime minister are as thick as bloody thieves. The special relationship between the two countries has never been stronger. O.K. so far?"

"Yes."

"Good. Now, look at it from the Russians' point of view. The president and the prime minister have cooked up a deal whereby we let the Americans base their cruise missiles here, and in return we get Trident missiles for our submarines, at a greatly reduced cost."

"But that missiles deal isn't finally settled yet."

"I *know* it's not settled!" Sally almost shouted. "That's the whole point! The deal is constructed around the personal relationship of those two men. If they die, the whole pack of cards will collapse."

"Well, I accept all that, but—"

"And another thing," Sally interrupted him. She was now at full gallop, and Ben recognized that a heave on the reins from him was not going to make much difference. "Consider the Russians' position at home. They've got a new leader, too— and he's no geriatric like Brezhnev and Kosygin. He's a volatile, impulsive bastard, and if I were in his shoes, and someone came to me and suggested wiping out the two outstanding Western leaders, I'm pretty sure I know what I'd do. I'd say yes, thanks, have a go by all means. We'll train you and guide you so that you can cause as much chaos as you like, but just in case anything goes wrong, keep our name out of it."

Sally leaned back in her chair to draw breath.

Ben felt as if he had been battered over the head with a cricket bat, but he was determined not to let Sally's assumptions go unquestioned. "But why here?" he said aloud. "Why should the plan be to kill the president here? And why the two of them together?"

"Simple. First of all, the president is bound to come to England before long. He and the prime minister need to talk over the cruise missiles deal, as you've said. There are rumors that he'll use his niece's wedding at the end of June as an excuse for a visit. And secondly, if the assassination does happen here, it will damage the special relationship that I've been talking about. Which would please the Russians no end."

Ben gave up all thought of arguing further. "Well, yes," he said with a sigh. "I suppose you're right."

"I *am* right," Sally insisted. "So you will do it, Ben, won't you?"

"Do what?"

"Run the computer search for me."

Ben sighed. "I don't seem to have much choice, do I?"

10

On Saturday morning Jane demanded to be taken to the small garage-*cum*-workshop which Gordon had rented (under an assumed name) in a small town some eight miles west of Winchester.

The garage was on the ground floor of an old stable block at the rear of a row of shops; the former hay loft above it had been converted to a small workshop. After making sure that the building was secure, Gordon had stored the sticks of gelignite there under the floorboards.

Then, for the next two days, he had spent most of his time in building a small but powerful bomb. The bomb was now almost ready, and Jane wanted to see how it was progressing.

When they arrived at the garage, Jane looked around with approval as Gordon closed the door after them: he had tidied up a great deal since her first visit, and had put iron bars across the two windows.

"Not bad, Gordon," she said with genuine admiration. "Not bad at all. Just make sure you get a lathe in here as soon as possible, or your cover story will begin to look a bit thin."

"Don't worry, I will."

"Now—where is it?"

"Upstairs."

Gordon led the way up a steep flight of wooden steps. He approached the workbench, switched on the overhead light, and drew a large leather briefcase toward him.

"Here it is."

Jane looked at the briefcase but she didn't touch it. She didn't like the look of it. "O.K., Gordon. Explain it to me."

Gordon pulled the top of the briefcase wide open. "Well, it's really very simple. Inside the briefcase is a radio receiver—the same kind they use in radio-controlled model aeroplanes."

"Where'd you get it?"

"In Winchester. They sell them in toy shops."

"O.K. So now you're a keen aeromodeller."

"That's right. I've got books on it."

Jane nodded. She had seen them at her house. "O.K., so we're covered on that, too. Is the receiver battery-operated?"

"Yes, and so's the transmitter." Gordon indicated a gray box standing on the workbench.

"Range?"

"Up to eight miles, but the closer the better."

"How does it work?"

"Well, most of the briefcase is packed with gelignite. And it's to be detonated by an electrical fuse. When we plant the bomb we shall leave it with the electrical circuit open. And then later on, when we want it to go off, we transmit a signal which completes the circuit.''

''How does it do that?''

''Through a servo.''

Jane remembered hearing about servos in various lectures in Libya. Unfortunately she couldn't remember what they did or how they operated, but Gordon must have sensed her uncertainty. ''A servo turns an electrical signal into a mechanical force,'' he told her. ''In this case a linear servo simply moves about half an inch sideways and completes the circuit.''

''O.K., I'll take your word for it. What about the wavelength?''

''Ah yes, that is a bit of a problem. We don't want the bomb going off prematurely when a taxi goes by.''

''No,'' Jane agreed with feeling. ''I don't think we do.''

''Anyway, the transmitter output is very precise and clean, because the people who build model aeroplanes have the same problem—they don't want their planes crashing because of other radio signals either. And I've also built some filter circuits into the receiver.''

''Good.''

''We can fix the precise wavelength later, when we know the site and what sort of radio noise is going on around it. Where's the site going to be, by the way?''

Jane walked away from the workbench. She didn't like to be too close to the bomb, although she knew that the detonator was not connected.

"This is just a pilot test," she said. "So in a sense it doesn't matter where we explode it. But since we're going to set it off anyway, we might as well achieve something useful."

"So?" said Gordon. "What's the target?"

Jane was longing for a cigarette, but she decided against lighting one. Smoking while building bombs was strictly an Irish habit.

"I've decided that it must be somewhere important. We must choose a target which will make news, so that when I report back to Klaus he'll be impressed."

"Report back to Klaus? What, the East German bloke, Klaus Flettner?"

"He, and no other."

"What the hell has it got to do with him?" Gordon's face clouded with anger.

Jane laughed at his naiveté. "But he's our contact, darling. He's a member of the SSD. We have to keep him informed."

"Why?"

"Because we do, that's why. He liaises with Moscow."

Gordon folded his arms and sighed with impatience. "Oh, all right, so it's to be a big target, and Flettner is going to come in his pants when he hears about it. But what's this big target going to be? That's what I want to know."

"I'm not sure yet," said Jane. "But it's got to be something nuclear."

Two days later they drove into London, where Jane explored part of London University.

She was amazed to find how easy it was to locate what she was looking for. Half an hour spent "getting lost" in an unfamiliar building, and she had found a site where a bomb would cause the maximum amount of public concern; furthermore, it was in a building where security appeared to be minimal.

But she didn't tell Gordon about it. Not yet.

Gordon was driving, and on the way home he asked if she would mind if he made a small diversion.

"What for?"

"Well, while we're in the district, I'd like to go and see my brother."

"Your brother?" A shiver of anxiety ran down Jane's spine; she wasn't quite sure why. Had she known that Gordon had a brother—or not? She couldn't remember.

"Yes. My younger brother. He's in a home for the mentally handicapped."

"Oh!" said Jane. And was reduced to silence.

Gordon drove on for another twenty minutes, and then turned down a drive which led to a converted country house. There was a sign at the front gate but Jane wasn't quick enough to read it: "Something House" was all that registered.

At the end of the drive Gordon pulled into a

small car park. "Will you come in?" he asked. "Or will you wait?"

Jane hesitated. She could see a few of the inmates of the home walking about in the grounds, and they were not an attractive sight; but there would be even more such creatures inside. She would never have admitted it to anyone, least of all Gordon, but mentally handicapped people frightened her, so she was forced to choose the lesser of the two evils.

"I'll wait here," she said.

"O.K. Please yourself."

Gordon left her in the car and went up the steps of the main house.

She was alone. Jane immediately locked all the car doors and closed all the windows. Then she searched for something to read, but all she could find was an old A.A. handbook. She wished now that she had told Gordon not to be long.

She lowered her head and began to read about hotels in Birmingham and garages in Luton. But the words soon became meaningless, and before long, what she had dreaded might happen, did happen.

One of the long-term residents of the home came over to talk to her. Or to try to talk to her, because Jane ignored him.

He was fully grown, but he had the mind of a very small child. And the persistence of a child. His nose was running copiously.

At first he came and stood in front of the car, smiling shyly and waving. He was a friendly soul.

Jane ignored him.

He approached the window beside her and leered at her, revealing substantial gaps in his teeth.

Jane still pretended not to have noticed, so the man pressed his distorted features against the glass, making them uglier than ever. She could hear him breathing.

It was all Jane could do to stop herself screaming out loud. She wanted to scream and scream and scream, and for a second she thought she might faint with panic. But somehow she managed to survive.

Eventually, after what seemed like hours, Gordon returned to the car. Without being unkind, he shooed Jane's admirer away.

When he got back into the driving seat Jane almost moaned with relief. She did her best not to show any reaction, but she was sure her face was giving her away.

Gordon looked at her curiously. "Are you all right?" he asked.

"Yes," she said. "Of course. Why shouldn't I be?"

11

Ben had not seen Sally for over a week, and he felt it was high time he did. He kept hoping that they would bump into each other in New Scotland Yard, but they worked many floors apart, and their paths never seemed to cross.

On Wednesday evening he phoned Sally at her flat. "Don't you think it's about time we had dinner again?"

"Yes," said Sally at once, "definitely. I want to tell you how I've been getting on with that printout you gave me."

"Oh, that, yes," said Ben. He had hoped that Sally might have forgotten the printout by now.

"And as far as dinner is concerned," Sally continued, "I think it's high time I cooked you a meal instead of eating out all the time. Have you eaten this evening?"

"No, not yet."

"Good! Come round now. I've got a casserole

in the oven and it'll feed the two of us—no problem.''

Half an hour later Ben arrived at Sally's flat. It was the first time he had ever visited her at home, and she explained that the house was owned by an old lady who let rooms only to the most respectable members of her own sex.

The flat was modest in size, but comfortably furnished. It consisted of a large bed-sitting room, with a kitchenette adjoining. The shared bathroom was along the corridor.

After he had been shown round, which didn't take long, Ben was given a can of beer to keep him going, and he sat himself down in an armchair.

"Now, this computer search you did for me is really very interesting," Sally began. "Very interesting indeed."

"So it should be," said Ben with feeling. "I tapped every blessed data base in the system. Quite illegally, of course—I hope you realize that."

"I do," said Sally. "I do. And I really appreciate it." She mouthed a kiss at him from across the room.

"And what have you discovered so far?"

"Well, if you recall, what I asked you for was a list of all those on your computer who matched up to certain criteria. First of all they had to be a man-and-woman team with possible terrorist connections. Secondly they had to be young, which we defined arbitrarily as under thirty-five. Thirdly, they had to have been abroad in the past year, and finally, any of those known to have been involved with explosives were marked with an asterisk for particular attention.''

"There were about a dozen of them, weren't there?''

"Fourteen. Out of a total of seventy-six, or thirty-eight couples. And I eliminated all fourteen of the starred names quite quickly.''

"How?''

"Well, some of them are no longer living together, or the airline records show that they haven't been abroad recently, or whatever. Most of the others on the list can be discarded for the same reasons.''

"Hmm,'' said Ben. "Have you done any *real* work this week? Or have you spent all your time on these unofficial inquiries?''

"Oh, I've given Special Branch a fair crack of the whip,'' Sally assured him. "Anyway, what it all boils down to is this. There are only two people on this whole printout who have spent a long period abroad in the past few months, and they're the ones who appeared on that Tunisian airport tape. The first job we ever did together. Do you remember?''

"Yes, I remember.'' Ben remembered it very well. It was only six weeks ago that Sally had walked back into his life after a gap of five years, and he had never forgotten the sheer delight of seeing her again after all that time. The realization had dawned on him, that very first morning, that if he played his cards right, he could spend the rest of his life with Sally. And the very thought of it had made his head spin.

What had struck him so forcefully that first day was how much happier Sally was than when he had last seen her. The inner serenity was what had made her so attractive. Now, six weeks later, some of the old strain had reappeared. But this time, instead of the obsession to win an Olympic gold medal, it was a determination to track down these two would-be assassins, who probably didn't even exist.

Ben suddenly realized that Sally would never let this matter drop until she got to the bottom of it. And the reason for this almost neurotic intensity of purpose was beginning to be obvious to him. Sally felt this way because in July 1980 the mighty Russian machine had crushed her into defeat. But she would not allow that to happen again: the will to win was too deeply ingrained in her character. She would rather die than be beaten a second time.

Ben became aware that Sally was talking again, and that he ought to be listening.

"One of the two people on the airport tape was a lecturer at the University of Hampshire, Dr. Jane Challoner. The other was a young man called Gordon Tate. Now, these two people are in the right age group, they have the right background, and around Easter they both spent a whole month in Tunisia, allegedly having a holiday."

"That's not a crime," said Ben.

"No, but I thought these two were sufficiently suspicious characters to justify going to see them again."

"Oh—so you've interviewed them again, have you?"

"Not yet, no. But I set out to. I went to see Tate first, but he'd moved. So then I went and kept watch on Jane Challoner's house for an hour or two, and spoke to one of the neighbors. And sure enough, I find that the two of them are now living together. So what do you think of that?"

"What do I think of living together? I think it's an excellent idea. When shall we start?"

"Not us, stupid. Them." Sally was not amused.

Ben sighed. "Well, I suppose they got to know each other in Tunisia, and decided to make it a more or less permanent arrangement when they got back here."

"Yes, that's one possibility. But if they were trained out there to act as a team, it follows that they *would* move in together on their return to England."

"Ye-es," Ben admitted. "I suppose it does." But he did wish Sally would stop going on about this and talk about something else. His own thoughts kept turning to food. It was hours since he had eaten, and his stomach was rumbling.

Sally stared at him. "You don't seem very convinced."

"No, I'm afraid I'm not."

Sally gnawed her lower lip. "What bits are you doubtful about?"

"Well, first of all, this whole thing could be a wild-goose chase. We have no way of knowing whether Natalie was telling the truth or not."

"*I* believed her."

"I *know* you did, Sally. But you passed the story on to British intelligence, and they don't agree with you. And another thing—I hope you realize that Challoner and Tate were thrown up by this latest computer search only because of the data which you filed in the first place?"

"Yes."

"Their only crime so far—correct me if I'm wrong—lies in sharing an airport lounge with a known Italian terrorist. Along with a couple of hundred other people. Do they have any record of violence?"

"No . . ."

"Have either of them committed any crime at all?"

"No."

"Well then, doesn't that suggest that you might be barking up the wrong tree?"

"No, not at all. It's precisely what I would expect to find. If I were the man in the Kremlin, and if I wanted to set up a small cell to cause the maximum havoc in the West, then that's precisely the kind of person I'd look for. Someone who is outwardly respectable but inwardly committed."

Ben gave up. He didn't want to fall out with

Sally, but he was getting dangerously close to it.

"Well, maybe these two are worth keeping an eye on," he told her grudgingly. But he didn't really believe it.

The buzzer on Sally's oven sounded, indicating that the casserole was ready. She gave him a warm smile, then stood up and took him by the hand.

"Come on, Ben. Let's eat."

12

Jane drove past the building slowly.

Today was Sunday, and the streets in this particular part of London were almost deserted.

"Do you see him?" she asked.

"Yes," said Gordon. He was looking back over his shoulder.

"What's he look like?"

"Oh, fiftyish. Plump."

"Good. Because we may have to take care of him."

"That's O.K. He won't be any problem."

Jane had not turned her head to look at the security guard. For one thing she was driving the car, and for another she was almost incapable of any but the most mechanical of movements.

The inner core of Jane's being seemed to be paralyzed: she could think, but she was aware at the same time that she was not seeing all the implications of a line of thought; and she could move, but her coordination was poor. She concentrated on looking for the entrance to the car park.

She had eaten nothing all day: no breakfast, and no lunch. She hadn't tried to make any excuses for not eating because she knew that Gordon could see perfectly well that she was scared shitless. He hadn't made any attempt to encourage her or to soothe her nerves, of course—but he had noticed her condition, and he had made the necessary adjustments.

Jane wanted to go home, wanted to go to bed, wanted to pull the covers up over her head and forget about everything. She just wanted to *sleep* and *sleep* and *sleep,* until at last, when she woke up, she would realize that it had all been a horrible dream.

But in the rational part of her mind she knew that she couldn't do any of that. She was too far committed. If she tried to quit now, they would kill her.

She shuddered.

I must control myself. I must!

She parked the car in a multistory car park in Gower Street. Today it was almost empty of cars, and completely empty of people.

She reached into the back seat and pulled a carrier bag towards her. From it she extracted a blonde wig and a pair of glasses. She put them both on. Then she picked up her handbag, which contained the revolver she had stolen from her young friend Nigel's father.

Gordon watched until she had finished. "Ready?"

"Yes." But her mouth was dry.

Gordon got out of the car and opened the boot.

There, packed carefully in place with several cush-
ions, was the briefcase containing the bomb.

Jane took a deep breath. "Easy does it, Gordon."

But he just laughed at her.

How can he possibly laugh?

"Don't worry, it won't go off till I tell it."

It had better not. Christ! Oh my God.

For a moment Jane almost fainted. She leaned
back against the car until she had regained her
balance.

Gordon slipped a steel jimmy up the left sleeve
of his zippered jacket. Then he held the briefcase
in his left hand and slammed the lid of the boot
with his right. Jane felt the shock of the slamming
deep in her belly, and she moaned with sheer
terror.

Gordon glanced at her. "O.K.?"

"Yes," she whispered.

But I can't move. I can't move!

"Come on then."

He set off, and not until he had gone several
paces did Jane try to follow him.

*I must not fall. I must catch up. Oh my God
please help me.*

Jane trotted along in Gordon's wake, holding
the wig on with her right hand.

They reached the street level and began to walk
towards their target.

"Weren't you supposed to bring a briefcase,
too?" Gordon asked. "I thought that was our
cover story—that we were both going to work in
the library."

"Oh! Yes! I forgot!"

"Well, never mind."

As they approached the steps of the building, Gordon took out a handkerchief; and as they went up the steps he lowered his head and pretended to blow his nose.

Jane was not supposed to look at the uniformed security guard either, but she did. She couldn't resist it. He was sitting in a little glass booth, reading the *News of the World*.

Gordon approached the lift and pressed the button. He used the handkerchief to cover his finger. The lift seemed to take an age to come, and Jane's knees were trembling so violently that she had to lean against the wall. What if someone else came to get into the lift at the same time as themselves? What if the guard came out of his booth? *What if, what if, what if* . . .

When the lift arrived, Gordon pressed button B for the basement, using the handkerchief once more. Then he put on a pair of gloves. Jane did the same.

The lift groaned down into the basement and Jane got out first. Gordon pressed the button for the eleventh floor, where the library was located, and then stepped out smartly as the doors began to close.

They were in a lobby at one end of a corridor. The entrance to the corridor was blocked by two doors.

Gordon approached them. The doors were fire-resistant; they had strong wooden frames with reinforced glass. They were locked. Jane was an expert on locks and security systems, but they had decided some days earlier that this was not a situation in which she should use her lock-picking tools: on the contrary, this was an occasion for brute force and ignorance.

Gordon put the briefcase on the floor, slid the steel jimmy down his sleeve, and set to work.

It took him four minutes to splinter away enough wood to loosen the metal frame which received the bolt of the lock. It was a lock which was designed to keep out honest men only. They passed through.

Jane led the way along the corridor, which was illuminated by a window at the far end. She counted to the third door on the left and then stopped. "Here," she said.

On the door which she had indicated there was a notice. It said: DANGER. RADIOACTIVE AREA. NO UNAUTHORIZED ENTRY.

Gordon looked at it. "Is there really any danger?"

"No. None whatever. It's just a general warning to keep out stray visitors." *I'm all right, I'm doing well, I'm under control.*

"Hmm." Gordon renewed his efforts with the jimmy. It took two minutes this time: the door seemed to be constructed mainly of old egg boxes.

When the lock was broken they went into the room.

"Well, there it is, Gordon."

"Yes . . ." he said. And after a moment: "What did you say it was?"

"It's a gamma-ray emitter."

"Oh. What's it for?"

"It's used for research into cancer treatment. They use it on rats and so forth."

Gordon walked around the mysterious machine, eyeing it curiously. It was painted white, and looked like a big photographic enlarger. "How did you know it was here?"

Jane was on firm ground now: she felt quite confident. "I read about machines of this kind in a newspaper. There are over a hundred of them dotted around the country. I just did a computer search in the library for papers on the use of these things. And when I found one by a man working in the University of London—bingo. After that it was easy."

"Hmm," said Gordon again. "Well, let's get on with it." He bent down to open the briefcase.

"It's mostly a lead shield," said Jane. "This white-painted bit. That's why it's so big." *Keep talking and you'll be all right.* "Somewhere in the middle there's a very small radioactive isotope, about two inches square I should guess." *He's got the briefcase open. Keep talking.*

"What will happen to it when the bomb goes off?"

"Not a lot. There certainly won't be any nuclear explosion, if that's what you're thinking. But with a bit of luck we shall crack the lead shield and expose the isotope. That will release quite a lot of radioactivity. And then when the media find out about that—well, the balloon will really go up. There'll be questions in the House, and so on."

Gordon made no comment. He had his head down, fiddling with a dial or something, something hidden deep inside the briefcase.

Jane couldn't help herself. She simply had to go and look. *Get closer*, she thought. *Get right above it. Then if it does go off it will kill you outright.*

The circuit required to detonate the bomb was designed to be completed by a radio signal from the transmitter which they had left in their car. But there was always the chance that it might be set off by a random radio signal of some other kind. A taxi. An ambulance. Or even, perhaps, a police car?

Jane giggled nervously when she thought of that possibility. And giggled again. And went on laughing hysterically until she lost control of her bladder and a warm feeling of release spread out from the center of her groin.

After a few seconds, she stopped laughing and sighed. Now that it had happened she felt better. There was no need to worry any more. And it didn't really show. She hadn't had a drink all day.

Gordon finished his adjustments and stood up.

I'm all right now. I'm all right now. I'm all right.

When they got back to the car Gordon put the aerial of his transmitter out of the nearside front window. To Jane it looked very much like one of those makeshift aerials which some people fit to make their portable radios work inside their cars.

Jane drove back to the main road and then

stopped opposite the opening of the side street down which they had walked a few minutes earlier.

Gordon sat with the transmitter on his lap. It was a small metal box, painted gray. Gunmetal gray, he called it. On the top of the box was a switch. He looked at her.

"Do you want to do it?"

"No," she said at once. *Too fast*.

He chuckled. "You couldn't, could you? Haven't got what it takes. Not when it comes to the crunch."

Jane didn't argue.

Gordon pressed the switch downwards, and there was a deafening, frightening explosion.

Part of the front of the university building seemed to vomit across the street. There was smoke. Orange flame. A tinkling of falling glass. More clouds of smoke.

Jane clung to Gordon, both hands gripping his clothing, pulling him fiercely towards her. She sat there open-mouthed, astounded by the damage they had caused.

"Bloody hell!" said Gordon.

13

Ben had spent all Saturday and most of Sunday writing a computer program. After finishing it he went out for some fresh air.

As he approached the front door of his flat he could hear the phone ringing. It went on ringing until he was within reach of it, so he put it out of its misery.

"Hello?"

"Ben, this is Sally."

"Oh, hello."

"Have you heard the news?"

"No, I haven't heard anything, I've been out for a walk."

"A bomb's gone off in Bloomsbury."

"Oh, Lord. Was it a car bomb?"

"No, it was in a building. Part of the University of London apparently."

Ben sighed. "Was anyone hurt?"

"Not as far as I know. But the interesting thing is that the police are looking for a young couple, a

161

man and a woman, who were seen going into the building shortly before the explosion.''

"Oh," said Ben, "I see what you're getting at."

"Yes. Anyway, I'd like to come round and discuss it. Can you spare me half an hour?"

Ben almost groaned but stopped himself just in time. This obsession with Natalie Zasulich's story of a double assassination was getting a bit hard to take. But aloud he said: "Yes, of course. Do you want to come here?"

"Yes, please."

"O.K., whenever you're ready."

Sally arrived five minutes after Ben had finished a shower. She pecked him briefly on the cheek, and marched straight past him into the living room. He watched her go, admiring her curvaceous figure.

"Have you heard a news bulletin yet?" she asked over her shoulder.

"Um, no, can't say I have." In point of fact, Ben hadn't even thought about turning on the radio. There had been far too many bombs in London in recent years, and he had never enjoyed hearing the details.

Sally sat down on the settee. "The target was apparently a laboratory containing radioactive materials of some sort."

"Oh, really?"

"Yes."

Ben could see that Sally was determined to talk about nothing else but this incident, so he tried to think of a sensible question. "Has anyone claimed responsibility?"

"Not yet, no."

Ben sat down in a chair opposite the settee and admired Sally's legs. Her dress was yellow, with a flowery pattern. It fitted loosely, with a generous amount of cleavage. Her bare arms were gorgeous to look at. Ben had never noticed before how beautiful her skin was: it glowed. He wanted to seize her, kiss her, squeeze her, lie on top of her . . .

Sally broke his chain of thought. "You know what I think? I think this bomb was a dry run for the plan Natalie Zasulich told us about."

"Yes, I gathered that."

"You see," Sally continued earnestly, "it stands to reason that these people are going to need a bit of practice. They need to be sure that they can construct a bomb which will work, one they can detonate at the right time, in the right place, and so forth."

"Hmm. And you still think your friends Challoner and Tate are responsible, do you?"

"Now, Ben, you really mustn't misquote me. I've never said that Challoner and Tate were guilty of anything. All I've said is, that of the suspects known to your computer, they seem to be the ones who should be investigated first."

"Well, O.K."

"But since you ask, yes, I do think they're worth checking up on. What I really want to know is what kind of people Challoner and Tate are—whether they're really capable of being hardened killers. So what I think I'll do is build up a character profile."

Ben watched Sally's lips as she spoke. It was as much as he could do to stop himself going over and kissing her, but he knew that the time wasn't right. Not yet. "How will you do that?" he asked, trying to sound interested.

"Well, I think I'll just pretend that they've applied for jobs which require security clearance. That's the sort of work I do anyway. In other words, I'll trot round to see their employers, their neighbors, school friends, and so forth, and find out a bit more about them."

"But isn't that a bit risky? You've been told not to take any further action on this Zasulich story. And if word gets back that you've been asking questions, Challoner and Tate might file a complaint against you."

Sally shrugged. "Let them."

Ben sighed. "Well, I don't know. I can't say I think it's a very good idea."

"Oh, dear," said Sally. "That's a pity, because I was hoping you were going to help me."

"Help you? How can I?"

"Oh, it's simple, Ben. You won't have to do very much. I promise."

Two days later they met again.

Ben had to work late that night, and after he left the office he had a quick snack at a pub. Then he phoned Sally from the bar and was invited to join her at her flat.

He arrived soon after eight o'clock. It was a warm summer evening, and Sally had the windows wide open. She looked delightfully cool herself, in a blue cotton frock with buttons all the way down the front. She gave him a chilled can of beer and settled him down beside her on the settee.

"Now," she said after Ben was comfortable. "You first."

"Well, it was all very straightforward really—"

"Just as I said it would be."

"Just as you said it would be," Ben acknowledged. "I did what you suggested: I rang Gordon Tate's landlord, or ex-landlord, a man called Peter Wren. And I told him the truth, basically, which was that my name was Meadows, that I worked at Scotland Yard, and that I wanted a bit of background information on young Mr. Tate."

"So you didn't have to tell any lies at all?"

"No, not really."

"There, you see, I said you wouldn't. What did he say?"

"Well, I asked what sort of a bloke he thought Tate was, where he'd worked, where he'd gone, that kind of thing. And I don't know what your friend Tate has done to his former landlord, but believe me, if Wren had his way, Gordon Tate would be behind bars for a very long time."

"He didn't like him?"

"He hated his guts! According to Wren, Tate was an idle, foul-tempered bastard, and the sooner somebody locked him away the better. He had no idea where he'd gone, and he didn't want to know, either. Despite the fact that he owed him four weeks' rent."

"I see. Well, that's very interesting. What about the other lead I suggested?"

"Ah well, that was a bit more nerve-racking. I couldn't do that on the telephone. It was a face-to-face job." Ben gave Sally a sideways glance and grinned at her. "You've got to remember that we computer wallahs aren't used to all this sleuthing."

"Never mind all that. Just tell me what you found out."

"Well, I found out from Wren that Gordon Tate used to be a student at the South-West London Polytechnic, and after a great deal of trouble I arranged to go and see his former tutor at lunchtime today. A chap called Gardiner."

"And?"

"Well, once again, in order to salve my conscience, I made a few general statements about how it's necessary to make checks on people who apply for jobs in sensitive departments, but I did *not* say that Tate had actually applied for such a job."

"You just implied it."

"Yes."

"Brilliant," said Sally. "Cowardly, but brilliant. And what did Mr. Gardiner say?"

"Well, after a bit of persuasion he got Tate's file out and Xeroxed it for me. And—" Ben picked up the orange folder which he had brought with him. "I have it here in my hand. It contains the names of 222 card-carrying members of the Communist party—"

"Oh shut up," said Sally, taking the file from him. "Just get on with it."

"Well, it's all in the file. Basically, Tate comes from what you might call a deprived background. His mother and father were killed in a car crash when he was quite young, and he grew up in a children's home somewhere. He wasn't all that brilliant at school, and he just managed to scrape into the Polytechnic when he was eighteen. He didn't do very well there, either."

Sally opened the file and began to leaf through the papers in it. "Character?"

"Not very impressive. Idle. Shiftless. Not above a little cheating. But ambitious, apparently. His politics were very left-wing, and he was a real barrack-room lawyer. His tutor obviously thought he was a great big pain in the arse. Tate seems to have spent most of his time in the gym—he was a physical-fitness freak."

"There are a lot of them about," murmured Sally.

"Yes. He was also dead keen on jazz. According to his tutor, the only decent work Tate ever did was in the shape of articles on jazz for the specialist magazines. He was very proud of them."

"Any involvement in violence?"

"Gardiner said no, not as far as he knew. But Tate was very keen on all the martial arts. Practiced karate all day long on the tops of desks."

"Hmm."

"In the end I just asked Gardiner whether he thought Tate would be safe to employ in a job which involved the security of the state."

"Oh—and what did he say to that?"

"Well, he wrestled with his conscience, and in the end said no, definitely not. As I say, dear Gordon was not above lying and cheating when necessary. By and large Gardiner didn't trust him."

"I see. . . . Well, I must say you did a first-rate job there, Ben. It wasn't as hard as all that, was it?"

"Not when you get used to pretending to be something you're not," Ben agreed. "And once you stop trying to think how you would explain your conduct if you were called upon to do so, it becomes quite enjoyable."

"Splendid! You may have a kiss as a reward."

Sally leaned over and kissed him warmly on the cheek. As she did so Ben had a glimpse of a nipple down the front of her dress.

"You're not wearing a bra," he said when she had finished kissing him.

"Of course I'm not, it's too bloody hot. I'm not wearing any knickers either, if you must know."

"Oh," said Ben in surprise. And then, since he couldn't think of anything else to say, he asked Sally how she was progressing with her own inquiries. She immediately became enthusiastic.

"I've had a really good couple of days, Ben, I found out a tremendous amount. Special Branch has a linkman in every university, so I had a word with our chap in Hampshire about Jane Challoner. Apparently she's pretty good at her job—young, but up and coming. She takes a women's lib line on most things, which gets up some people's noses, but other than that she's well thought of. No involvement in politics at all, so far as he knew."

"Well, that doesn't sound too much like a red-blooded revolutionary. Sounds fairly normal to me."

"Yes, that's what I thought—suspiciously normal—so I tried a different approach."

Ben did his best to concentrate on what Sally was saying, but his mind was wandering. Not only no bra, but no knickers either. Was she trying to tell him something? If so, what? That it was unseasonably hot for June? Or that she wanted him to make love to her? He could see her nipples quite clearly through the dress. Not only could he see them but he wanted to reach out and grab them with both hands. It was more than flesh and blood could stand, really it was.

"Are you listening, Ben?"

"What? Oh, yes, of course. You were trying a different approach, you said."

"That's right. Our man at the university gave me the name of the boarding school Jane Challoner used to go to—a very exclusive one, by the way. So I rang them up and by a variety of devious means got them to tell me where her parents used to live."

Very casually, Ben put his left arm round Sally's shoulders. She made no objection. "I *see*," he said, as if she had just said something very significant.

"Yes. And then I went round to this address and had a look at it. The Challoners don't live there any longer, of course. Her father's dead, for one thing. It's a big house. . . ."

"Is it?" said Ben. With his right hand he began to stroke her left arm.

"Yes. And they were obviously a very wealthy family. Now, the thing about big houses is that you have to have help in cleaning them. . . ."

"Yes, yes, you do."

"So I rang the doorbell and told the old gentleman who answered it that I was trying to trace the lady who used to do the cleaning for Mrs. Challoner, who lived there before him, et cetera, et cetera. I made out that I was from a firm of solicitors, and that she'd inherited some money—you get the idea."

"Yes, I do. You're very good at inventing stories like that." He continued stroking her arm.

"So, surprise, surprise, the old gentleman gets his wife and she tells me that she still has the same cleaner as Mrs. Challoner had, and that she's a Mrs. Nelly Gaul. So, yesterday evening, I went round to Mrs. Gaul's council flat, armed with a bottle of gin."

"Good thinking, Sally. Callers armed with bottles of gin are seldom turned away."

"Well, you'd be surprised. This old bird was very suspicious at first. I told her the gin was a present from Mrs. Challoner, which she didn't believe because she said Mrs. Challoner would have drunk it herself in double-quick time, so I had to change that story. Anyway, after a while, and after we'd had a couple of large glasses each, Mrs. Gaul started to warm up. And eventually she told me some very interesting stories."

Ben himself was certainly warming up. He had an erection which was positively painful, and he moved his legs as unobtrusively as possible to straighten it out. God, that was better.

"And what did she tell you?" he asked. His sole aim was to keep Sally talking so that she could continue pretending not to notice that he was stroking her beautiful warm, round, delicious left breast through the thinnest of thin material.

"Well, to cut a long story short, Mrs. Gaul had known Jane Challoner since she was about ten years old."

"And?"

"Well, Mr. Challoner, now deceased, was apparently a very nice man indeed. A businessman of some sort, and well connected. Lord This and Sir John That used to come to dinner. And—guess what—the present prime minister was a regular caller, too!"

"Oh. Very interesting," said Ben. He could contain himself no longer and kissed her passionately on the mouth. Sally responded but after a moment she broke away.

"Yes. And then, when Jane was about fifteen or sixteen, her father lost all his money."

"Oh dear." Ben couldn't have cared less, but Sally went on talking at an increased pace.

"Yes. His company went bankrupt, and the prime minister and Lord This never came round any more, and Jane was very upset and had big crying fits, and Mrs. Challoner began to get drunk at regular intervals."

"Oh," said Ben again.

"Yes." Sally stroked his hair. She had her arms locked around him, holding him close. "Yes," she said again. "So what do you think of all that?"

Ben kissed her hard. His body longed for her. "Tragic," he said. "Very sad. . . . But as it happened to someone else, and a long time ago, I can't get too upset about it."

"No," said Sally. "Neither can I."

Ben buried his face in the side of her neck, and continued kissing her as he unbuttoned the front of her dress.

"She was a wild, rebellious girl," said Sally distantly.

Reminds me of you, thought Ben. *Fat lot of notice you take of the authorities.*

"Jane went slightly crazy after her father died. He committed suicide, you know. She ran wild. Got drunk—took drugs, probably. . . . Boyfriends, sex in the afternoon, you name it, she did it."

Ben had opened the dress all the way down the front. He spread it open and stroked her from knee to shoulder, admiring the beauty of her curves as he did so.

"She knew him, you see," said Sally dreamily. Her eyes were closed. "The prime minister, back in the old days, when he was just an M.P. He came to her house often, and then, after a while, he didn't come any more. . . ."

She pulled Ben's head down so that his mouth closed over hers, and he touched the inside of her thigh. Her legs opened and she moaned gently.

Ben stayed the night at Sally's flat. She insisted.

In the morning, when he opened his eyes, he found that Sally was fully dressed. He looked at his watch: it was half past six.

"Where are you off to?" he mumbled.

"I'm going to work," she told him. "I've got a lot to do. And this evening I'm going to interview Jane Challoner and Gordon Tate, so you won't be seeing me again till tomorrow." She blew him a kiss. "Mind how you go."

And she closed the door behind her.

Huh! So much for a romantic lie-in, thought Ben.

He sat up in bed and tried to work out how he felt. In the end he decided that he felt much as a woman must feel when her lover turns over immediately after having had sexual intercourse and begins to snore.

He sighed and scratched his head. Would it always be like this, he wondered—or would she one day treat him like a person and not a sex object?

14

The bombing at the University of London left Jane feeling shaky. She went to bed early that night and slept for twelve hours.

The following morning she went to her office at the university as usual. It was the height of the exam season, and she had more than enough work to occupy her mind. Which, as it turned out, was just as well.

The newspapers all carried extensive reports of the damage caused by the bomb: the explosion had cracked the lead shield of the gamma-ray emitter, just as she had intended. The level of residual radiation was said to be high, and the whole block would remain cordoned off for some time.

All of which was precisely what Jane had predicted would happen, and precisely what she had *wanted* to happen. So why, she asked herself, why didn't she feel even remotely pleased about it? Why did she feel so tense and nervous, and even *guilty* for Christ's sake?

She didn't feel any greater sense of achievement as the week went on. After the first night, when exhaustion took over, she lay awake with a mind full of horrible memories and frightening fantasies. Gordon, on the other hand, fell asleep every night without difficulty.

On Wednesday afternoon, Jane came home from the university at about five o'clock. She fed the cats, made a meal for herself and Gordon, and began to wash up. Then the doorbell rang.

Jane answered it, still wearing her apron and rubber gloves.

Standing at the door was an extremely attractive young woman in her mid-twenties: blonde, blue-eyed, and dressed in a stylish trouser suit. Jane knew that she had seen her before but for a moment she couldn't place her.

"Good evening, Dr. Challoner. My name is Denning—Detective Sergeant Denning."

"Oh. Yes," said Jane. *Shit! The law!* She remembered now where she had seen this girl before, and her knees went weak. *The bitch from Special Branch!* Jane clutched the front door tightly, and tried not to let her emotions show.

"You remember me?" asked the blonde girl with a polite smile.

"Oh, yes, of course I remember you." Jane tried to smile back, but all she could produce was a nervous twitch of the lips. And she despised herself for failing to control her fear.

"I wonder if I could ask you a few questions. . . ."

Questions! Christ! A wave of panic flooded

through Jane like a slam in the arm from a hypodermic. She knew only that she had to get right away from the door to pull herself together.

"Yes, yes, of course," she gasped. "But would you just excuse me for a few moments? I'm right in the middle of something."

Jane rushed back into the kitchen. Her heart was pounding in her ears and her breathing felt constricted.

Oh God, control, I must regain control!

She breathed as regularly as she could, counting each movement of her lungs until at last some semblance of normality returned. Then, forcing herself not to hurry, she took off her apron and gloves and walked into the living room to check her appearance in a mirror.

Well, at least I don't look too terror-stricken. Just a little bit harassed. And why shouldn't I look harassed? Doesn't every suburban housewife look knackered at this time of day?

Sergeant Denning was still standing patiently at the front door when Jane returned. "May I come in now?" she asked.

Jane gave her a frosty smile. "Is that really necessary?"

"This may take a little time," the sergeant told her, and stepped inside.

Jane gave in: to fight such a simple request would arouse suspicion. "Oh, very well," she said, and led the way into the living room. She wondered where Gordon had got to. He always buggered off when there was any washing-up to do, so he was probably upstairs in the loo, as usual.

Jane sat down and the visitor did the same.

"Now—what is it you want?" Jane had decided that it was important to take the initiative. "The last time you came to see me it was something about typhoid, wasn't it?"

"Legionnaires' disease."

"Oh. Well, whatever. What is it this time—bubonic plague?"

The policewoman smiled. "No. Much more mundane, I'm afraid. It's about an explosion."

"Oh." *Think*. "What did you say your name was?"

"Denning. Detective Sergeant Denning."

"Oh." *Knock her off balance*. "Can you prove that?"

"Oh, yes."

The blonde girl opened her handbag and handed over a plastic card. Jane tried to concentrate on it but all she could take in was the fact that her fingers were shaking. She seized a pencil and paper and wrote down the details without really being aware of them.

"I see," she said when she had finished. "Well now, Sergeant, am I being cautioned?"

"Certainly not. This is just a general inquiry. I'm sure you'll want to help."

"If I can, of course." *Stay cool. Keep your head*.

"I expect you heard about the bomb which went off in London last Sunday?"

"The bomb? Oh, yes, yes, I did." Rampant fear seethed through Jane's mind. *She knows.*

No, she doesn't. How could she?

She does! She does! She knows!

No.

But on the surface she managed to remain calm. "What do you want to know?"

"Well, it's like this—your car was seen in London last Sunday."

"My car?" Jane's throat was so dry that she was afraid she would croak.

The sergeant's smile persisted. "Yes. You see, whenever a serious crime is committed, the police monitor all traffic leaving London by the major routes. We do it through television cameras which feed the car numbers into a computer."

"My word, that is clever." *Too fucking clever by half. If it's true.*

"Yes, it is, isn't it? And as I say, it appears that you were in London last Sunday as well."

"Along with about nine million other people."

"Yes!" Happy little smile. "So—what were you up to in London?"

"Oh, we just sort of . . . mooched around."

"We?"

"Yes. My friend and I." Jane paused. "I have a friend who lives with me," she volunteered. *Fool! You needn't have said that.* "We went to London together last Sunday. We spent most of the time in the National Gallery."

"Ah, yes. I see. That explains it." Sergeant Denning closed her notebook. "Well, that's all I need to know, thank you. Obviously it was just coincidence that your car was seen at the relevant time."

"Yes, I can assure you it was. Pure coincidence." *Christ, you don't sound very convinced yourself.*

Sergeant Denning stood up to go, and Jane wanted to cry with relief. She stood up, too, and she felt the muscles of her face relax as the tension flowed out of her. She led the way to the front door and opened it. She could breathe quite easily now.

"Oh, just one other thing," said Sergeant Denning.

The words hit Jane like a blow. "Yes?"

"This friend of yours who lives with you—what did you say his name was?"

"I didn't—I didn't say." *Oh my heart stop beating she will hear oh my heart.*

"It wouldn't be Gordon Tate, would it?" And she smiled, so knowingly.

Jane wanted to cry. She wanted to scream and shout and get all this poisonous shit out of her system. "That's really not any of your business, is it?"

The smile again. "No, it's not, I agree. But I am right, aren't I?" The blonde girl was reasonableness itself. How could anyone deny her an answer?

"Yes, you are right. Gordon does live with me. Now, will you please go?"

But the sergeant didn't go. She came closer. Her manner became . . . intimate. Almost sexy.

"You met him on holiday, didn't you?"

"Yes."

"In Tunisia."

"Yes." *Please go*.

"It's a funny thing about that holiday of yours. The assistant manager at the hotel can remember you very clearly. But no one else who stayed there can remember you at all. Now isn't that odd?"

"Yes, very." *Now please please go I can't stand it any longer I hate you I loathe you, you must go if you stay I may kill you slash you hurt you destroy you go.*

Sergeant Denning left without another word.

She walked down the garden path, and when she reached the gate she turned and looked back. And she smiled again.

15

Ben was wondering whether he should eat now or wait for Sally. She had said that she would be at his flat by six o'clock, but now it was five past seven and there was no sign of her. Where was she?

Problems, problems.

In the end he just said the hell with it and made himself a large omelette and coffee. If Sally was upset because he hadn't waited, too bad, she would just have to put up with it.

Well, no, that wasn't quite right. If she was offended he would apologize. In fact, he would not only apologize, he would grovel. He would go down on his knees and beg forgiveness, if only she would let him make love to her again.

Ben sighed. He had to admit it: he was now obsessed with Sally. He couldn't stop thinking about her all the time he was awake, and when he was asleep he dreamed about her.

Ever since he had unbuttoned Sally's dress all

the way down the front, the image of her naked body had imprinted itself on his brain. The intensity of the desire which gripped him was disturbing. He couldn't wait for her to come in through the door of his flat, and when she did appear he didn't want to do anything except take her clothes off as fast as possible.

The doorbell rang and Ben jumped with surprise.

Sally was late, and she disliked being late. Whenever she was late she felt obliged to hurry, and when she hurried she got hot and uncomfortable.

So she did *not* like being late.

What she liked even less was the thought that Ben might be annoyed with her. All day long she had found it difficult to think of anything else: it had been Ben Ben Ben, every minute on the minute. But now that she was about to meet him again she felt unsure of herself.

She paused outside his flat and checked her appearance in a mirror. She tucked a few wayward strands of hair into place and pressed the doorbell. And because the door didn't open instantly, she began to suspect disaster.

He's gone out. He couldn't wait. I'm an hour late and he wouldn't stand for it. Got fed up. Pushed off oh my God come on Ben I've lost him. . . .

The door opened and Sally almost fell forward into the flat. It was as if she were seeing Ben for the first time ever: he was exquisitely desirable and she wanted to grab him with both hands and devour him, make him hers, all hers. . . .

They made love immediately and lengthily and Sally was quite shocked at the words she used, at the things she did to excite him and begged him to do to her, to stroke her, kiss her, tease her, love her.

Eventually they were forced to rest, and after a while Sally got up and brewed a cup of tea to revive them.

"Do you want to eat?" Ben asked.

"No, not at the moment. Later."

Ben sat up in bed. "Well, if we're not going to eat, and we've finished doing the other thing, you'd better tell me what you've been up to. I haven't seen you for a whole thirty-six hours."

"Ah, yes, well, I've been busy."

"Did you interview Challoner and Tate?"

"Oh, I don't want to talk about that now."

"Well, I do. I went to a lot of trouble to help you with this inquiry, and I want to know what's going on."

"Oh, all right. Well, yesterday evening I went down to Winchester and saw Dr. Challoner. Tate was hiding upstairs, I think. I heard him moving about."

Sally went on to give Ben a quick summary of the questions she had asked, and Jane Challoner's answers.

"Hmm," said Ben thoughtfully. "So what are you going to do now? Have another go at persuading Mr. Fitch to take some action?"

"No, no, that would be a waste of time. He wouldn't listen to me when we were just back from East Berlin, and he won't listen now. No, what I'm going to do next is try to find some *direct* evidence that they're up to something. Something really incriminating—documents, letters, or sticks of gelignite."

"How are you going to do that?"

"I'm not sure. It's going to be difficult. I couldn't find anything in their house the other night."

"In their house?" Ben almost spilt his tea. "You mean you've actually searched it?"

"Yes."

"When?"

"Yesterday evening, after they'd gone out."

"With or without a search warrant?"

"Without, of course."

"Bloody hell!" said Ben.

But Sally just laughed at him. "It's the only way, Ben. And they *are* up to something, I know. I could feel it. They're not just an ordinary couple."

"Well, maybe. But I repeat, how are you going to settle the matter, one way or the other?"

"Well, I shall just have to keep an eye on them in my spare time, that's all. Follow them when they go out. See where they go, who they meet."

"Oh. Well, I hope you're not intending to do that this weekend, because I have other plans."

"Oh—such as?"

"Well, I thought we might go away together."

Sally snuggled up to him in delight. "What, have a real dirty weekend?"

"Yes, if you insist."

"Oh, great! That's a marvelous idea. Thanks a lot, Ben, I can't wait."

And it was true. She couldn't wait. She was thrilled to bits at the thought of spending a whole weekend with Ben. But she also felt guilty, because she would be enjoying herself at a time when she ought to be watching Challoner and Tate. And that bothered her.

She had seen Natalie Zasulich die—and she did not want the Russian girl to have died in vain. She knew damn well that Challoner and Tate were involved in *something* illegal. But she also knew that she had not yet managed to convince Ben that she was right. So for the moment she said nothing. She just hugged his arm and kissed the side of his face.

16

Jane Challoner was reading *The Guardian* over breakfast. Vinca and Claude, her two cats, sat expectantly at her feet, waiting to be fed.

Page one of *The Guardian* carried a fresh report about three men who had handled the radioactive cylinder after the explosion in London. All three were suffering from the early stages of radiation sickness and were stated to be "rather poorly." Two of the men had had to have some fingers removed by surgery.

In an editorial, *The Guardian* came to the conclusion that there was altogether too much radioactive material in the country, and that insufficient attention was being paid to the risks involved.

Unfortunately, Jane could derive no more satisfaction from that morning's newspaper than she had from those of previous days. In fact, if she was honest with herself, she had to admit that the report sickened her.

At that point Gordon came into the kitchen from

the hall. "Postcard for you," he said, and handed it over.

Jane looked at the card in surprise. On one side was a picture of Buckingham Palace; on the other there was a brief message: "Dear Jane— How are you getting on with your research? Don't forget the deadline! See you at the wedding. Love, K."

The postcard, coming on top of the news in *The Guardian*, was more than Jane could cope with. She put her elbows on the table and covered her face with both hands. Her cheeks felt clammy, and it was as much as she could do to keep down her breakfast. Her forehead throbbed.

On the other side of the table Gordon was humming a tune as he tucked into a large bowl of cereal and bran. He was reading the *Daily Mirror*.

Jane wondered if she should try to get to the loo before she was sick, but after a moment she decided that the slightest movement would be disastrous. She remained where she was, breathing deeply until the nausea subsided.

Gordon didn't seem to have noticed her distress, and she wasn't sure whether to feel relieved about that, or annoyed with the selfish bastard for not taking the slightest interest in her.

She realized that these moments of sheer panic were becoming more frequent, and she didn't know how to deal with them: she knew only that they were terrifying, and that they left her feeling weak and useless.

She reached down and picked up her beloved Vinca. She stroked the thick, sleek fur until Vinca purred in ecstasy. Jane smiled. The cat's response helped to calm her.

After a few minutes she picked up the postcard from Klaus Flettner and read it again. She sighed. The card reminded her that she had once been lunatic enough to volunteer to carry out a mission for Moscow, and that once you made a deal, Moscow would expect you to deliver. And that, of course, was what had set off the latest attack of nerves.

She decided to snap out of it. She set Vinca down on the floor and stood up. "Gordon! It's time we had a talk."

Gordon looked up at her. "What about?"

"About what to do next."

"Oh, O.K. I'm listening."

Jane began to pace about the room. Her legs felt a bit wobbly but her stomach had settled down.

"The pilot test seems to have worked," she began. "It proved that we can make a bomb, and it proved that we can damage the public morale. What we have to do now is to strike an even greater blow with an even larger quantity of gelignite. Something that will really shake the world."

She was addressing Gordon as if he were a public meeting, but she soon became aware that he was not impressed.

"What you mean," he said, "is that it's time we actually killed someone."

Jane blinked. "Yes. That's correct."

"So, who are we going to kill?"

Jane gave him a faint smile. "That's what I want you to tell me."

Gordon's eyes seemed to glaze over. *Got you*, she thought triumphantly.

"Come on, Gordon. Who's going to be our next target? It's got to be someone important. Someone whose death will not only shock the nation, but will alter the balance of power. . . . Come along, boy, don't keep me waiting."

Gordon frowned, as if thinking was a painful process. "How about a member of the royal family?"

"No good at all. The object is to divide the nation, not unite it in grief."

Gordon scratched his head. "It's got to be someone famous, has it?"

"Of course."

"And someone with political power?"

"Yes."

Gordon's face registered the birth of an idea. "How about our local M.P.?"

Jane opened her mouth to give Gordon the biggest bollocking of his life, but then it occurred to her that he might be pulling her leg.

After a moment's thought she abandoned the idea. Gordon had never yet demonstrated a sense of humor, and she didn't think he was about to grow one now.

"No, Gordon. Not our local M.P. Try someone a little further up the scale."

No response.

"Number ten? Downing Street?"

"Oh, you mean the prime minister." Gordon thought for a moment. "Yes, that would shock people all right. And he has got a lot of power. I suppose . . . But it would be difficult, though. And in any case, I don't think we should do anything." And with that, he returned his attention to the *Daily Mirror*.

Jane was seized by a spasm of rage. She crossed the room in three strides and ripped the newspaper out of his hands.

"God damn and blast you, you gutless, cowardly shit!" she screamed. "What do you mean, we shouldn't do anything?" She trembled with fury, her eyes bulging.

Gordon turned pale. "Well, exactly what I say."

"And what the fucking hell is that? *What* do you say, Gordon?" The spittle flew from her lips and her fingernails cut into her palms as she clenched her fists.

"What I say," Gordon told her calmly, "is that we must be much more careful what we do from now on."

Jane folded her arms. "Oh? And why so?" Her knees trembled.

"Well, for one thing, we had the police round here only the night before last."

"Police?" Jane sneered. "She was just a girl. She knows nothing."

"You didn't think so at the time. She got you worried, I could see. And I say we've got to be careful."

Jane turned away. *Control! I must regain con-*

trol! She paused before facing him and speaking again.

"All right. So we've had a visit from a girl in blue. But so what? It didn't mean a thing, Gordon. Every time a bomb goes off, every Special Branch officer in the country goes out and interviews a couple of hundred lefties. We're just on her list, that's all."

"Well, maybe so. But if we kill the prime minister there'll be one hell of a manhunt."

"Of course. But we'll cover our tracks. We're professionals."

She went round behind Gordon and began to massage his shoulders: he liked that.

"What we've got to do, Gordon, is to compare ourselves with surgeons."

"Surgeons?"

"Yes. Just think how hard it must have been, years ago, to steel yourself to cut off a leg to save a patient's life, when there were no anesthetics. It must have been a very hard thing to do. But it would have been the *right* thing to do. And it's the right thing for us to do *now*."

The muscles in Gordon's shoulders began to relax.

"We have to shift the world to the left, Gordon. Sharply to the left. Not because that's a perfect system, but because it's a *better* system. You do agree, don't you?"

Gordon smiled. "Oh yes. I agree all right."

"Good."

She leaned down and kissed his neck. How

simple he was to lead when only she put her mind to it. She kissed him again.

"Yes, Gordon, that's what we'll do. You and I. We'll pull this off together, you see if we don't." And after a while; everything began to seem possible once more.

It was only later that night, when she was lying awake in bed, that her doubts launched another attack.

Why had Gordon agreed to her proposal so readily? He hadn't really argued with her at all. It was almost as if . . . well, almost as if he'd known all along what she was going to say. But that wasn't possible. Was it?

Jane turned over in bed and looked at Gordon's shape in the gloom. Was it really possible that Moscow could have told him what she was planning? If so, the implications were that he was not just there to help her—he was also there to watch her. To test her, judge her, and, if she was found wanting, to wipe her out.

She thought about this possibility for all of thirty seconds, and then decided that the idea was unthinkable.

She turned over and went straight to sleep.

The next day they went to London and became tourists.

Jane discovered that Gordon's grasp of the geography of the city was poor, despite the fact that he had lived in London for years, so they went on the sightseers' bus tour which began and ended in Piccadilly Circus. It took two hours.

In the afternoon they wandered down Whitehall and looked at Downing Street and the Houses of Parliament.

Throughout the day they paid particular attention to the security precautions, and they soon came to the conclusion that the protection provided by the police was deceptively casual. At the entrance to the Houses of Parliament, for instance, near the tunnel to the Members' car park, there was just one uniformed policeman, lounging about and looking bored. But that couldn't possibly be the whole of the story. There were undoubtedly closed-circuit television cameras, and probably a number of plainclothes officers scattered about in the crowd.

At the end of the afternoon they had a cup of tea, and when she was sure that no one could overhear them, Jane got down to business.

"Well, Gordon, are we going to be able to do it in London or not?"

"No," said Gordon immediately. "We can't. Not here."

Jane agreed, but she wanted to know his reasons. "Why not?"

"Well, for a start, we're going to have to use a car to transport the bomb. Right?"

"Right."

"Well, it would obviously be impossible to get a car anywhere near our subject in London. Downing Street is hopeless, and so are the Houses of

Parliament. The only alternative is to just park the car in the street and try to time the explosion for the precise moment when our man's car goes by. But the odds against that working must be enormous. Not to mention the slim chances of getting away afterwards.''

Jane was relieved, because Gordon was confirming her own judgment.

"Yes," she said, "I'm sure you're right. London is impossible."

"So, where do we go from here? We have to do it somewhere."

Gordon's words shocked her. He was right, of course, but it seemed strange to hear her own thoughts in someone else's mouth. Could it be that Gordon understood that he could not back out of the contract either? If so, he was brighter than she had thought.

"Yes," she agreed. "It has to be done somewhere."

"So where does that leave us?"

"Well, I think it leads us into the country. . . . But not tonight. Tomorrow."

That evening they checked into the Ritz Hotel. Jane had always wanted to stay at the Ritz, and she had recently seen an advertisement for weekend breaks there at surprisingly modest rates. More to the point, she also wanted to see whether Gordon was still intimidated by posh hotels, as his Libyan file had suggested.

He wasn't. She could detect no sign that he was

nervous at the reception desk. In fact he was quite
impatient with the clerk on duty, who was a for-
eigner of some sort.

They went upstairs, and discovered that the room
they had been allocated was beautifully furnished.
But the novelty of opulence soon wore off, and
after half an hour Jane demanded to be taken out
to dinner.

They ate that night at a small Italian restaurant
in Soho. After a couple of pre-dinner cocktails,
and most of a bottle of wine, Jane felt the need for
entertainment, so after the meal she dragged Gordon along to the Revuebar.

The programme consisted of a succession of
beautiful girls stripping themselves naked in time
to music. Occasionally, for variation, there were
two or three girls on stage together, and there was
also a handsome male dancer; he too performed
naked, demonstrating that nature had been generous to him. Jane loved it all: she hadn't enjoyed
anything so much for ages. She liked the nude
girls even better than the boy, though he was very
dishy.

Halfway through the show, she glanced at Gordon while a real blonde was spreading her legs
apart and pointing her toes at the roof. Gordon was
watching with evident enjoyment, so Jane slipped
her hand into his groin.

Nothing.

"Doesn't even this turn you on?" she asked in
amazement.

"I am enjoying it," he told her cheerfully.

"You could have fooled me. Jesus Christ, you're inhuman. It's making me feel unbelievably randy, and I'm a woman! And there's a man four rows behind me whose cock is so stiff it's poking me in the back of the neck."

Jane noticed that Gordon couldn't sleep that night either. Perhaps it was the Ritz bed. Whatever the reason, he seemed ready to talk well into the night.

They talked business mostly: about The Project and how to carry it out. And they talked a great deal about the prime minister.

"You don't like him, do you?" said Gordon after a while. "You go a bit funny whenever you mention him. As if there was something personal."

Jane was silent for a moment, wondering how much to say in reply; but then she decided that it would do no harm to tell the truth.

"I knew the man, years go," she said. "Long before he was prime minister. He was a business associate of my father's."

"Really?" Gordon was impressed.

"Yes."

"But why don't you like him?"

"Because he's a hypocrite."

"Oh. You mean he fucked you and enjoyed it, but then he wouldn't admit it afterwards?"

His comment hurt Jane more than she cared to admit. "Something like that."

Gordon chuckled. "How old were you at the time?"

"Fourteen, fifteen."

"Oh!" said Gordon knowingly.

"What do you mean by that?"

"Well, I can imagine what you were like when you were fourteen. The biggest little cock-teaser God ever invented."

Jane brought her right fist down hard on Gordon's chest. She tried to hurt him, but she wasn't strong enough. He just grunted with amusement.

"It wasn't like that at all!" she said.

"Wasn't it?"

"No. It bloody well wasn't." She rolled over in bed. "I was an innocent fourteen-year-old girl, believe it or not." She could hear the pain and anguish in her own voice, and she knew she was exposing herself, but she didn't care. "I was a *virgin*, for Christ's sake. Fourteen years old, and he seduced me. He was the first."

"But you enjoyed it."

"Of course I enjoyed it! But that doesn't alter the fact that he's a ruthless bastard. . . . He's a fascist, Gordon, don't you understand? That's why he has to be killed. As long as he's in power we shall never have justice in this country. Never." Tears came into Jane's eyes and she was glad the room was in darkness.

"He told you he loved you, did he?" Gordon's voice sounded far away.

"Yes . . . He did as a matter of fact." And in her mind she could still hear the words. She could hear his lies again: just like all politicians' lies.

You're the most beautiful girl in the world, Jane.

Do you think so?

Yes.

Will you really marry me?

Of course. In a few years' time, when you're older.

Gordon grunted doubtfully. "Hmm. It's hard to believe you were that stupid."

"Yes, it is, isn't it?" The tears rolled down Jane's cheeks in the blessed blackness of the night. "And I suppose I *was* stupid. I was very, very green then. Very naive. But I never will be again. Never. Never. Never. . . ."

Jane wiped the tears away with the back of her hand.

"And I'll tell you something else. I'm going to kill that fascist bastard before long. I'm going to kill him if it's the last thing I ever do."

The next morning Jane was awake early. She left Gordon sleeping, and went and had a shower in the luxury of a Ritz bathroom.

It was while she was in the shower that she realized at last what the postcard from Klaus Flettner had meant. And once she realized that, everything else fell into place.

Gordon woke up soon afterwards, and after breakfast they checked out of the hotel and drove down to Sussex to look at the prime minister's country house.

It was public knowledge that the present prime

minister did not use Chequers, the house which had been a rural retreat for prime ministers ever since 1912. Instead he used his own house in Stokely, a small village on the edge of Ashdown Forest.

Jane and Gordon spent the morning driving round the district adjoining the house. They considered the various routes which the prime minister might take when coming down from London, and talked of culvert bombs on the IRA model. They also explored the village in which the house was situated.

After lunch at the village pub they walked across a patch of open ground to gaze into a tree-lined stream.

"Well, it would be a whole lot easier out here than in London," commented Gordon.

"Yes. Much."

He turned to look up stream, through the trees. He pointed.

"That church over there must be the one where the prime minister's daughter is going to get married. Did you read about that in the papers?"

"Yes, I did." Jane felt as if she were dreaming. How easy it was all going to be. How inevitable. But then it was all supposed to be inevitable, wasn't it? Marx had said so.

"Let's go and have a look at the church," Gordon suggested.

"All right."

The church stood at the end of a narrow lane, with no houses in the immediate vicinity. It was

...t of gray stone, and appeared to date from the
thirteenth or fourteenth century.

When they reached the church they went inside,
welcoming its coolness. It was deserted.

Gordon moved ahead to explore, but Jane just
sat down in a pew at the back of the church. She
had needed only one glance to make up her mind
as soon as she came in through the door. After that
it was a bit like a game of hunt the thimble: all she
had to do was to tell Gordon whether he was hot
or cold.

After a while he came back. He spoke in a
whisper.

"This is more like it! It would be dead easy in
here."

"Yes. It would."

"This is the PM's country church. He comes
here every Sunday when he's at home."

"Yes. I know."

"And you remember what you were saying about
political impact. . . ."

"Yes?"

"Well, I read in the paper today that the American president is going to attend this wedding as
well."

"That's right."

Gordon's eyes gleamed. "Now, just think—if
we were to plant the bomb in here, we could wipe
out the pair of them! And God knows how many
other VIPs! We've got more than enough gelignite
to reduce this whole place to a pile of rubble. And
if we could pull that off, that would have more

than enough political impact to satisfy Moscow—
wouldn't you say so? It would be a coup that
would shake the world!''

Jane gave him a brief smile. ''Yes, Gordon,
you're right. Wiping out the pair of them, as you
put it, would guarantee peace for a generation. But
where would you put it, Gordon? That's the point.
Where is the bomb going to go?''

Gordon didn't answer. He frowned and began to
pace about. After a while he came back.

''Are there any cellars underneath here?''

''It's called a crypt.''

''O.K., but is there one?''

''Yes.''

''Well, how about there?''

''No good. It will be searched and searched
again.''

Gordon looked around. ''What about in the
organ?''

''No.''

''In the altar?''

''No.''

He wandered off again, scratching his head and
scheming. Jane smiled; she had never seen him
work at a problem like this.

Eventually he came back. ''We must be able to
put it somewhere.''

''Yes. That's true.''

''Have you any ideas?''

''Yes.''

''Well, where then?''

Jane stood up. ''Follow me.''

were two rows of massive stone pillars set
ar intervals down the center of the church.
Halfway along, between two of the pillars on the
left, was a stone tomb.

According to the inscription, the tomb housed
the remains of one William Tayler, a merchant,
born 1550, died 1590. On top of the tomb was an
effigy of the merchant carved in pitted stone; his
hands were crossed on his chest. The whole monu-
ment was about six feet long, two feet wide, and
three feet high.

Jane paused and put her hand on the merchant's
shoulder.

"Here, Gordon. The bomb will go in here."

17

On Friday night Ben and Sally set off to spend the weekend at a hotel near Eastbourne.

It proved to be one of the happiest short holidays Ben could remember, and he was left in no doubt that Sally thought so, too.

On Sunday morning, Ben suggested that on the way home they should call on Sally's father and stepmother in Guildford. Sally agreed, and they arrived at the Dennings' house soon after four o'clock.

It was the first time Ben had met Max Denning since the Moscow Olympics, and he was shocked by the change in Max's appearance. His hair and moustache were now white, and his face had lost its fullness. He claimed to be as fit as could be expected for his age, but Ben suspected that the older man was considerably less robust than he made out. However, he didn't pursue the subject, and they talked about judo instead. Max had maintained his keen interest in the sport, and he was anxious to hear about up-and-coming youngsters and recent matches.

After a while they came to a gap in the conversation, and Max began to speak with some diffidence.

"How—er—how did you come to meet Sally again, Ben? After all, it's been quite some time since Moscow."

Ben explained about his job at Scotland Yard, and the videotapes which he and Sally sometimes had to work on together.

"Ah yes, I see." Max nodded. "I'd heard you were in computers. Have you—er—have you been seeing much of Sally then?"

"Yes, a fair bit, over the last couple of months."

"Oh . . ." Max sat and digested that piece of information. "Well, you see more of her than me, then. She doesn't come home very often these days."

"She's too busy, I suppose."

"Well, yes, perhaps. But to be frank, Ben, Sally doesn't see eye to eye with my wife, Paula. Daughters never do like their fathers to marry again, and then, of course, the two of them are from different generations. Still, there we are. Can't be helped."

Ben drew a breath. He could see that Max was anxious about his daughter, foreseeing a time when fatherly advice would not be available, so he tried to provide some reassurance.

"Max, don't misunderstand me," he began. "I haven't said anything to Sally yet, because it's only fairly recently that I've got to know her again—

but how would you feel if in the course of time I were to ask her to marry me?''

Max's eyes brightened; he leaned forward in his chair, his hands on his walking stick. ''Why, I'd be delighted, Ben, delighted. I can see at a glance that she's happy with you, and personally I'd be very glad to see her settled down—that's what every father wants. And I couldn't ask for a better son-in-law than you—I know you of old.''

Max paused, and put his head on one side.

''But I think you're right not to rush things,'' he added. ''After all, she can be a bit of a handful at times, you know!'' And he grinned mischievously.

''Yes,'' said Ben. ''I'm beginning to think you're right!''

On the way back to London Sally seemed depressed and said very little, so Ben stopped at a riverside pub and bought her a drink. Every man in the bar turned to look at her as they walked in, but Sally herself seemed too preoccupied to notice.

They took their drinks outside and sat on a bench on the river bank. Sally had brought the *Sunday Times* out of the car, and she became engrossed in a section which Ben was pretty sure she had read before.

He peeked over her shoulder and saw that her interest was focussed on an article about the president of the United States. It had now been formally announced that he would be coming to England in two weeks' time for talks with the

British government; he would also be going to Paris and Rome.

"Does that worry you?" Ben asked.

Sally lowered the newspaper and frowned. "Yes, it does. It's just what I was afraid would happen. And what really worries me is that no one is taking Natalie Zasulich's story seriously."

"You are." *Perhaps too seriously.*

"Yes, I am. What we really need to do is set up twenty-four-hour surveillance on Challoner and Tate, tap their phones, and so on. Really check them out."

"That seems a bit extreme, Sally. Supposing they're just an ordinary, law-abiding couple—"

"They're not."

"Well, perhaps not. But so far you haven't a shred of evidence to suggest otherwise."

Sally ignored this comment and gazed into the distance. "What I really ought to do is harass the life out of them, every hour on the hour for the next two weeks, so that if they are planning anything they'll become so nervous that they'll abandon the whole idea."

Ben groaned inwardly. "You can't possibly do that—you've specifically been warned to stay away from them."

"I know what my orders are better than you do," Sally snapped at him. Her frown deepened. "Those two are up to something, damn it. I know bloody well they are. And they're not going to get away with it."

Ben thought it best to say nothing; he had not

seen Sally so upset for a long time. Not since—well, not since Moscow.

After a few moments Sally got up and walked back to the car, leaving her drink unfinished.

Ben sighed heavily but stayed where he was. It would be best to let her cool down alone for a minute or two.

One thing was certain, he decided: he hadn't yet found out how to argue with Sally without upsetting her. Perhaps he never would. What was particularly unfortunate was that the weekend had been idyllic up to now—it had gone so well, in fact, that he had even been thinking of asking her to marry him!

Well, this was obviously not the right moment. And when you came right down to it, perhaps there were just too many differences between them for marriage ever to work at all. Perhaps the right moment to propose never would come.

18

It was all very well for Jane to decree that the bomb must go into a sixteenth-century tomb—and Gordon agreed that in practice that was the only place it *could* go—but converting that decision into a reality was not so easy.

On Monday afternoon Gordon visited the church again. He went armed with a tape measure and a book about architecture to provide him with cover.

As he had expected, the church was almost empty: there was just one old lady arranging some flowers. She soon departed, and Gordon sketched out a detailed plan of action.

As far as he could see, the carved effigy of William Tayler was placed in position just like the lid of a box: it looked as if it would lift straight off the stone structure which formed the bulk of the tomb. The problem therefore reduced itself to one of lifting the lid.

Gordon couldn't even guess how much the effigy weighed, but he doubted if it could be more than the engine of a car, and car engines were lifted readily enough with the aid of a block and tackle.

He made a few measurements, and decided that he would have to erect a strong steel bar, several feet above the tomb, to support the block and tackle. One end of the bar could be rested in an angle where an arch met a pillar in the nave. The other end would have to be supported on a triangle formed by three pieces of scaffolding and held in position by rope. Once the block and tackle was in position, it would then be a matter of securing a rope at each end of the effigy in order to lift it.

In theory that was all quite straightforward. In practice, the work would have to be done at night, in almost total darkness.

When he raised the matter of money, Jane told him that she still had thousands of pounds of her grandmother's legacy left, so on Tuesday morning Gordon was able to buy all the equipment he needed. By the middle of Tuesday afternoon he was ready to carry out the next stage of his plan, later that night; in the meantime, he decided to work off his nervous tension by attending the weekly judo practice at the university.

He drove to the gymnasium and began to change. As he did so, he noticed that the building was curiously quiet, and when he went out onto the floor of the gym he found to his surprise that he appeared to be alone. There were two mats set out for practice, just as he had expected, but there was no sign of any participants.

Well, this is a bit odd.

Suddenly a voice rang out from behind him: "Looking for a fight?"

Gordon turned.

"Did I scare you?"

He blinked. "No, I was just a bit surprised to see you, that's all."

"I bet you were."

It was that copper, Gordon realized. For a moment he hadn't been able to place her, but now he remembered. It was that blonde girl who had interviewed him in Bayswater, the one who had made Jane so jumpy only last week.

Stay cool. There's nothing to worry about.

"You look as if you were expecting to see the judo class in here."

"Yes. I was. So were you, by the look of it." The girl was wearing white trousers and a jacket, exactly like his own.

"It's cancelled. Because of the exams."

"Oh."

The girl stood there with her hands on her hips, staring at him. She had an amused expression on her face, as if she didn't rate him too highly. Gordon made up his mind to show how cool he really was.

"Don't I know you?" he asked. "Haven't we met somewhere?"

"Yes. I'm with Special Branch. I interviewed you in London two months ago."

"Oh. Yes. I remember. . . . Legionnaires' disease, wasn't it?"

"Something like that."

The blonde girl smiled, and Gordon was forced to admit that fuzz or no fuzz, she was a really nice piece of crumpet.

"Well? Do you want to fight or don't you?"

The remark struck Gordon as strange. It just wasn't the sort of thing judo players said to each other. But best not to show surprise.

"Well, yes," he said. "If you like."

"Good."

The blonde girl led the way out onto the mat, where they bowed to each other courteously. Then, without further ado, she seized him by the lapels and threw him with *tai-toshi*.

Gordon hit the mat hard, and for a moment the wind was knocked out of his lungs. He took his time getting up.

Shit but this girl is good! He had every physical advantage over her, but the blonde girl's technique was superb.

Gordon climbed back to his feet and decided to be more careful. They stood, head to head, gripping the other's jacket and moving their feet for position. And then, to his amazement, the girl began to whisper to him.

"I know what you're up to, Gordon! I know what you're planning to do. . . ."

What the *hell* was she talking about?

While he was busy thinking, the blonde girl threw him again, with *hane-goshi*.

This fall hurt him even more than the first, and Gordon began to feel cross. God damn and blast

the little bitch! She was obviously trying to humili-
ate him. And not doing a bad job of it, either.

He hauled himself to his feet yet again. His left
shoulder was a spangle of pain. He seized her
angrily by the jacket.

"I know what you're planning!" she whispered
in his ear. "I know what you're trying to do!"

Gordon panted, raucous breaths heaving in and
out. Half of the panting was caused by exertion,
but half was the result of blood-racing panic. How
the hell *could* she know? How *could* she *possibly*
know?

He hit the mat a third time and cried aloud with
pain and frustration. He was *not* going to be thrown
around like a mouse being tossed by a cat.

He snarled with rage and leapt up without paus-
ing to draw breath.

Which was all wrong, he knew that. But by God
this lousy, stinking, pox-ridden whore was not
going to do this to him!

Gordon put everything he had into *osoto gari*,
but she avoided it easily, shifting her weight so
that he couldn't even begin the throw. He tried
hiza garuma, and she defeated that, too.

"You see, Gordon," she hissed in his ear, "I
understand you. I can see through you! I can tell
what you're trying to do. And I won't let you. I
won't let you do it, Gordon! I won't!"

And then, at last, he understood.

She was talking about judo.

Of course.

She had to be.

Judo.

She couldn't be talking about anything else.

How could she?

It was impossible.

It was secret.

"Gordon!"

He ignored his name. He wanted to throw this girl, throw her hard. Fall on her, crack her ribs, crush her, smash her.

"Gordon!"

The screeching cry came again from the spectators' gallery above the floor of the gym.

"Gordon!"

He paused reluctantly in the struggle for position.

"Just a minute," he said to his opponent. He disentangled himself from her grip and looked up. "What do you want?" he said impatiently.

Jane was standing above them. She stared down with glistening eyes, her lips bared and her face contorted with rage.

"What the hell do you think you're doing?" she screamed at him. She could scarcely articulate the words.

"I'm . . . practicing."

"Well, stop it! Stop it at once!"

And then Jane hesitated, as if realizing that her passion was out of all proportion to the situation. "It's time to go," she said in a quieter voice. "It's time . . . to go."

Reluctantly, Gordon accepted that she was right. He excused himself and went and got changed.

He and Jane drove home separately, and when

he arrived he found Jane at her desk in the living room, still muttering under her breath.

"I'll kill her! I'll murder her! I'll crucify the miserable little bitch. How dare she! How dare she!"

Jane took out a sheet of paper, wound it into her electric typewriter, and began to clatter away.

Gordon waited until she had finished before he asked what she was up to.

"I've written to my M.P.," Jane told him with evident satisfaction. "When that little blonde tart was in here the other day I took her name and number off her warrant card, and by God I'm going to make life hot for her. You see if I don't."

"But I don't get it," said Gordon. "Why are you writing to a Member of Parliament?"

"To complain, of course! Why the fucking hell do you think?"

Gordon considered the matter. And the more he thought about it, the less he liked it. What had this young policewoman done, precisely? All she had done was interview him once and Jane twice, in the normal course of her duties. She had also practiced judo with him and been a bit rough in the process. And, finally, she had whispered sweet nothings in his ear. So what?

"I still don't get it," he said at last. "What are you complaining about?"

Jane paused in the middle of typing the envelope. "I am complaining, Gordon, about the fact that this nosy little cunt is harassing us without any justification whatever."

"No, she's not."

"What?" Jane's voice rose about an octave. "What did you say?"

"I said, no, she's not."

He stood up and approached her. Jane held the letter and the envelope close to her chest, as if afraid that he intended to snatch them.

"And what's more, I'm against you writing that letter. It can do no good, and it may do harm."

"How?"

"It'll draw attention to us. And that's the last thing we want to do. I think you should forget it."

"Oh you do, do you? Well tough shit, Gordon. Tough shit."

"I'm against it," Gordon repeated, "and I want you to remember that. I can't stop you sending that letter, not if you really want to. But I don't think you should. And the next time you report to your East German friend, you can tell him that. From me."

Jane looked at him. And Gordon saw that for the first time in their relationship, he had managed to frighten her.

At half past eleven that night they went upstairs and changed into dark-colored clothes. Then they retired to the garage, where they ran through a checklist of equipment.

Finally Gordon took the bulb out of the roof light in his car and fitted false number plates on the front and the back. The false registration numbers would not be much help if the police checked them against the national computer, but they were a safeguard against the possibility of some nosy little boy writing the numbers down in his notebook.

By midnight they were ready to go, and by 1:30 they had driven seventy miles to the Sussex village of Stokely. There they drove down the tree-lined lane which led to Holy Trinity Church; they parked well out of sight under an ancient oak, switched off the engine and lights, and waited.

It was necessary to wait in order to get their eyes accustomed to the darkness, and also to see whether a police car would come and investigate what they were up to.

Gordon wasn't sure what to expect in the way of security checks. It was public knowledge that in twelve days' time the church would be the scene of a fashionable wedding which would be attended by the president of the United States, the British prime minister, and numerous other bigwigs. The question was, how soon would the police start to keep a special eye on it? Gordon's guess was, not until a couple of days beforehand. But in the meantime it was best not to rush ahead too quickly.

Nothing happened, so fifteen minutes later they blackened their faces with boot polish and put on tight-fitting gloves. Then they prepared to transport their gear into the church.

To Gordon's relief, the heavy door on the south side was unlocked: he had been half afraid that Jane would have to pick the lock. He laid two pencil torches at crucial points in the nave of the church, and then began to unload the scaffolding from the roof rack of his car.

He did all the work himself because it was much easier that way. None of the equipment was impossibly heavy, and he knew exactly where it should go. All Jane had to do was to hold the church door open and keep out of the god-damned way.

It took him forty-five minutes to fix the block and tackle above the tomb of William Tayler, and to check that all the scaffolding was roped firmly in position. When he was ready he located Jane in the shadowy half-light.

"O.K.?" he whispered.

"Yes," she said, but without much conviction.

"Good."

He got Jane to hold a pencil torch for him, and then scraped all the way round the joint between the effigy of William Taylor and the stone base of the tomb beneath it. Not many particles came away, which pleased him, because it suggested that the effigy would lift off easily.

So much for hopes.

When he applied a lifting force through the block and tackle, he found that, in accordance with Murphy's Law, the bloody thing simply would not shift at all.

Gordon swore and cursed, strained and sweated, pulled and tugged and kicked and spat on it—but all to no avail.

Shit.

Jane said not a word throughout the whole of this performance. It was as if she was afraid to open her mouth for fear of the reply which might come her way.

After a minute Gordon decided that there was nothing for it but to put a crowbar under the lid and to prise the bloody thing loose.

He went round to the end of the tomb where the late Mr. Tayler's feet pointed upwards, and jammed his crowbar into the joint between effigy and base. Then he placed all his weight on the free end of the bar, and pushed downwards.

What happened next he wasn't sure. But suddenly something came loose: the crowbar flew through the air, landing on the stone flagstones of the nave with the most appalling clatter, and Gordon himself went sprawling flat on his back.

The ringing sound of steel against stone seemed to echo round the church for ever. Gordon had never heard such a din in his life.

After a moment he sat up.

He glanced at his watch: it was 3 A.M. A time when all good citizens were fast asleep. And in any case there weren't any houses within a hundred yards. So what the hell was he pussyfooting around for? No one would have heard—and if they had they would simply turn over and go back to sleep again.

Jane tried to help him to his feet, but he pushed her away. He fitted the crowbar into the same crack again, and exerted pressure with more caution than he had used the first time.

And, sure enough, something began to move.

After that it was all straightforward. Twenty minutes later Gordon had hoisted the lid of the tomb two feet clear of the base, and he and Jane were able to shine a lamp into the interior.

There was a space about six feet long, two feet wide, and eighteen inches deep.

It was empty.

"What happened to Mr. Tayler?" asked Jane.

"God knows."

"Yes," said Jane. "I expect he does." And they both fell about laughing for at least a minute and a half. After that they felt a good deal more relaxed. And when it came right down to it, Gordon decided, they *were* in a ridiculous situation. What on earth would they say to anyone who found them here now? "Well, actually, we're very keen on brass rubbings." It was hardly a convincing story.

When they had recovered from their fit of hysterics, Gordon went over to the car and brought in his radio receiver unit. He placed it inside the tomb and lowered the lid.

Together he and Jane then drove three miles south, to a point on a high hill overlooking the valley in which the church lay. From here, in daylight, the church was clearly visible below them. At the moment all they could see were a few lights twinkling in the inky blackness.

Gordon walked forward a few paces to the point where the hill began to drop away. To their left, a tall tower was just visible in the moonlight.

"What's that?" asked Jane.

"Oh, I don't know. Some kind of old windmill or something."

"It doesn't *look* like a windmill."

"Well, on the map it's called Smith's Folly."

"Oh, it's a folly, is it?"

"That's what it says. If it makes you any the wiser."

"You know what a folly is, don't you, Gordon?"

"No." He fiddled with the transmitter.

"It's a building with no specific purpose. Never did have one. It was probably built to give unemployed men something to do—or to enable a rich man to get a better view of his land. Something like that. They were very keen on them in the nineteenth century."

Gordon grunted as he checked the last connection. "Well, we could use it as our base on D-day if you like. It's got a door and windows. Do you think you can make us a key?"

"Sure. Why not?" Jane sounded more confident than she had for some time.

"Now," said Gordon. "I'm ready."

In the previous week he had put together a more sophisticated version of the radio-controlled detonating mechanism which he had used for the London bomb. He had bought a more sensitive transmitter/receiver combination, and had also incorporated a microprocessor as a safety lock. It was only when he fed in a series of numbers, in the correct sequence, that the receiver would accept the signal to detonate.

He pointed the transmitter down the valley and punched in the code on the numbered keys. Each digit sounded a musical note, and Gordon pressed the buttons at unequal intervals so that they played a little tune. They played the first six notes of

"God Save the Queen," which Gordon thought was amusing. Jane didn't appear to notice.

"Is that it?" she asked when he had finished.

"Not quite." He groped in the gloom for the metal switch on his transmitter box which would send the signal to fire. He clicked it downwards. "There. That's all."

He felt very tired now, and anxious to be done with the night's work as soon as possible. Apart from his weariness, there was another reason for haste: it would be dawn before long.

They drove back to the church, parked in the same place, and went inside. Gordon half expected a couple of dozen policemen to pounce on them, but there was no one there. Everything was just as they had left it.

They opened the tomb and looked inside. Gordon could see at a glance that the servo had moved the lever to the right, just as it was supposed to do.

"Has it worked?" asked Jane anxiously.

"Yes."

"Are you sure?"

"Yes! Of course I'm sure!" And he made her feel with her finger, to prove that the lever actually had moved.

"Gordon!" she said breathlessly. "That's fantastic!"

"Yes," he said. "Isn't it."

They arrived home soon after six o'clock in the morning.

Gordon slept until noon. Then he got up and

drove back, yet again, to the village which he and Jane had left only a few hours earlier.

He parked his car near the post office this time. Then, armed with the usual book on architecture, he walked back to the church.

When he arrived he entered cautiously. The atmosphere was totally different now from that which he had experienced in the middle of the night, but he still felt apprehensive and on edge.

The building was filled with warm light which filtered through the stained-glass windows. Slowly Gordon walked around, examining this, showing silent approval of that, miming to an unseen audience. One lesson which had been dinned into him in Libya was that American Secret Service agents in particular were pathologically suspicious, so it was always possible that even now the church was under scrutiny through closed-circuit television. He was ninety-nine percent sure that it wasn't—but you could never be absolutely certain, so he devoted a little time to play-acting.

In the end he decided that everything was safe so he felt free to examine the tomb.

Fortunately, he couldn't see a scratch on it. Well, not a *new* scratch. It was covered with the scratches and scars of nearly four hundred years—but there was nothing to show that the tomb had been tampered with recently, and that was what he had wanted to check.

In the next few days Gordon tried to complete his work as quickly as possible, because the nearer the wedding of the prime minister's daughter approached, the more likely it was that the church would come under tight security.

His first task was to construct a number of metal boxes which would fit into the coffin-shaped space inside the tomb. He made four of these boxes so that individually they would not be too heavy: each one took him a whole day.

His plan was to fill all the boxes with explosive. Part of the contents would be gelignite, and part would be the IRA's so-called "co-op" mix, a deadly mixture of sugar and weedkiller which could be prepared by anyone with access to the local "co-op" or grocery store. The boxes would eventually be linked by detonating wire, and they would all be tightly sealed to prevent them being detected by sniffer dogs.

The co-op mix looked innocuous enough when it was prepared, but Gordon knew from his training in Libya that it packed a massive punch. He prepared fifty pounds of it, to be added to an equal amount of gelignite.

Jane too was busy throughout the rest of that week: it was the exam season, and Gordon hardly saw her except in the mornings and at bedtime. Occasionally her commitment to the university annoyed him; but Jane argued that it was essential to maintain her profession as a cover, not only until the day of the wedding, but also until well after it. It would be foolish to arouse suspicion unnecessarily.

After a certain amount of grumbling, Gordon accepted the situation. After all, there was little he could delegate to her, and it was not as if she would be particularly good company: she looked gray-faced, strained, and tired, and she was sleeping badly.

By the Friday evening of that week, after many hours of nonstop work, Gordon felt that he deserved a break from his labors, so towards nine o'clock he went over to the university gym for a work-out.

Most students had finished their exams by now, and the gym was crowded. This time it was no surprise to find the blonde policewoman among those practicing judo, and with a jerk of her head she again invited him onto the mat. But he was wise to her this time, and, by attacking at a moment when she wasn't expecting it, he threw her hard almost at once: threw her so hard, in fact, that she landed off the mat, and was clearly bruised and shaken.

"Oh dear," he said solicitously, as he helped her to pick herself up. "I do apologize. I hope I haven't hurt you." And the blonde girl looked so shocked by the ruthlessness of his attack that for a moment he was almost sincere.

19

After the judo practice Sally went into the changing-room and sat down heavily.

Tate was no ordinary man where judo was concerned, and if she had not been fit and highly skilled, she would have ended up in hospital, there was no doubt about that.

He deliberately tried to injure me. The thought ran around in Sally's head. And not only had Gordon Tate tried to hurt her, which was disturbing enough in itself, but he had also succeeded—which was worse! Olympic silver medallists were not supposed to be thrown by just any-old-body who happened to be hanging around the gym. But Tate had done it. She could still feel the pain, and she was annoyed with herself.

Sally took a shower and tried to work out what this experience meant.

In the last few days, she had begun to think that perhaps Ben was right—perhaps Challoner and Tate really were clean and decent. After all, she had searched their house and found nothing. She had spent every available evening sitting in her car waiting for them to go out—and when they did go out it was only to buy cigarettes or fish and chips.

Gradually Sally's suspicions had begun to fade.

But forceful contact with the floor of the university gym had changed all that. For if there was one thing she was sure of, it was that law-abiding people do *not* throw other law-abiding people in the way Gordon Tate had treated her. So she was back to being convinced again.

But convinced of what, precisely?

Well, she might as well face it. She was *certain* that Challoner and Tate were the couple who had been described to her by Natalie Zasulich. Not *might* be, but *were*.

And why did she believe that?

Well, because she had met them, and studied them. And because she had compared them in her own mind with others who were known to be violent in pursuit of their political beliefs; and the comparison had told her that these two really were potential assassins.

The problem was to find some evidence. And that meant watching the house and following them whenever possible. And that made her angry. Very angry indeed. Because Gordon Tate and Jane Challoner were screwing up her life completely.

Here she was, having fallen in love with a man whom she had worshipped for years but had always thought was beyond reach, and all she wanted to do was to concentrate on strengthening her relationship with him.

And what was happening?

What was happening was that she was being prevented from doing what she really wanted to do by an overdeveloped sense of duty.

Anyone else would let Challoner and Tate go to hell, Sally told herself. *But no, not you. You're too professional to do a sensible thing like that.*

For one wild moment Sally did consider solving her problem by asking Ben to help her. But she realized at once that she couldn't. For one thing he was busy with his own duties—and, moreover, he didn't even believe she was right.

Sally sighed. It was enough to make you weep. *"Shit!"* she said. And meant every word of it.

The next morning, Saturday, Sally was up early. She drove to Winchester and began looking for a room to rent.

What she was looking for was a room with a window which overlooked Dr. Challoner's house. It didn't have to be close to the house, because she could always use binoculars, but the room had to have an uninterrupted view of the front door and the garage. Fortunately, since Dr. Challoner's residence faced a hillside covered with Victorian terraces, there was a good chance that she would find what she wanted.

As a first step, Sally began looking for news agents' shops. Most of these had a few cards in the window offering accommodation, and the third shop she called at proved to have just what was needed: it was a small flat on the floor above the shop itself, with its own entrance at the side of the house, on the corner of a street.

The shopkeeper was hoping to find a long-term tenant, but after some spirited haggling she agreed to rent the room on a weekly basis. For cash, in advance. Sally also had to agree to pay the cost of any telephone calls.

The deal was expensive, and Sally thought twice before accepting it, but at least she was now the occupant of a flat which would meet her needs.

Next, Sally went into the town and stocked up with food and drink for the weekend. Her credit card bought her a portable radio and a pair of binoculars.

After that she stayed in the flat and peered out of the living-room window for nearly forty-eight hours without a break. She made only brief visits to the bathroom, and allowed herself only a few hours of sleep. Apart from that, she watched and waited, waited and watched, and grew steadily more bored and frustrated.

I must be crazy, she thought, several times. *Completely and utterly crazy.*

Gordon Tate and Jane Challoner came home at about six o'clock on Saturday evening; she had no idea where they had been before that.

On Sunday morning Tate left the house at about nine. As soon as she saw him open his car door Sally rushed down to her own car and tried to follow him. But he was three streets away from her, and by the time she reached the house he had gone.

He stayed out until eight o'clock that night.

At 11 P.M. the lights went on in the front bedroom. Jane Challoner pulled the curtains across the window, and at half past eleven the chink of light between the curtains disappeared.

That was all that happened.

On Monday morning Sally drove back to London to start work at the usual time. She was feeling tired and bad-tempered, but at least she had proved one thing; she had proved that what she was trying to do on her own was impractical. If Challoner and Tate were to be tailed effectively, it would have to be done by experts.

There was nothing else for it: she would just have to have another try at persuading her boss, Walter Fitch, to give the necessary orders.

20

The bomb was finished.

At the moment, the four metal boxes were stowed in the back of Gordon's Talbot Alpine, so he drove carefully.

For once in his life he felt optimistic. Everything was going to be all right, he decided. It really was. The business of putting the bomb into the church was going to be difficult, yes. But they had lifted the lid of the tomb once, and what you had done once you could always do again. So it was all going to be O.K.

He arrived back at Jane's house, parked his car in the drive and locked it carefully; then he let himself in at the front door.

He walked down the hall and turned right into the living room.

And there, sitting in the chair facing him, was the East German, Klaus Flettner.

Gordon stood still for a moment, and the conversation came to an end as both Jane and Flettner became aware of his presence.

230

Jane spoke first. "Well, don't just stand there like a lemon. Come on in."

Gordon glanced at her. She had a glass of orange juice in her right hand. It was almost certainly well spiked with vodka or gin, because her face was flushed and her voice was plummy. She was also smiling that cocky little smile of hers, the one which always made him want to give her a fucking good kick up the arse—

Flettner rose to his feet. He was wearing a double-breasted suit. His hair was brilliantined and his shoes were freshly polished. He looked like a typical victim of too many good lunches and not enough exercise.

"Gordon, my dear fellow. How nice to see you again."

He came across the room and held out his hand.

Gordon ignored it. "What the hell are you doing here?" he asked.

Jane seemed both amused and embarrassed by his rudeness. "Gordon, really . . ."

Flettner withdrew his hand and stuck it in his trouser pocket. He gave Gordon a quizzical look.

"I said, what the hell are you doing here?" Gordon repeated.

Flettner grinned. "Well, since you ask, my name is Heinrich Braun, and I'm over here on business. I export dyes, for the wool trade. Jane here is a friend whom I met on holiday in Ireland last year. You, I gather, are her live-in lover."

"Well, sort of," said Jane, and giggled.

But Gordon was not amused. Adrenalin flooded his veins. He could taste the gall in his mouth.

"O.K., so that's your cover story. But what are you *really* here for?"

Flettner smiled, a sophisticated man-of-the-world smile. "To supervise, Gordon, of course. To make sure that nothing goes wrong."

"Nothing will go wrong. The bomb will work. I know. I built it."

"I'm sure it will, Gordon. But I'm sure that you will also admit how important this project is to all three of us. If it goes well—our reputations are made. If it goes badly . . ." He shrugged. "You must understand that, surely?"

"I understand all right. You let us do all the work without any help, and now that we're on the point of succeeding, you want to claim all the credit. I understand all right. You don't fool me, Flettner."

The East German remained unruffled.

"Gordon, my dear fellow. You have been working nonstop for days—I know, Jane has told me. You are hot and tired. Why don't you just go upstairs and have a shower, and then come down once more. And we will start this conversation again. Now, what do you say?"

"What I say," said Gordon, "is go fuck yourself."

21

Late on Monday afternoon, when Sally had finished work, she took the underground to St. John's Wood, and after a few minutes' walk rang the doorbell of Ben's flat.

"Oh!" he said as he opened the door.

"Hello, Ben," said Sally wearily.

She kissed him on the cheek and walked past him into the living room. Ben followed her, looking concerned.

"What's the problem?" he asked.

Sally sat down. "Oh, I don't know. I'm just tired, I suppose. Have you got a drink?"

"Only a beer."

"That'll do."

Ben opened a can of light ale and poured half of it into a glass. "I rang you over the weekend," he said, glancing at her thoughtfully. "But you didn't seem to be in."

"No. I was out."

Sally was conscious that she was not being very responsive, but she felt both fatigued and depressed.

"I want to talk to you, Ben. Seriously."

"O.K." He sat down opposite her. "I'm listening."

"It's about this assassination business. . . . I'm sorry to go on about it, and I'd like nothing better than to forget the whole thing, but I can't. It's too important. . . . It's my belief that Challoner and Tate really are the couple Natalie Zasulich told me about."

The street—the Mercedes—the scream of the brakes . . . Sally could see Natalie dying all over again, even as she spoke.

"If Natalie was right, then Challoner and Tate are planning to kill both the president and the prime minister together, with a bomb, on either Friday or Saturday of this week. Now—I have tried several times to get my boss to put these two suspects under constant surveillance."

"But he won't do it."

"No. You're right. There've been dozens of threats of violence since the president's visit was announced. Plus all the usual problems with the IRA, the PLO, and the lunatic right and left. So, he's not convinced that this one needs special attention."

"No. And I gather you got an official reprimand for your pains," Ben added.

"How do you know that?"

"Oh, people talk."

"Well, yes, of course, you're right." Ben's

comment made Sally even more depressed than
ever. "Challoner complained about me to her M.P.,
so I got my knuckles rapped. The reprimand doesn't
bother me, but it does make things easier for
Challoner and Tate, because I've been told, yet
again, to stay away from them in future."

Ben nodded. "Well, that's what you'd better do
then. And I really don't see why you're so worried. You're concerned about the P.M.'s and the
president's safety, and that's reasonable enough.
But as far as I can see, they're going to be pro-
tected to an almost excessive extent. He and the
prime minister will hardly be able to blow their
noses without someone checking the handkerchief."

Sally had to make an effort not to lose her
temper. Like most laymen, Ben understood absolutely nothing about security. "The problem, Ben,
is that unless our leading politicians remain locked
in a fortress, it's always going to be possible for a
determined man or woman to take a shot at them.
And the best defense against that is to keep a very
careful eye on those who might want to assassinate
them."

She looked at Ben to see if she was getting
through to him, and obviously she wasn't, but she
ploughed on.

"What I'm saying, Ben, is that Challoner and Tate
ought to be watched constantly between now and
next Sunday morning. And preferably their house
and telephone need bugging as well."

"But Fitch has already said that he won't do
that," Ben protested. "Which is scarcely surpris-

ing, because as you told me yourself, Dr. Challoner's only crime to date is that she once got the better of you in a public debate. But you never forgive anyone who beats you, Sally—not in judo or anything else. And I think you ought to bear that in mind.''

That really got Sally going: her fatigue began to disappear.

"I know what Dr. Challoner's crimes are!" she snapped back at him. ''And if Fitch won't do anything officially, I shall do what's necessary myself—unofficially.''

Ben frowned, and Sally looked away from him. She couldn't bear to see him frown.

"Just what are you going to do?"

"Well, for a start I've rented a room. It overlooks Jane Challoner's house. And what I'm suggesting is that you and I should watch the house in turns—twelve hours on and twelve hours off, for the whole of this week.''

Ben groaned, and she could tell from his expression that he thought the whole idea was absurd. "How can we possibly do that?"

"You just sit there and bloody well watch!" Sally told him. ''It's not difficult—and when they leave the house you try to follow them, and see where they go.''

"But there's no way we could even begin to do that," said Ben. He was frowning again—fiercely.

Sally felt as if she wanted to cry. "Why not?"

"Well, because we both have jobs to do—we can't just abandon them.''

"We could take leave."

"No, we can't! That's a ridiculous idea. We couldn't possibly take time off—not this week, of all weeks. Everyone in the entire force is working flat out, preparing for the president's visit."

"Well then, we could phone in sick," Sally suggested. But even as she spoke she knew Ben would never accept that.

"Don't be so bloody stupid!" He sounded disgusted with her. "The whole thing is totally impractical from beginning to end, Sally, and I'm surprised you can't see that."

"What's the matter?" asked the person who was using Sally's voice. It was a stranger to her, whoever it was: a stranger conceived of fatigue and born of disappointment. "Are you scared of losing your job?"

"No, of course I'm not scared!" Ben was furious now—she could scarcely have offended him more. "But as for losing jobs, the way you're going, you'll lose yours before the week's out. If you've got any sense at all you'll just forget about your two suspects and get on with the job you've been given."

Sally's body began to tremble. She stood up in an attempt to control it.

"Very well. If you won't help me, I'll do it myself." And she began to walk towards the door.

Ben caught her by the arm. "Just a minute—do what by yourself?"

"Keep watch on Challoner and Tate."

"Oh, for Christ's sake! I won't even let you try."

Sally ripped her arm free of his grip. "You won't what?"

"I won't let you!" Ben repeated. "If you disobey orders, this week of all weeks, you'll throw away your entire career—and I won't let you do that."

"Oh, you won't, won't you?" Sally spat out the words. "Well, let me tell you this, Ben Meadows—you don't own me, and you never will. And nobody tells me what I can and can't do—not you or Walter Fitch or anyone. I make my own mind up."

She began to move towards the door again, shouting at Ben as she went.

"And as for being stupid, you're right, I am stupid! I was stupid enough to think that you cared for me, and would want to help me. Well, that's one mistake I shan't be repeating!"

She reached the front door of the flat and pulled it open.

"And don't bother ringing me up next week to ask how I got on. I never want to speak to you again!"

She slammed the door behind her with a crash which shook the whole building, and she ran towards the stairs in case Ben came rushing after her.

But even as she ran down the stone steps of the block of flats, she was aware that Ben was *not* rushing after her.

She was listening for the sound of the door opening, listening for a call, a sound, *anything*. She didn't want an apology, she would settle for an insult—

But nothing came.

Nothing happened.

When she reached the bottom of the stairs she stopped.

She turned.

She listened again.

But the door of Ben's flat remained shut.

22

Gordon's mind whirled. He fought to control the fury which raged within him.

Who did it? he asked himself. *Who really held this operation together? Me. Not you. Not either of you. Not you, you po-faced whore. And certainly not you either, you fat-bellied lump of German dog-shit. Me. I did it. I was the one. And I deserve some credit.*

The question was, would anyone give him any? Gordon had begun to doubt it, and the doubt gnawed at his soul. He was going to have to do something to correct the situation, but as yet he wasn't sure what it would be.

After dinner, Klaus Flettner asked to be shown details of the bomb and the church, so Gordon went through everything. In detail. He explained where everything would go, why it would go there, and how it would work. And at the end of the exposition Flettner began to ask questions.

He asked about the age of the gelignite, the

proportions of the co-op mix, the choice of detonator, the radio wavelength, the site for transmitting the firing signal, the choice of the church as the location for the bomb, the choice of the tomb within the church, the construction of the metal boxes, the voltage of the batteries, the design of the transmitter, the clothes Gordon had worn when constructing the bomb, the renting of the workshop, and so on and so forth.

It was clear from the outset of Flettner's tirade that nothing was right.

Absolutely *nothing* was right. Flettner criticized everything, and in the end Gordon's patience ran out.

"O.K., Flettner," he said, "if this is all such a great big disaster, I tell you what—I'll get you a ticket for the wedding next Saturday morning, and you can go and sit next to the tomb of William Tayler and watch. How would you like that?"

Flettner smiled an oily smile. "It is not so much a question of whether I will be there. The real question is whether the president of the United States will be there."

Gordon suddenly felt sick. Was it possible that he could have misunderstood something as elementary and simple as that? He could scarcely splutter a reply. "Of course the president will be there. What the hell are you talking about?"

Flettner smiled again. "But how can you be so sure? His itinerary has not yet been announced."

"Listen, dimwit, the girl getting married is the prime minister's daughter, and the president's niece.

It's only because of the wedding that he's coming over here in the first place.''

Flettner laughed. ''I doubt it. I doubt whether presidents fix their schedules so that their wives can wear pretty hats.''

''Oh, well, that's all you know,'' said Gordon with total contempt. ''You've been out in the desert so long you've lost all your marbles. I'm telling you, Flettner, it's precisely because of the wedding that the president *will* be in England at that time. That's the only thing that will get his picture in the paper and his face on the television screens. It's called human interest, but of course a Marxist like you wouldn't know anything about that.''

Flettner remained unmoved. ''Very well. Let us assume, for the moment, that the president is going to attend the wedding. But how can you be sure that the bomb will kill him? And the prime minister, too?''

''Because I've *been* there, that's why. Because I've looked at the structure of the building, and because I know that with the bomb placed where it is, it will bring the whole fucking roof down. No one who's in there will get out alive.''

''I hope so, Gordon. For your sake, I really hope so.''

Jane had finished the washing-up as they talked, and she was now sitting on the settee. Gordon noticed that her eyes shone with sadistic pleasure, as if she were relishing the fact that they were fighting over her. Which they weren't—at least, not yet.

With the discussion about the bomb at an end, Flettner moved across to the settee to sit beside Jane. She welcomed him with a seductive smile. She crossed her legs, tossed the hair out of her eyes, and laughed.

Flettner smiled back, and Gordon felt sick with disgust at the pair of them. He couldn't imagine now why he had ever felt the slightest respect for Flettner, or allowed himself to be intimidated by Jane. He was surprised that he had been so slow to recognize that Flettner was precisely what he was pretending to be: a typical German businessman, overweight, greedy, and smug. Jane, on the other hand, was simply a four-star bullshitter: she talked a good fight, but when it came to the crunch she was inclined to wet her knickers and cry like a baby.

So the hell with both of them.

At eleven o'clock they all changed into dark clothing and began the long night's work.

After they had loaded up Gordon's car they drove to Stokely, arriving at half past midnight.

Gordon made for his usual parking place, under the trees at the back of the church, and they waited for their eyes to grow used to the darkness.

The delay gave Gordon time to clarify his mind about Flettner. He had to decide whether he was justified in resenting the East German's presence, or whether his anger was just a form of childish jealousy which he ought to ignore.

Eventually he decided that he *was* right to feel bitter. Flettner could lift and carry, but nothing would be done tonight which would not have been done in his absence.

But there was another source of irritation rubbing away at a raw place on Gordon's consciousness: he realized now that he himself had simply been used as a pawn. That wasn't surprising, really. It was the way these people worked. But Gordon understood now that the intention to kill the president of the United States had been there all along. Jane had taken him to the church deliberately, and he had not singlehandedly dreamed up the idea of killing the West's two leading politicians at one blow. On the contrary, the double assassination had been at the heart of Moscow's thinking right from the very start. It was just that no one had bothered to tell young Gordon.

Well, he thought, *we'll see who's really smart before the night's out. We'll see soon enough.*

Fifteen minutes after their arrival, timed to the second on his digital watch, Gordon got out of his car and led the way across the grass of the graveyard to the south door of the church.

It was locked.

"What a good start," said Flettner. "Congratulations."

"Shut your fucking mouth," said Gordon. "On this operation we don't say a word unless we need to, and when we do need to speak, we whisper. Understood?''

Flettner laughed. "Understood," he said in a stage whisper. "But how do we get into the church?"

"We use a key," said Gordon. "I thought even a German would know that."

He flicked his fingers and Jane stepped forward and unlocked the church door. Even Flettner was reduced to silence by this demonstration of British efficiency.

For the next hour Jane kept watch outside the church while Gordon and Flettner worked inside. Despite Gordon's warning, Flettner continued to talk, and without lowering his voice. Most of what he said was sensible enough: he asked practical questions about what should go where, and how it should be fixed.

At first Gordon was irritated by this prattling, but after a while he gave up worrying. It was obvious that Flettner was just a natural-born doubter and pessimist—and besides, the man was frightened.

The two of them worked fast, and after an hour everything was in position. They lowered the top back onto the tomb, dismantled the block and tackle, brushed the floor, and checked every inch of it with the flashlight.

Gordon felt more relaxed now. He was happy about what he had been doing so far, and even happier about what he was going to do next.

They loaded everything back into the car. Everything except a steel crowbar, which Gordon held in his gloved right hand.

After they had finished, Jane relocked the church door, and with evident relief she ran ahead of the two men towards the Talbot Alpine. Gordon and Flettner set off side by side across the grass.

The moon was brighter tonight, and they could pick their way among the gravestones without difficulty.

As they passed one particular gravestone Gordon fell back a pace to let Flettner go ahead of him, and as the East German stepped forward, Gordon swung the crowbar back with both hands. He lifted it high above his head and brought it plunging down with enormous force onto the top of Flettner's skull.

The force of the blow splintered the bone and inflicted damage directly onto the brain below. Gordon felt it through his hands. The contact jarred him to his heels.

Jane must have heard the sound of Flettner's death as she stood by the car. She turned to look as the East German's body swayed on its feet. And then, as the dead man fell, she whimpered in terror.

The crowbar hung down beside Gordon's right leg. It was heavy now.

He felt tired: the event he had been anticipating for an hour or more was over. He sighed.

"Come here," he said to Jane. Not loudly, but loud enough for her to hear. "Come here."

Jane responded, but she came slowly, as if she

were both too frightened to obey and too frightened not to.

"I'm not going to hurt you," Gordon told her. "Just help me to get him in the car."

"But you—you killed him!" Jane sobbed.

"Yes."

"But why? Why?"

"Because I felt like it, that's why. Now help me get him to the car."

At noon the next day Gordon returned to the house in Winchester. He hadn't slept for nearly thirty hours, but apart from a smarting sensation in his eyes he felt perfectly O.K.

He let himself in at the front door of the house and went upstairs to the bedroom. Jane was deeply asleep, but eventually he managed to rouse her.

"Go in the bathroom and wake yourself up a bit," he told her with a smile. She hesitated. "Go on." He pushed her on her way.

Jane staggered into the bathroom. As usual, she had been sleeping naked. He heard her running some water and splashing it on her face. Then she came back. She sat down on the edge of the bed and groaned.

Gordon chuckled. "Are you awake now?"

"Yes."

"Yes, what?"

"Yes, Gordon."

He took hold of her chin and made her look at him. "Try again."

Jane gazed at him blankly.

"Yes what?" he repeated.

"Yes . . . Yes, sir?"

Gordon smiled again. "That's better," he said. And it was. He sat down on the stool in front of Jane's dressing table, his back to the mirror. "I thought I'd better tell you what I've been up to. First of all, I unloaded all the gear. And then I rang that number you gave me—the emergency drill, remember?"

"Yes."

"Good . . . Yes, I rang this famous number that's so bloody secret you were only supposed to ring it if Father Christmas came down the chimney or something. Anyway, I rang it and spoke to Flettner's friends. Have you ever met them?"

Jane shook her head. Her naked breasts also shook, the pink nipples trembling. Gordon was struck by the fact that she was really very sexy.

"Yes," he said thoughtfully. "I rang this secret number and spoke to them. It turns out there are two of them. A big one and a little one. The little one is the boss. They're foreigners of some kind—East Germans, I suppose. Anyway, I arranged to meet them in Windsor Great Park. I covered Flettner up with a tarpaulin and took him with me."

Jane's eyes opened wide. "And what did they do?"

"They took him from me. Just took the body, tarpaulin and all, and went. Leave it to us, they said, so I did."

"But what did you tell them? I mean, how did you explain about Klaus?"

"I told them the truth. I told them that he came with us when we laid the bomb, that he rubbed me up the wrong way, and that I hit him to teach him some manners. What did you expect me to say?"

Jane's voice was shaking so much she could hardly get the words out.

"But—you—you know what this means, don't you? He was their best man, and you killed him. That means they'll kill you—and probably me as well."

"Oh, you think so, do you? Well, that's all you know. The impression I got is that I did them a favor. Did you know he wasn't supposed to be here at all?"

Jane's eyes answered for her: she hadn't known.

"Well, it's true. He was supposed to stay well away from us. So I was right. He *was* just trying to muscle in on the action. And they weren't very pleased about it, I can tell you."

"Did they say anything else?"

"Not much, no. They just wanted to be sure that the project was going according to plan. Just so long as that bomb goes off on Saturday, that's all they care about."

He looked into Jane's eyes, but she turned her head away. He wondered how much she had cared for Flettner. Not a lot, he decided. Not really.

After that he got undressed and climbed into bed with her.

He pulled her towards him and she came readily, wrapping her arms around him. She was clearly frightened out of her wits, and he held her tight while she sobbed.

"It's all right," he told her. "It's all right. You'll be quite safe with me."

He ran his hands up and down her body, smoothing away the tension. And as he did so he realized that from now on she was going to do exactly what he told her.

Eventually Jane's panic subsided. And when it did, she too became aware of the change in their relationship. She reached down into his groin.

"Gordon! You're as hard as a rock!"

He chuckled at her surprise. "Yes," he said. "I always told you there was nothing wrong with me."

And a few minutes later, when she was quite ready, he pushed her over onto her back and entered her very gently.

23

Sally wept all the way home from Ben's flat. She sat in a dark corner of the underground train and sobbed. No one took the slightest notice.

She had made a fool of herself, she decided. Not for the first time, and probably not the last. That didn't matter, but the problem was, would Ben ever forgive her? She would apologize, of course, once the dust had settled. But would he ever feel the same about her again? He might say he did—but would he? How could he?

Oh, God, what a disaster: things would never be the same after this.

Sally tried to put Ben out of her mind and think about something else. But she kept coming back to the source of all the trouble.

What she really had to decide was what to do about Challoner and Tate. Because it was Challoner and Tate who were the cause of this whole bloody row in the first place.

It was all their fault, she decided. Everything.

251

Without them on her mind she would never have fallen out with Ben, and for that reason alone she would have preferred to forget all about them. But she couldn't forget. They were too important. And having pursued the matter all this way she certainly wasn't going to let it drop now.

Part of Sally insisted that she ought to go straight back to Winchester, right now, on the grounds that if she really believed what she had been saying, she ought to be using every moment to keep Challoner and Tate under observation. But she was exhausted, and for the moment the exhaustion won. She went home instead.

When she arrived she had a large glass of gin, and after that she could barely summon enough energy to undress before she fell into bed.

The next morning Sally overslept and arrived at work almost an hour late. All the other members of her squad seemed to be far too busy to have missed her, and she spent the rest of the morning ploughing through the heap of files on her desk.

On her way to lunch she bought an early edition of the evening paper, and found that details of the president's itinerary had now been announced.

The newspaper started Sally's mind buzzing again. She had spent her morning checking the bona fides of a few perfectly innocent little typists and switchboard operators, and yet here were the president's movements set out for all to see! If Challoner and Tate *were* going to make a move, they could now time it to the minute. The whole thing was bloody ridiculous; it made her hopping mad.

She sat and read through the newspaper report again as she finished her tuna sandwich. And over coffee she made up her mind what to do.

It was all very simple. Either Challoner and Tate *were* involved in a plot to kill the president and the prime minister, or they weren't. If they were, it was vital that someone should watch them until they began to make a move. If they weren't, then the absence from normal duties of one member of the Special Branch wasn't going to make much difference.

Sally didn't even go back to the office. She just phoned the personnel department to say she was sick, and went home.

She was right. She knew she was right. Ben wasn't convinced, her boss wasn't convinced, and nobody else was likely to listen to her, but she herself knew she was right, and she was going to do something about it.

After packing her suitcase with enough clean clothes to last her until Saturday, Sally backed her faithful Mini out of its mews garage and drove straight to Winchester. Once there, she let herself into the flat which she had rented the previous Saturday, and set up her binoculars on a tripod. Fortunately, the window had lace curtains over it, which disguised the fact that she was being inquisitive about her neighbors.

After that she began a long and tedious vigil. Nothing much happened throughout the afternoon and evening. At eleven o'clock, the lights went off downstairs and came on upstairs. And after a while, the bedroom light went off again.

Sally decided to get some sleep while she could. She was well aware that Challoner and Tate could leave the house at any moment, in either of their two cars, but they certainly appeared to have gone to bed. There was a certain sixth sense which operated on a surveillance job, and she would just have to hope that the distant sound of a car being started would wake her up.

She lay down on the settee, and tried to sleep.

She awoke several times in the night, but on each occasion, whatever it was that had woken her proved to be a false alarm: she could see Dr. Challoner's house in the light of a street lamp—and nothing had changed.

At 6 A.M. Sally made herself some breakfast.

Soon after eight the curtains at the front bedroom window were drawn back, and at nine Dr. Challoner came out of the house, carrying a large briefcase. She drove away in her car, a blue Ford Escort.

Sally debated with herself whether she should follow Jane Challoner or not, but in the end she decided against it. The odds were that the lecturer was just off to the university, so there was not much point in going after her. It seemed preferable to wait and see what Gordon Tate would get up to.

Unfortunately, Tate did very little. Sally caught a glimpse of him at the living-room window at about half past nine. He had a newspaper in his hand,

and he glanced up and down the street. Was he looking for suspicious loiterers? Or just waiting for the postman? It was impossible to decide.

For a few minutes Sally wrestled with the possibility that she might be wrong about her two suspects after all. Perhaps she was wasting her time.

She sighed.

Ah well, it wouldn't be long before she knew the answer, one way or the other.

24

Jane sat with her two cats in her lap.

The days were passing slowly.

Slowly, because she focussed upon every minute.

In the back of her mind Jane knew that this heightened consciousness of reality was prompted by a fear of death; but it was also prompted by a new-found love of life.

To her amazement, Jane realized that she was happy now, and that she had never been happy before. For the first time since her adolescence she had fallen in love!

She laughed aloud when she thought about it. What a bizarre thing to happen, and to her of all people! She had thought she was above such romantic tosh. Nevertheless, bizarre or not, she *was* in love. And she was happy because she knew what she was doing, believed it was worthwhile, and was doing it with someone who cared for her.

Yes, he did. Gordon cared for her.

Jane didn't want to inquire too closely into the

change in Gordon, but something important had happened to him. What it was she didn't know, and didn't care. But Gordon could now make love again, and did so frequently, as if making up for lost time. And Jane herself enjoyed it passionately, too. There was something deeply satisfying about feeling Gordon swell and throb inside her—and afterwards he was so gentle and so apologetic about his own abandon that often she had to laugh. All of which emotions were unfamiliar to her, and yet delightfully warm and pleasant. Yes, she was happy at last. She looked at Gordon and smiled.

Gordon smiled back. Then he closed his eyes.

He was wearing a set of stereo headphones that evening, and he felt as relaxed as the cats in Jane's lap. He was listening to Charlie Parker. The track was called "K.C. Blues," and at the end he could actually hear Bird turn away from the microphone as he led his fellow musicians into the coda. *Fantastic*, he thought. *Amazing*.

The track ended and Gordon became aware that Jane was shaking him by the arm. He took off his headphones.

"Telephone," she said.

"Oh." He picked it up. "Yes?"

"Hello, Gordon, this is Alfred."

Alfred. Alfred? Oh, yes, the little guy.

"Oh, hello, Alfred. How are you?"

"I'm fine," said the voice. "Just a slight touch of laryngitis."

That was the code word—laryngitis. Gordon began to search through his memory for the appropriate answer.

"Oh dear, I'm sorry to hear that. I won't keep you talking long then." That was the reply—thank God he had remembered.

"There's been a slight change of plan, Gordon. A slight delay. The way things stand now, I shan't be arriving until eleven twenty-one."

"Eleven twenty-one," Gordon repeated. He knew that the time must be important, but he couldn't yet see how. He would have to think about it.

"Yes, that's right. Eleven twenty-one exactly. And you mustn't be late, Gordon. I want you to be on time to the second—do you understand?"

"Yes, sure, I understand."

"Good. Cheers then, Gordon. See you."

"Yes, see you. Bye."

His caller put down the phone, and the dialing tone purred in Gordon's ear. He lowered his own receiver.

Eleven twenty-one.

It was something to do with Saturday morning, he knew that. Something to do with the timing of the bomb.

"Who was that?" asked Jane. Her face was anxious.

"It was one of our East German friends."

"What did he want?"

"I don't know. . . . I'm not sure."

He crossed to the television set, picked up the *TV Times* and turned to Saturday's programmes. And after a moment he understood.

He shuddered.

The wedding of the prime minister's daughter

was to be a private affair—or at least the ceremony itself was. But from 10:00 to 10:30 there would be live coverage of the arrival of guests at the church. Then from 10:30 to 11:20, there would be an episode of "Kansas City," the season's most successful soap opera. After that, live coverage from the church would resume, with the wedding ceremony expected to end at 11:30. Quite a number of nations, including the American networks' breakfast shows, would be tuned in to see the bride emerge into the sunshine.

Alfred's intention was clear. No, not Alfred's—Moscow's. The plan was so chillingly simple: it was to explode the bomb at a time when all the world would be watching. Perhaps fifty different countries would be taking the television picture, live, in full color. About half a billion people would be sitting in front of their cathode-ray tubes, looking at that picturesque little doorway. And as they watched, the church would explode and die.

Jane stared at him. "Gordon, you've gone quite pale. Are you all right?"

"Yes," he said after a moment. "Yes, I'm all right."

25

By Thursday evening, Sally's spirits were at a low ebb. It was hot and stuffy in her rented flat, and she was stiff from sitting in the same position for hours on end; her head ached and she had forgotten to buy any aspirins.

But bodily discomfort was not the main problem. What made Sally's misery acute was the wretched feeling of doubt which threatened to overwhelm her. What the hell was she doing here anyway? Who in their right mind would watch Challoner and Tate for even two minutes? And so on.

Above all, she found herself longing for Ben to be there beside her. Even a few words from him would be better than nothing, and there were many times when the telephone seemed the most tempting object she had ever seen. She could hardly restrain herself from dialing Ben's number, just to hear his voice as he answered—to say *hello, how are you, I love you*. But it would be a mistake to speak to him now. Best to wait a few days, until after the weekend.

Sally knew that the critical time was approaching. She had studied the president's itinerary, and she knew that he was coming nowhere near Winchester—so if Challoner and Tate were to try to assassinate him, and if they were to use a command-detonated bomb, they would have to leave the house some time on Friday or Saturday. Probably sooner. They would need to be within sight of the president if they were to detonate the bomb effectively.

Press the button. Press . . . Must watch. Must watch Challoner and Tate. Follow them . . . Must. If they leave, follow them. . . .

Sally pulled herself upright with a jerk. She had almost fallen asleep. And she must *not* fall asleep! Not for a long time yet. She must remain awake, because she had nothing to give her a warning if Challoner or Tate drove away in the early hours of the morning. Nothing except the evidence of her own eyes. And for that she had to be awake. Awake. Awake . . .

Despite all her good intentions, Sally slept for a couple of hours that evening, and was disgusted with herself when she finally awoke. It would not happen again. It would *not!* Surely she could go without sleep for a day or two. After all, by Sunday the whole thing would be over. No more presidential visits for several years. No more warnings. No more unauthorized searching of houses. No more worrying about harmless lecturers and students. No more falling out with the man you love.

The phone rang.

The sound was so unexpected that Sally jumped with shock.

"Hello?"

"Hello, Sally, it's me—Paula."

For a second Sally didn't recognize her stepmother's voice.

"Oh—oh, yes, of course—I'm so sorry, Paula, I didn't realize who it was for a moment. How did you get this number?"

"Your landlady gave it to me."

"Oh. Yes, yes, of course. I did tell her where I would be."

"I'm ringing about your dad."

"Oh?" Sally clutched her forehead. "Is anything the matter?"

"Yes. I'm afraid he's in hospital."

"Oh!" Sally sat down. "Is it his heart?"

"Yes. Yes, it is." Paula's voice sounded distant and faint. "He's had another coronary, and I'm afraid it's rather serious."

Sally found herself short of breath. "Oh. Oh dear," she said lamely. "It's such a terrible shock."

She could see him across the barrier. There, said Ben, can you see him now? A small man. A man with a pipe. Your father. Yes.

"I think you ought to come and see him straight away. He's asking to see you."

Sally covered her eyes with her left hand, and made an effort and kept her voice even.

"Yes. Yes, I'd like to see him, too."

"I'll tell him you're on your way then, shall I? I'm at the hospital now."

"No!" said Sally. "No, I'm afraid I can't come just at the moment."

"But—why not?"

"Well . . . well, because I'm on a special assignment. It's to do with the president's visit. I don't think I can really get away till it's over."

There was a shocked silence at the other end of the line. "Are you sure? Can't someone else relieve you?"

"Well—I'll try, of course. But it won't be straight away."

"Well, you do your best then. But I should have thought the president could survive without you to look after him—and your father would certainly like to see you."

"Give me the details," said Sally abruptly. She felt more controlled now but she didn't want to discuss it any more. At Paula's dictation she wrote down the name of the hospital and the ward. "O.K. Now listen: tell Dad I'll be with him just as soon as I possibly can—but it won't be tonight. I'm sorry, but I'm sure he'll understand."

Paula said nothing.

"Paula? Is that all right? Will you tell him?"

"Oh yes," said Paula. "I'll tell him. But I can't say it's all right. Because it's not all right at all."

26

Jane woke up with a start. Someone was screaming.

Screaming, screaming, screaming.

"Jane! Wake up! Wake up!"

She became aware that Gordon was shaking her by the shoulders. And then she realized that she herself was the one who was screaming, and she stopped in the middle of a breath.

After a second's silence she clapped her hands to her face and began to sob. Gordon put his arms around her, and she clung to him frantically in the darkness, her cheek clamped against his chest, her tears wetting his skin.

Eventually Jane became calmer and Gordon lay her down on her back again. She noticed that the alarm clock showed 4 A.M.

"There," he said. "Is that better?"

"Yes. Yes, thank you, Gordon. Thank you." She closed her eyes and squeezed his hand.

Gordon settled down beside her. "Do you want to tell me about it?"

"No. It was too horrible."

"Tell me anyway," he said. It was an order.

Jane turned her head to one side and stared into the darkness. "It wasn't very nice."

"Nightmares never are. Tell me anyway."

"Well. I was dreaming. About a bomb going off."

"In the church?"

"No. Somewhere . . . underground. I went down some stairs. It was dark, and there were flames flickering everywhere. And over in one corner I could see something moving. So I went towards it . . . and it was a body. The arms and legs had been blown off—and it was naked. And the head was just a dark, shapeless blob. But it was screaming, screaming, screaming. . . ." She sighed. "And then I woke up."

Gordon held her close, stroking her back. "It was a nightmare," he said. "You must forget it."

"Yes, I know."

She felt cold, in spite of the sweat on her body. She pulled him closer to her, and she began to feel safe again.

"It's going to be all right, you know," Gordon assured her.

"Yes. I know it is."

"What we're planning to do is justified. I'm sure of that now. I had my doubts at first, but you've explained it to me, and now I can see what a lot of good it will do. And we're going to do it together. . . . We've been pretty hard on each other, you and I—knocked some lumps off each other.

But we've got over that now. We're a team, aren't we?''

"Yes, Gordon, we're a team. We really are." She hugged him with all her might.

"Neither one of us could do it without the other." He was silent for a moment. "And I've been thinking about afterwards."

"Afterwards?"

"Yes."

Jane began to feel drowsy. She felt completely secure for the first time in many years. "What are we going to do?" she said sleepily. "Afterwards."

"Well, carry on as we are now, more or less. You'd like that, wouldn't you?"

"Yes. I'd like that very much."

"You can go on being a lecturer. And I shall be—well, I don't know what I'll be, but I'll do some sort of work with my hands. Be a technician, or a metal worker, something like that. After Saturday we'll have made our contribution—let someone else make the running for a change. And I tell you what—"

"Yes?"

"I'll take my brother on a holiday. Somewhere warm and sunny. Would you mind?"

Jane squeezed him tighter. "No, of course not. I'm sorry I was so horrible that time you went to see him. But it frightened me."

"Yes," said Gordon, "I know. It frightens me, too. It could have been me, you see. It could have been me."

27

Sally hadn't slept much. She had spent most of the night wondering whether she should drop everything and go to see her father, and only two things had stopped her from doing so. One was the stubborn side of her nature, which insisted that having started this surveillance job she should see it through to the end, come what may. The other factor was a reluctance to admit that her father was as ill as all that. He couldn't possibly be on the point of death. He was much too tough to die.

He was, wasn't he? *Wasn't he?*

Soon after eight o'clock in the morning Sally rang the hospital and spoke to one of the doctors. She found him helpful but not very reassuring. In principle there was apparently no reason why her father shouldn't recover from his latest heart attack and resume a normal life—but at the moment he was still seriously ill, and the next few days would be critical.

Sally gritted her teeth. Well, things didn't sound

too bad, did they? No need to get up and go to the
hospital right this minute. But on the other hand
things didn't sound so bloody marvelous either.

After a moment Sally put her head in her hands
and had a damn good cry. She had never felt so
miserable in all her life.

Sally cried for about five minutes. After that she
felt better, and half an hour later she had recovered
her sense of perspective. She decided that she
would keep on ringing the hospital, and if her
father's condition got really bad she would go
there. But in the meantime she would finish what
she had started. All she had to do was to keep
Challoner and Tate in her sights from nine o'clock
this morning, when the president arrived at Heathrow,
until about six o'clock tomorrow evening, when he
was due to fly to Paris.

Towards midmorning Jane Challoner came out
of her house, carrying the usual briefcase, and
drove away in her Ford Escort.

Sally let her go. It just didn't *feel* as if anything
dangerous was happening.

Soon after twelve noon, Gordon Tate emerged
from the house and began to get his own car out of
the garage. This time Sally was able to run down
to her car and catch up with him just as he drove
away.

Tate went into Winchester, where Sally followed him on foot. He had lunch at an Italian
restaurant, wandered around the shops for a while,

and finally spent a couple of hours in a cinema, watching a reissue of *Jazz on a Summer's Day*.

Sally now became just as uptight about her assessment of the situation as she had been earlier. Were these *really* the actions of a Libyan-trained professional who was planning to kill the American president? Or was this just the way any victim of unemployment would behave? The latter seemed more and more likely.

Soon after five o'clock Tate drove home, and Sally returned to her flat. She noticed that Jane Challoner's car was now back in the drive also.

Sally's head ached and she took three aspirins with a glass of milk. She wasn't quite sure whether the headache was caused by the oppressive weather, or by the depressing circumstances—but she suspected the latter.

She telephoned the hospital yet again, and was told that her father was as well as could be expected, whatever that meant.

Sally returned to her observation post at the window. She passed some time studying detailed maps of the areas which the president would visit, but by seven o'clock she was bored and restless once more. She had trouble staying awake. What made it worse was that absolutely nothing was happening outside.

Then the doorbell rang.

Sally sighed. She was tempted to ignore it.

But whoever was there was persistent. The bell rang again, and it was obvious that it was not going to stop ringing until she took some action.

Sally swore and went downstairs. It was probably some salesman trying to sell an encyclopedia.

But it wasn't a salesman. It was Ben.

"Oh! My God!" said Sally.

"No," said Ben with a grin. "Just me. Can I come in?"

"Oh—yes, of course."

She stepped aside to let him in, and Ben moved past her. He was carrying a paper bag which smelled good.

"I've brought a Chinese meal with me," he said as he went up the stairs. "Do you fancy some?"

Sally was still at a loss for words. "Well—yes, please."

"Good."

Ben carried on up the stairs, so she closed the door and followed him. When she returned to the living room she automatically went to the window and looked through the binoculars again.

"Still watching?"

"Yes. That's the idea."

Ben was poking around in a cupboard, looking for plates; he soon had everything ready.

"Knives and forks rather than chopsticks, I think?"

"Yes," Sally agreed. "That'll be easier."

Ben smiled, and she smiled back at him as she took the offered plate. She didn't quite know what to say or do, so she went and sat on her usual chair by the window, with the plate on her lap. Ben sat beside her.

They ate in silence for a minute or two. Sally was hungry: she had gone without a proper lunch.

"I had a call from Paula," Ben said after a moment.

"Oh, yes?" Sally tried to keep her voice calm, but inwardly she could hardly cope with the emotions which were hurtling about inside her.

"Yes. She's a bit worried about your father."

"Well, so she should be."

"Yes . . . Anyway, Sally, she's very worried about you, too. Your dad keeps asking to see you, but Paula says you have this vitally important mission which means you can't get to the hospital."

"Yes, that's right." Sally kept her eyes on her plate. "It's not easy to get away just at the moment. But it won't last long now. Just another twenty-four hours and that's it."

Ben paused, toying with his food. "Paula asked me if I could help."

"How do you mean?"

"Well, the idea is to keep an eye on Challoner and Tate, isn't it?"

"Of course."

"On the assumption that if they are planning to detonate a bomb somewhere, they'll have to leave home to do it."

Sally felt her cheeks flush. "It's not a matter of *if*, Ben, it's a matter of *when*."

Ben raised a hand in acknowledgement. "O.K., so it's a matter of when. And 'when' will have to be either tonight or sometime tomorrow."

"That's right. Probably tomorrow."

"All the better. So why don't I keep watch for you for a couple of hours tonight, while you go and see your father?"

Sally stopped eating. "Would you do that, Ben?"

"Of course. That's why I'm here."

Sally thought for a moment. The president was at a dinner at Number 10 Downing Street tonight, and that didn't allow much scope for trouble. Furthermore, if her two suspects had been going to try anything today, they would surely have left home by now.

"O.K.," she said. "You're on. And, Ben . . ."

"Yes?"

Sally hesitated. "I don't really know how to say this, but I know people like me can be very tiresome at times."

Ben grinned. "I can't *imagine* what you mean."

"Well, you know me—you know what I'm like. I'm one of those people who can't bear to let go of anything once they've got their teeth into it."

"Yes, you're quite right," said Ben cheerfully, "you can be pretty intolerable at times."

Tears came into Sally's eyes, and she blinked them back. "But I have tried, Ben. I have tried to cure myself of it—really I have—and I can't. It's just the way I'm made."

Ben laughed. "I know," he told her. "I know

all about the way you're made. I trained you, remember? I helped to make you the way you are, and I wouldn't have you any other way. Now— just tell me what I have to do while you're out.''

After Sally had gone, Ben settled down and tried to make himself comfortable. He had been forbidden to wash up or even go to the bathroom while she was out, so there wasn't much to do except peer through the binoculars.

Unfortunately, there was very little to see, either with the binoculars or without them, and before long Ben was just as bored as Sally had been.

After twenty minutes a movement caught his eye. It was dusk now, and Ben refocussed the binoculars to get a better view. Sure enough, the front door of the Challoner house was open and Gordon Tate was loading suitcases into the boot of the Ford Escort.

Blast! It looked as if Challoner and Tate actually *were* going away for the weekend.

Well, his instructions from Sally were quite clear: he was to follow them wherever they went, and to phone in and report as soon as he got the chance.

Ben grabbed a piece of paper and wrote: *Following their car. Will phone*, and then hurried downstairs to the street.

He started his MGB first time, and accelerated away from the curb with a satisfying roar. He drove into the quiet avenue where the Challoner house was situated, and parked about seventy-five yards away on the opposite side of the road.

Two minutes later, the blue Ford backed out of the drive and came up the road towards him. Ben bent down under the dashboard until the car had passed. Then he reversed the MGB and set off in pursuit.

He drove for about twenty miles, keeping what he hoped was a suitable distance between himself and the Ford. It was dark by that time, so he felt there was little risk of the driver in front realizing that he was being followed, even if he was thinking of that possibility. And Ben considered that most unlikely.

After about forty minutes the Ford's left indicator came on and the car pulled into a lay-by. Ben thought it would be risky to do the same himself, so he carried straight on for another hundred yards and then came to a halt at the side of the road, under some trees.

He turned off his engine and lights and wondered what he should do now. Just wait, presumably. Dr. Challoner and her friend had probably decided to take turns at driving. Or maybe they were studying the map. Fortunately, there were no side roads between them and him, so they would have to come past him eventually. And when they did, he would simply follow them once again.

Ten minutes went by.

Then twenty.

And by that point Ben was beginning to worry. In fact, it was a long time since he had felt so anxious about anything. He was keen to do this job properly, so that Sally would think well of him, and the last thing he wanted to do was lose contact with the people he was following, even if they were just off for a weekend in the country.

Every time a car went past he studied its shape and read its registration number. So it wasn't possible that they could have gone by without him noticing.

At least, he didn't *think* it was.

After twenty-five minutes Ben could contain his impatience no longer. He felt he just had to know what was happening. Had their car broken down? Had they turned around and gone back the other way? Or what? He decided he would walk back along the road and find out.

Ben got out of his car. Out of sheer habit he started to lock the door.

As he did so he heard a footstep behind him. He began to turn to see who it was, but before he could do so the world exploded as he received a tremendous blow on the head. Huge clusters of multicolored stars flared in his brain.

For a second Ben clung to the door handle; his mouth was open and he gasped a great cry of pain. But then a second blow smashed down on the other side of his skull and the lights faded to blackness.

Sally was no stranger to hospitals: she had been in more casualty departments than she cared to remember, and had a six-inch scar on her left arm to remind her of a drunken Cypriot.

There were six patients in the Coronary Care Unit, and her father's bed was the second on the left. He was asleep.

Sally smiled at one of the other patients, who was sitting up in bed reading, and sat down at the bedside.

The hospital was quiet now, beginning to settle down for the night. Sally sat and waited.

Her father seemed quite peaceful—at least he wasn't in any pain—but his face was pale. She wanted to hold his hand, but she thought it might disturb him, so she settled back in her chair.

After about ten minutes her father woke up. "Hello, Sal," he said unexpectedly.

"Oh, hello!" Sally leaned forward and kissed him. "How are you feeling?"

"Not too bad," he said, and his voice sounded strong enough for it to be convincing. "And all the better for seeing you."

Sally took hold of his hand and pressed it against her cheek. Her eyes filled with tears.

"You've been busy," said her father.

"Yes." The tears overflowed and wet her cheeks. "Yes, I have. But it's all right now, Dad. It's all right now. I'm here."

After about half an hour Sally left the hospital and drove back to Winchester.

It was dark when she arrived, but she noticed at once that Ben's car was no longer parked in the street, and that alarmed her. She ran up the stairs two at a time and groaned when she read his note.

Damn and blast. This was the last thing she had wanted to happen.

She sank into a chair and tried to persuade herself that the situation was not as bad as she feared. After all, her boss was convinced that she was wrong about Challoner and Tate, so there probably wasn't anything to worry about. Ben would just follow this very ordinary couple to a pub or a restaurant, get thoroughly bored hanging about waiting, and then he would be back here by eleven or twelve, complaining about being sent out on a fool's errand.

That was the way it would go.

Wasn't it?

No, it wasn't.

Sally knew perfectly well that Challoner and Tate were not just another bourgeois couple going out for a night on the town. They were dangerous, and wherever they had gone they would be watching for anyone following them. And Ben was not a professional. He was a computer expert, for God's sake. O.K., so he was fit and strong, and able to look after himself in a fight—but that wasn't the same thing as being able to outthink a couple of trained killers.

Sally stared at the telephone. What she needed was a call from Ben, saying where he was and what was happening. When she knew that, she could join him, and between them they might well be able to cope. But without someone to help him, Ben was vulnerable.

She looked at her watch. It was ten o'clock already. Then she looked at the telephone again: it was sinister and silent. Why didn't it ring?

She stared at it hard, willing it to transmit the message she wanted.

Come on, damn you—ring.
Ring!
Ring!
Ring!

28

It was Saturday morning. Jane was awake early, but not neurotically early, just a few minutes before the alarm clock was due to go off. She lay in bed and thought about how she felt.

Tense. Anxious. But controlled. Able to think clearly. She knew that everything was going to be all right. She could function.

At seven o'clock she got up and had a shower. Later, while Gordon was washing, she packed their suitcase. Then they went downstairs to breakfast.

They were almost alone in the hotel dining room, with only one middle-aged businessman in a far corner. Gordon ate his usual substantial meal: porridge, kippers, toast, and coffee. Jane was less enthusiastic, but she made herself take some protein in the form of a dish of cereal.

As she ate, Jane read a morning paper. The president's talks with the prime minister were apparently going well; a communiqué would be is-

sued later. This morning the president would be
having breakfast with the foreign secretary. After
that, he would be attending the wedding of his
niece, and in the afternoon he was expected to
have tea at Buckingham Palace. In the evening he
would fly to Paris. The whole schedule, commented the *Daily Telegraph,* constituted a security
man's nightmare.

Jane smiled.

She searched the newspaper carefully, but could
find nothing about a man being found dead on the
A272. Well, maybe no one had found him yet. Or
perhaps he had been found too late for the early
edition of the paper. Either way she wasn't too
worried. In fact, the more she thought about it, the
more certain she was that the man had not been
tailing them at all. He had certainly been following
them, in the sense that his car had stayed behind
theirs for mile after mile. And when they had
stopped, he had stopped. But on the other hand,
Gordon had found nothing in the man's car to
suggest that he was any sort of professional.

Well, so much the better. Jane decided to forget
all about the man on the A272; and judging by the
way he was eating, Gordon had forgotten about
him already.

After breakfast they went back upstairs to the
bedroom. Jane opened her shoulder bag and
doublechecked that her revolver was loaded. She
was pleased to find that her hands were steady.

Gordon picked up their suitcase and they went
downstairs to the lobby. At the bottom of the

stairs, as they turned left to walk towards the reception desk, they saw two uniformed policemen talking to the manager.

For a moment Jane was stunned. She felt as if her heart had stopped beating.

Stay calm. It's probably nothing to do with you.

Gordon approached the reception desk and Jane stood beside him, her heart pounding. The girl on duty smiled at them.

The manager and the policemen went on talking. Jane tried to hear what they were saying but she couldn't make it out.

Gordon smiled back at the receptionist as he paid the bill. Jane watched, like a dutiful wife, but all the time she was expecting to feel a hand on her shoulder. Her modest breakfast curdled in the pit of her stomach.

But no hand came.

Gordon put away his wallet and picked up the suitcase. They both turned to go out of the door. As they did so, Jane saw that the policemen had left the lobby.

She looked back at the receptionist. "Why were the police here?"

"Oh, there was a break-in last night in the bar," said the girl. "Nothing serious. Just a couple of bottles of whiskey stolen."

"Oh," said Jane. "I see."

29

Sally woke up at frequent intervals, all through the night. Each time she hoped she would see Ben on the far side of the room, and at one point she imagined she had heard his car—but she was always disappointed.

It was daylight now, so she got up and looked at Jane Challoner's house through the binoculars. But of course nothing had changed: there was no car in the drive and no sign of life at the windows.

Sally went into the bathroom and had a quick shower. Then she put on clean clothes and brushed her hair. After that she forced herself to eat some breakfast.

Her head still ached, and the nerves in her limbs tingled with fatigue. She had brushed her teeth but her mouth still felt as if it were lined with flannel. And all the time she conducted a running debate with herself about what could possibly have happened to Ben.

There were times when she managed to per-

suade herself that there was nothing at all to worry
about. Perhaps Challoner and Tate had gone to a
nightclub. So Ben had followed them there and
had fallen asleep in his car. He was only human,
after all. He had fallen asleep at, say, two o'clock
in the morning. And it was only seven now. So
what the hell was she worrying about? Ben just
hadn't woken up yet, that was all.

That particular hypothesis calmed Sally's nerves
for almost five minutes. After that she lost confidence in it. It was true that Ben wasn't a professional; but he was a conscientious and sensible
man, and he wouldn't have fallen asleep. And he
would surely have phoned her or gotten a message
to her by now. So there must be some other reason
for not having heard from him.

She went out and bought a morning paper from
the news agent's shop below the flat. She came
back up the stairs slowly, promising herself that
the phone would ring before she reached the top
step.

But it didn't. When she reached the room the
phone was just as silent as ever.

Come on, damn you. Ring.

She turned on the radio while she read the paper. Nothing much seemed to be happening in the
world, apart from a fashionable wedding. A pop
star had been arrested. The dockers in Liverpool
were on strike again. And on the radio, the bride's
hairdresser was discussing what kind of condi-
tioner she recommended.

Time drifted by. The radio was irritating but she

kept it on. It seemed important to keep in touch with the outside world.

Sally sat quite still, staring out of the window. She would have preferred to go out and start searching. But where would she go, where should she look? She had no idea.

She felt numb, and her mind began to wander backwards and forwards through her memory. She thought of the victims of the last big IRA bomb attack, whom she had seen at first hand two years earlier. Those furthest away from the blast: ruptured ear drums. Those nearer: lungs blown open; dead. Those closest to the explosion: limbless, the tops of their heads removed by the blast entering through their mouths. And the man who had been at the site of the explosion had the very flesh stripped off his backbone.

Sally could see the carnage as vividly now as on the day it had happened. That particular bomb had been an experience which she had pushed into the deepest crevice of her memory, and she had seldom cared to think about it. But today fatigue allowed the images to creep out once more—and now she realized why: unless she took the right action, those same terrible injuries would be inflicted on other people today.

But how could she possibly prevent it? She was powerless sitting here, and yet she couldn't think of anything else to do.

The nine-thirty news bulletin began.

Sally listened halfheartedly at first, but the final item brought her to attention. A thirty-five-year-old Scotland Yard computer expert, Mr. Ben Meadows, had been found unconscious beside his car in Sussex. He had apparently been struck on the head and had been admitted to hospital with a fractured skull. Police were investigating. And now back to—

Back to nothing. Sally turned off the radio with a snap. She picked up her maps and her handbag and went down the stairs three at a time.

She drove with the window wide open, letting the air whip through the Mini. But she didn't really need the breeze to wake her up. All she had needed was some kind of proof—proof that she had been right all along. And now she had it.

O.K., so it was bitter proof, and it might yet cost Ben his life. But at least the doubts were ended. She hadn't yet got any evidence which would convince her boss—she couldn't prove any connection between Challoner and Tate and Ben's injury—but Sally herself was now *sure*, and that made all the difference.

She drove with ruthless speed, blasting other drivers out of the way with her horn. With her left hand she took the Special Branch radio communicator out of her handbag and switched it to "Receive." There was nothing but static at present, but as soon as she got within range of today's action she would begin to learn what was happening.

30

Jane drove her car towards the folly on the hill overlooking the church; Gordon sat beside her. She was approaching the hill from the south to avoid the traffic jams around Stokely.

From time to time she glanced at Gordon in the passenger seat beside her. He was fidgety and pale, but she guessed that she herself might not be looking too relaxed.

Gordon seemed to guess what she was thinking; he squeezed her hand and smiled.

When they reached the top of the hill, Jane parked her car under some trees, well away from the tower and in a position where it was almost hidden by thick foliage. She had expected to see a number of other cars up here, but the hilltop was deserted.

She unlocked the car boot and took out a pair of binoculars. Gordon reached for an SLR camera; his cover story today was an interest in photography. Then he lifted out an aluminum box of the kind used to hold photographers' lenses.

As they approached the folly, Jane glanced around again, and only when she was satisfied that they were not being watched did she take out the key which she had made a week earlier. She slid it into the door of the tower and unlocked it. The door was heavy and slow to move, but on their previous visit she had oiled the hinges, so at least it now swung silently.

Inside the tower the atmosphere was gloomy and damp; a few shafts of sunlight filtered down to struggle against the shadows. Jane closed the door behind them and locked it from the inside.

"O.K.," said Gordon. "Let's go up."

The tower was shaped like a windmill, with a wooden staircase climbing around the curved inner wall. They went up the stairs, crossed a small landing, and pushed open a second heavy door.

The room at the top of the tower had two windows, one overlooking the valley to the north, and one looking south.

Gordon moved to the northern side of the room and swung open the window, which gave a squeal of protest. The incoming air was fresh and clean, in contrast to the dusty smell of the room. From here they had a clear view of the approach road to the folly, and they could also see the church, some three miles further on.

Jane watched as Gordon unpacked his aluminum box. First he took out the transmitter, which like the rest of the box's contents had been cocooned in polystyrene; he put it on the two-foot-wide window ledge. Then he removed a battery-powered television set with a three-inch black-and-white screen.

He switched the set on, and tuned in to an episode of "Kansas City." The wedding guests had been shown arriving at the church earlier on, but there would be no further coverage of the wedding until 11:20, when viewers would return to Stokely in time for the bride to be seen leaving the church.

While Gordon was preparing his equipment, Jane rested her elbows in the window ledge and peered at the scene below through her binoculars. The churchyard was surrounded on all sides by a great throng of spectators, held back by uniformed police. Television cameras and security men with rifles vied for the vantage points on nearby buildings.

After a few moments she turned to see what Gordon was doing. He extended the telescopic aerial on the transmitter and directed it carefully down the valley. Then he rubbed his hands on his trousers to dry them.

"Now," he said. "I'm going to prime it."

Jane's hand went up to her mouth. Gordon touched her arm to reassure her.

"It's all right," he said. "Really it is."

"Why don't you wait?" Jane asked. "It might go off before you want it to."

"No, it won't. It will go off when I press the switch, at 11:21, and not a moment before."

He reached out and keyed in the six digits which

would prepare the radio receiver in the tomb for its final signal. And as he pressed the numbered buttons they played their little tune. *Dah dah di dah di dah*. When he had finished, Jane looked up and saw that the church was still intact.

She exhaled with relief. She hadn't realized how tense she was.

Gordon laughed at her. "There, you see! O ye of little faith. Now—all we have to do to detonate the bomb is just press that switch there." He pointed.

Jane nodded her head. "Yes. I understand." And she also understood that Gordon was going over these things again because he could see how nervous she was.

"Good. If necessary we can set the timer so that it will go off automatically." He indicated the timer switch and the two sets of digits on the vertical face of the transmitter. The upper one, which was stable, read 00.00.00. The lower one, which was showing the actual time in seconds, read 10.57.51.

52, 53, 54 . . .

Jane suddenly felt a shudder of panic. She clutched Gordon's arm. "Let's set it and go," she begged.

"No." Gordon shook his head. He put his arms around her and held her close. He felt solid and dependable, and she fed on his determination, injecting it back into her soul.

After a few moments he made her look at him.

"It's not easy," he said. "It's not an easy thing

we have to do. We've known that all along. But we've done everything right so far, and we'll do this bit right, too. O.K.?''

"Yes," she said. She smiled through some ridiculous tears. "Yes, you're right, Gordon, of course."

"Now, I tell you what we'll do. You keep watch at the back, and I'll keep an eye open at the front. We won't have to wait long. Just another twenty minutes or so."

Jane turned away and went to stand by the other window, looking south. When she glanced round at him, Gordon had picked up the binoculars and was staring down at the church.

31

Sally drove hard. She was convinced that it was important to be where the prime minister and the president were. What she would do when she arrived she wasn't sure—but the main thing seemed to be to get there.

As she approached her destination, the traffic began to thicken, and before long the line of cars slowed to a crawl. Soon it stopped completely.

Sally swore and consulted her map. She was now only about two miles away from the church, but at the present rate of progress she wasn't going to get there for another couple of hours. She switched on her headlights, pulled over to the wrong side of the road, and drove on.

That particular maneuver carried her another mile, at which point she discovered that traffic was being diverted into a temporary car park in a field. Not even her Special Branch credentials could get her past the uniformed officers on duty at the roadblock.

Well, fair enough.

Sally left her car and began to run towards the center of the village.

She guessed that it was about a mile to the church—and she ran at a pace which she felt she could keep up all the way. Crowds of sightseers were making the same journey, and she overtook them by the hundred.

In her hand she held her Special Branch radio communicator. She had an idea she might need it.

The day was warm and sunny, and trails of sweat were soon running down her face. Fortunately, she was dressed for running: jeans, a T-shirt, a light nylon jacket, and rubber-soled shoes tied with laces.

Her body asked her to stop running please, it was hot and tired. She ignored the messages and made herself run faster still.

As she ran, she tried to think about her next move. Challoner and Tate were not going to be hanging about in public, just waiting to be arrested. No—they were going to be tucked out of sight somewhere, so that they could detonate their bomb at just the right moment. So what she had to do was to look for the places where a bomb might possibly be located. Then, somehow or other, she would have to check those locations out, or get someone else to check them out, or direct the president and the prime minister away from them.

How she was going to do any of those things, she hadn't the faintest idea. But the first thing to do was to arrive.

It was a long mile, and Sally was glad to stop running. Once she reached the edge of the main throng she pushed her way to the front of it. For the most part people let her through good-humoredly.

She reached the stone wall of the churchyard and wiped the sweat out of her eyes. Her heart was still pumping at a tremendous rate, and her mouth was full of hot saliva.

The wedding ceremony was being relayed over loudspeakers, and the people outside the church were hushed and attentive. And while she was getting her breath back Sally paused to think.

Natalie was quite precise. It was to be done by a bomb, and it was to be done while the president and the prime minister were together.

Sally thought about the implications of that. The president and the P.M. were together at the moment: they were inside the church. But after the wedding they would ride in separate cars to the prime minister's country house. There they would be together again until the middle of the afternoon, when the president would drive to London.

Sally examined the alternatives carefully. If she were intending to plant a bomb of her own, which would she consider the easier target—the church, or the country house?

No contest. The choice was obvious. Sally just could not believe that Challoner and Tate were capable of infiltrating a bomb into the prime minister's own residence. They were good, but not that good.

The church, on the other hand, was a different

matter. This was the first time it had ever been in the public eye, so it was not one of those buildings which were subject to continuous surveillance. It would have been searched, of course. Searched three times, probably, by separate teams of sniffer dogs and experts of one kind or another. But if anyone wanted to plant a bomb in a church, where would they leave it?

The crypt? The font? Under the floor?

Now there was a possibility.

Suppose a determined couple took up some flagstones, laid their bomb underneath, and carefully replaced them—how about that? Was that feasible?

Well, yes. It could be done.

The next question was, where would you go to detonate such a bomb by radio command? It would have to be somewhere close, say within five miles, and preferably in a direct line of vision.

Sally began to look around. The village lay in a long valley, with sides to the east, south, and west.

Sally's eyes raked the hills to the east, and a wave of depression washed over her. There were *dozens* of houses overlooking the valley, and any one of them would be perfect for the purpose she had in mind. No wonder all the dark-suited Americans looked so jumpy.

Sally turned and looked to the west. The same was true there. There were fifteen or twenty houses visible, so there must be a number of roads, too, where you could just park your car and press a button. But they were all fairly close at hand. Perhaps a bit too close to make your getaway unnoticed.

She turned to the south.

Nothing.

To the south she saw nothing, except a line of wooded hills on the distant horizon, two or three miles away. Nothing but an unbroken—

Just a minute. It was not an entirely unbroken line of trees. There was a tower sticking up on the ridge.

Sally remembered noticing the tower on the map she had been studying that morning. It was a folly—Smith's Folly, to be precise. What about that?

She glanced up at the church tower above her. Sure enough, it was thronged with hot-looking security men. The tower was the obvious place from which to control security at the wedding, so what better place than a tower from which to detonate your bomb? Especially if it was far enough away to be safe from instant roadblocks.

Sally looked at her watch: it was eleven o'clock. The ceremony would be over in half an hour, if not less. So there were two choices: either she could stay here and assume that nothing would happen; or she could try to reach Smith's Folly and check it out, just in case.

It didn't take her more than about two seconds to decide what she would do.

Everything hurt. Her feet hurt, her legs hurt, her arms, lungs, heart. Every muscle she possessed seemed to have been tested past the point of destruction. But she didn't stop. She kept on running.

She turned in through the gate of the car park, reached her car and fumbled for her keys. Her heart was beating so hard it disturbed her vision: the image presented by her eyes vibrated in time with her pulse.

The engine screamed as she entered each gear at the point of maximum torque. With her left hand she opened the map on the passenger seat beside her, but her visual memory was good and she only needed to glance at it once.

After five minutes' hard driving she came to a turning to the right. At the junction was a signpost which read: SMITH'S FOLLY—NO THROUGH ROAD.

Sally slowed down and went up the hill as quietly as she could. As soon as she rounded the final bend, and caught sight of the tower perhaps a hundred and fifty yards ahead of her, she stopped. She rolled the car a few yards back down the hill, and got out.

She stuffed the radio communicator into the left-hand pocket of her jacket. She might need it later to summon help.

Then, taking advantage of the trees to give her cover, she set off up the hill.

32

Jane was looking out of the window.

She was admiring the view, and trying hard not to think about what was going to happen soon. She wasn't succeeding though, and her pulse was racing as a result.

Suddenly she saw something unusual. A movement. Then she saw it again. It was someone running through the trees on the hillside below.

Whoever it was had stopped now, obviously trying hard not to be seen. But now he—no, she— had moved again. Yes, it was definitely a woman. A woman in jeans.

Jane tried to speak. Failed. Caught her breath. Tried again. "Gordon . . ."

No answer.

"Gordon!"

"Yes?"

Jane kept her eyes on the trees, but she stepped back, out of the sunlight, so that she herself would not be seen. "Come over here, quick." Her heart thumped in her chest.

Gordon came to her side.

"Look." She pointed. She couldn't seem to breathe properly. "She's here!"

"Who is?"

"That girl! That policewoman! The one you practiced judo with."

Gordon pressed himself close, raising his head to look out of the window without betraying his presence. Jane couldn't put the thought into words, but she was thankful that he was here beside her. She couldn't survive without him.

The girl moved again. "There! See?"

"Oh. Yes!" said Gordon. "Yes, there she is!"

He pulled Jane away from the window. She looked up at him; her eyes were so wide open that they hurt.

"How did she get here?" *Please, Gordon, please—tell me it's all a mistake.*

Gordon frowned. "I don't know, damn it."

"Does this mean they're on to us?" *Please, please say it doesn't.*

"No." Then he hesitated. "No—it doesn't mean that at all. . . . If they were on to us we'd have been arrested weeks ago, or there'd be a thousand troops out there. . . . No, it's just this one girl who's been smart enough to figure out that we might be here, that's all."

Jane almost fainted with relief. Yes, that was it. The girl *was* on her own, after all. Thank God for Gordon's common sense. "But what are we going to do now?"

"We're going to keep our heads, Jane. That's

what we're going to do. We're going to keep our heads, finish our job, and then leave.''

Jane took a deep breath. Her mouth fell open with relief.

''But what about the girl? Do you think she'll try to get in?''

Gordon thought for a moment. ''Yes, probably. And if necessary we'll have to kill her. You've got your gun, haven't you?''

''Yes.'' She produced it.

''Good. Now, here's what you do. Go downstairs and unlock the door. If she's here to investigate the tower, she'll probably come right in. When she does, wait until she's shut the door, and then shoot her.'' He paused. ''Do you think you can do that?''

Jane thought about it. ''Yes, I'm sure I can.''

''Good.'' Gordon patted her arm and smiled.

''What about you?''

''I'm going to stay here. There's only about five minutes to go.''

Jane nodded. ''All right.''

She went out onto the landing and hurried down the stairs. She unlocked the tower door, without opening it, and then hid herself behind one of the four buttresses which divided the lower floor into quadrants. When she was in position she looked up at Gordon and gave him a sign to show that she was in full command of herself.

He clenched his fist in salute, blew her a kiss, and went back into the upper room.

33

Sally could see no sign of Jane Challoner's blue car, so probably there was no one up here at all. But she decided to play safe.

At the back of the tower was a door with a window about twenty feet above it. Just once Sally thought she saw a flicker of movement at the window, but it might have been imagination. To be on the safe side, she kept as far to the left as she could, out of sight of the window.

For the last fifty yards before the tower there was nothing but bare grass, and she ran across it fast, crouching low. She was conscious of the fact that any ordinary person who was watching would think she was completely crazy. But so what? This was no time for a girl to stand on her dignity.

Sally stood with her back pressed against the wall of the tower. The stone felt hot, even through her clothes. She found herself panting, partly to get her breath back after the run and partly through sheer tension. The door was to her left.

The next step was obvious. It was to turn the iron handle and see if the door would open. If it did—well, she would go in. If it didn't . . . she would have wasted her time. Made a fool of herself. Got it wrong. Again.

Sally shook her head to rid herself of this stupid self-pity and doubt. She was not wrong. Never had been.

And yet she didn't want to try that door handle. *Why not? You must.*

I can't.

You can! You will!

Oh, God . . .

Sally groaned and swore under her breath. How she loathed that peeling brown door. It seemed somehow dangerous, even in the sunshine.

She reached out and took hold of the circle of iron. She turned it, slowly, clockwise.

With a snick the latch moved upwards. The *snick* reminded her of other doors, other gates, other times. She shook her head again. *Must concentrate.*

She pushed the door open, stepped inside, and closed it gently behind her.

It was dark in the tower: cold, and musty. She shivered.

For a moment she could see nothing. Then her eyes began to adjust.

There were stairs, she could see that. And a landing above. Down here, on the lower floor, there were what looked like dividing walls. And everywhere there was rubbish: piles of old timber, metal drums, sacks, cigarette packets. Someone had found a use for Mr. Smith's folly after all: it was a rubbish dump.

The tower seemed totally silent, and yet why should the door be open? *Danger!* There was nothing for it but to go upstairs and see if there was anyone up there.

Sally moved towards the bottom of the flight of wooden steps, and as she did so she caught a glimpse of movement out of the corner of her eye.

Too late.

There was a tremendous boom, and the boom hurled her backwards into the wall. She bounced off the wall, fell forward onto the ground, and rolled over, flat on her back. She felt numb.

Lie still! Don't move! Hold your breath!

The pain began but she welcomed it. *Sign of life.*

There was more movement now. Heavy feet on the landing. She could hear but she kept her eyes closed.

"Jane?"

"Yes?"

"Are you there?"

"Yes! I'm O.K.! I got her!"

"Great! Marvelous! Well done!"

Sally recognized those voices. She knew their owners well, and she had known all along that they would be here. She had a date with them.

See? Doubters! I was right!

The pain in her chest intensified. The numbness passed and a tearing sensation wrenched at her left side. She almost screamed, and she almost moved, but she forced herself to lie still.

Don't move don't gasp say nothing. Don't even breathe.

She half opened her eyes, and through the veil of her eyelashes she could see Jane Challoner coming towards her. She had a gun in her hand.

Come to me, my beauty. Come closer, I love you, I hate you. Come closer, I want you I need you.

"It's nearly time," said Gordon from above. "I'm going back into the room."

"O.K."

Come closer I need you I love you.

And then, through her shaded eyes, Sally saw Jane pause, as if in doubt.

She willed her to come nearer, and slowly, very slowly, Jane advanced across the floor.

You must come. You will come. You have to. You have to look at me. You have to be sure that I'm dead.

Jane appeared through the dust and the gloom. With the gun still in her right hand she knelt down and leaned forward. It was true, then: she did need to be sure.

Silently, Sally came up off the floor, bending at the waist. The pain in her chest cut into her as if she had been slashed with a knife.

She ignored the wound and went for her targets. Two targets: the gun and the throat.

With her left hand Sally grasped Jane's right wrist. She crushed the fragile bones with her thumb, forcing the gun to drop away almost at once. And with her right hand she seized Jane's beautiful, white-skinned throat. Not the neck: the throat. She took a grip at the front—a handful of delicate flesh—and she twisted it, tore at the sinews and the muscle. Because in the next few seconds one of them had to die.

Neither girl made any sound. As soon as the gun had gone, Sally moved once, and once only. She wrapped her own legs round those of the other girl, pinning them, so that no matter how great the agony Jane could not kick or drum her toes on the floor. And with her right hand Sally maintained that malignant grip, mercilessly clenching her fist.

At first, Jane flailed with her free hand at Sally's face, gouged at the eyes, sought a grip of her own. But then the hand ceased to attack and began to defend—it moved upwards, trying desperately to remove the fingers which were closed in a bulldog grip.

The pain of the physical effort was piercing Sally's lung. She could feel the tissue tearing because of the force which she was applying through her hands. But it didn't matter. She knew that to live is to feel pain, and she was determined to live. The pain didn't matter—it would soon be over.

In the room on the upper floor Gordon was watching his miniature television set. "Kansas City" was coming to an end. The heroine was having a row with her rich uncle, and any minute now the final credits would roll. Soon the cameras would be returning to coverage of the wedding, and then he could fire the bomb.

He looked at the clock. It was 11:19:05.

06, 07, 08.

Sally turned Jane over onto her back. She was lifeless and horrible.

So what? Nothing new. You've seen death before. Get up and get moving.

Sally rose to her knees.

There was a rattling sound from her nylon jacket. She put her hand into the pocket and found that her radio communicator was smashed irreparably. Perhaps the bullet had hit the communicator first and deflected into her lung afterwards. Either way it didn't matter much: the communicator was smashed and her lung was punctured. She could feel the blood bubbling into her chest cavity.

She pulled herself upright and looked up the stairs.

Nothing. Nobody. But the stairs swayed in the air.

Mustn't sway. Mustn't wobble. Must go up. But wait—need the gun.

She bent down and picked up Jane's revolver. She almost lost her balance as she did so.

Must go up the stairs. Take gun.

Sally groped for the handrail and pulled herself unsteadily onto the first step. It seemed such a long way to go.

She watched her feet intently, placing them one after the other, first on one step, then on the next.

I can make it. I really can.

It suddenly occurred to Gordon that there was a
strange silence downstairs. Why the hell wasn't
Jane back up here? Had her nerve failed? He went
out onto the landing to have a look.

What he saw staggered him for a moment, and
he almost gasped out loud. But he had the presence of mind to cover his mouth with his hand and
to come straight back into the room.

Jesus Christ! He could hardly believe it. But he
knew what he'd seen. There was no mistake. Jane
was lying stretched out on the floor, and that
bloody policewoman was coming up the stairs.

Holy shit . . .

The blonde girl was coming upstairs with the
gun in her hand! And he was going to have to do
something about it. Fast . . .

Gordon glanced at the television screen. They
still hadn't returned to the church. Christ, but that
fucking soap opera was lasting all morning. Well,
there was only one thing to do.

He crossed to his transmitter box and adjusted
the figures on the timer to read 11.21.00. Then he
pressed the switch which brought the timer into
effect.

There. It was done. The bomb would now go
off automatically at the required time, and he would
be free to kill that bitch on the stairs.

He went and stood behind the heavy wooden
door, ready to slam it if his enemy was foolish
enough to step over the threshold.

He clenched his fists in fury: he just couldn't wait to get his hands on her. Whatever had happened to Jane, whether she was alive or dead, there was one thing he knew for sure: the blonde girl was going to die.

The stairs were steep. It wasn't fair to make stairs as steep as that.

Sally felt breathless, and every movement cost her a huge effort. But she was nearly there.

She reached the landing and paused. The door to the upper room was almost closed: there was just a three-inch gap. But Gordon Tate was in there somewhere. She knew that, because she had heard his voice.

She glanced down at the gun in her hand. It looked as if it was loaded, as if it would fire when she pulled the trigger. It had already fired once, after all.

Must be quick, though. Time running out.

Gently she pushed open the door with her left hand.

Wide open.

On the far side of the room there was a window. On the window ledge were two boxes. One seemed to be a clock, and the other was a small television set. But there was no sign of Gordon. That was odd.

Come along, Gordon. Where are you?

She stepped forward into the room, and as she did so the door came whipping around on its hinges.

Of course! He's behind it!

But although Sally realized what was happening, her body could not react fast enough. The door formed a massive club, and the weight of it trapped her against the door frame. The impact made her feel as if she had been shot in the lung all over again. Her skull cracked against the hard edge of the wood and she screamed aloud—screamed and clutched her side.

Which was all wrong. *Weakness. Stupidity— leaving yourself exposed.*

He was on to her at once. He forced her right hand back against the wall and knocked the revolver out of her grip just as professionally as she had shaken it free from Jane. It slid across the floor into a corner and he tried to go for it, but she clung to him, seized his shirt and swung her feet round so that she was between the gun and him.

He broke free of her hands and backed off, eyeing her warily. She stared at him, baring her teeth, sucking in oxygen to bankroll the coming demands on her body. Each intake of air seemed to burn a hole in her lungs.

He came at her with a downward karate slash. She swept it away with an open-hand horizontal, and he backed off again, thoughtful and wary. He had tested her and found that her reflexes were still operating.

She tried to think how to kill him. *Never done it. Never thought about it. Never been trained.*

He aimed a front-of-fist blow at her head, and she parried it with the heel of her palm, deflecting it across her body. Pure reflex.

Ben's voice, from years earlier, echoed in her head: *If you're ever in real trouble, life-and-death trouble, go for the septum.*

O.K. Try.

He kicked her with a forward stamp high, right on the bullet wound. She screamed and bent double in agony. He connected with a side-snap kick and she fell to the ground, blinded by pain.

The gun was behind her on the floor. She sensed it rather than saw it, and reached back for it with her left hand.

He stamped down on her forearm; she felt the bone break.

He bent for the gun himself.

She rolled over and clubbed him on the left temple with her right fist, striking with all the momentum she could muster.

There wasn't much force in the blow, but Gordon was knocked off balance and sprawled in a heap.

Both of them got up slowly. Neither could reach the gun. He held his temple. Her left arm hung oddly.

"You rotten, lousy whore!" Gordon was almost weeping with fury and frustration. She had punched him and inflicted pain. Stopped him from doing what he wanted to do. It wasn't right, his face seemed to say. It wasn't fair.

Good. Out of control.

"You filthy, dirty bitch!" he screamed at her. "I'm going to tear your fucking head off!" And he hurled himself at her throat with both hands eagerly outstretched.

Good. Let him come.

Sally welcomed his reckless attack. She saw him hurtling towards her and drew him lovingly in. She stepped across with her right foot, and used his momentum to augment a *tai toshi*.

It was a pathetic throw on her part, weak and sloppily executed. But it was all she could offer.

Gordon landed flat on his back and Sally followed him down: she fell on her knees beside him. And as a continuous part of that downward movement, she drove the heel of her palm directly towards the base of his nose, at an angle of forty-five degrees.

Ben's voice: they were talking after a training session, Ben and a group of girls. Talking about street fighting and self-defense. *The septum is a bone shaped like a needle.*

Sally aimed the heel of her right palm downwards, aimed it far beyond the floor, right down into the darkened room below.

Behind the septum is a hole, and behind the hole is the brain. If you strike the septum at the right angle, you will force three inches of pointed bone directly into the brain.

Sally gave her body a twist, adding power to the flexing of her good arm. Everything she had was behind that blow, and when it connected there was no sense of coming up against an obstacle. Just a clean, pure movement which completed its natural course.

Gordon Tate's body arched on the floor beneath her, and his mouth opened wide. After a moment his eyes filled with blood. He gave a great groan of pain, and then the life passed out of him.

Sally leaned over Gordon's body, gasping for air. She was so exhausted that the saliva dribbled out of her mouth. Each movement of her rib cage seemed to stab her in the chest. She needed to breathe but it hurt, and she moaned each time it happened.

A few seconds later she sat back on her haunches. *Must get up. Must . . . get . . . up.*

Her body longed for rest. It longed to lie down and do nothing more. But she knew that there was more to do. She wasn't sure what, but there was something.

Something to do with the clock.

She turned to look at the window ledge. Yes, there it was: the clock—two clocks actually—with the seconds ticking away.

Sally pulled herself to her feet, using the wall for support.

Nice little clock. Two sets of figures: 11.21.00, and 11.20.43.

44, 45, 46 . . .

Nice little clock.

She approached it, swaying on her feet. Two sets of figures. Two switches. *Nice little box. Gray.*

48, 49, 50 . . .

Have to stop it. Must stop it. Which switch?

52, 53, 54 . . .

Two switches. One switch for off, one switch for fire. Which switch?

56, 57, 58 . . .

Sally flicked up the switch on the right.

58, 58, 58 . . .

Which switch . . . Right switch.

The numbers on the front of the box began to dissolve, and she watched with fascinated interest as the floor rose up to hit her.

34

In late September of that year there was an Indian summer in England: there were long days of glowing sunshine, and an atmosphere of calm settled over the countryside.

On the last Saturday of September the prime minister attended another wedding in his village church. There were no crowds this time, and the prime minister felt much more relaxed than at his daughter's wedding, because this time he didn't have the worry about what might go wrong.

He watched at a distance as the bride entered the church on her father's arm. The bride's father walked slowly, as if he were not a hundred percent fit, but he was obviously a proud and contented man.

Once the bride had gone into the church, the prime minister entered on tiptoe and sat in a pew at the back. There were plenty of guests, on both sides of the aisle, but there was more than enough room for an uninvited spectator.

At the end of the ceremony, the bride and her new husband walked up the aisle together. They looked as happy as all couples should in such circumstances, but the prime minister noticed that as they drew level with a tomb on the left-hand side of the nave, they paused for a moment.

They glanced briefly into each other's eyes, as if they shared some kind of secret. And then they moved on, passing the last of their guests.

As they came towards the west door, the bride and groom suddenly became aware of the prime minister, who was waiting alone in his pew.

The prime minister raised his hand in salute, and after recovering from their surprise, the bride and groom both acknowledged his gesture with a smile. And then, arm in arm, they walked out through the door of the church.

MORE SCIENCE FICTION FROM BART

THEIR LIVES, THEIR LOVES, THEIR LEGENDS

Their movies still delight us, their romances continue to thrill us and their tragedies hurt as deeply as those that happen to members of the family!

Here they are! **MARILYN**, **ELVIS** and **JIMMY**—each in a handsome magazine packed with informative articles and glorious color photographs, many not seen in years!

Plus, each magazine contains 8 giant color pin-ups, which unfold to become 16" x 22" posters. Rare! A collector's item!

50 pages + pin-ups. 8" x 10 7/8" flexible cover.

MARILYN MONROE $9.95   ELVIS PRESLEY $5.95
JAMES DEAN $10.95